# ESCAPING THE FUTURE

I0773536

# ESCAPING THE FUTURE

ADAM CROZIER

ESCAPING THE FUTURE
Copyright © 2022 by Adam Crozier
All Rights Reserved.
www.adamcrozierbooks.com

This book is a work of fiction. Names, characters, businesses, organizations, places, events and incidents either are products of the author's imagination or are used fictitiously. Any resemblance to persons, living or dead, events, or locales is entirely coincidental and not intended by the author.

All rights reserved. No part of this publication may be reproduced, stored in a retrieval system, or transmitted in any form or by any means electronic, mechanical, photocopying, recording or otherwise without the prior permission of the author, except for the use of brief quotations in critical articles or reviews.

Cover Design by: Best Page Forward

Editing by: Invisible Ink Editing (Developmental), Joe Pierson (Copyedit), and Sarah Casman (Proofread)

ISBN: 979-8-9864656-0-9 (Paperback)

First Edition, 2022

# CONTENTS

*To my wife, Carrie, for without her
unwavering love and support, this adventure
would have remained untold*

# CHAPTER 1
# ONE LAST ADVENTURE

*Saturday, July 9, 2022*

They say that moving is like cleaning up the past in order to prepare for the future, but twelve-year-old Nic Walker never liked cleaning, and he knew that his future was better off where he was. It wasn't his choice, though, so he folded in the flaps of his last cardboard box, ran packing tape over the top, and sealed away the memories of his childhood.

Finally done packing, Nic flopped down on the carpeted floor of his room and agonized over how unfair it was that he and his family had to move. Nic lay there silently waiting for his mom to return with the U-Haul. Once she did, he could go meet up with his two best friends, Tate and Sophia. Nic was spending the night at Tate's house, playing Dungeons and Dragons with them for the last time, but it wasn't enough. It would be the last time he got to see his friends, at least whenever he wanted. If he was lucky, their families might meet up again in a year, but it didn't seem likely.

Tomorrow, he would move to San Jose, up in Northern

California. His new house may be bigger, but there was enough wrong with it that his dad joked about making a carpenter out of him. Nic didn't know anyone up there, and the thought of moving away from the friends he knew since he was a baby made his stomach churn. Despite his parents' assurances that he would make new friends, Nic knew he could never make friends like the ones he had here, who were like family.

Ten minutes later, the front door slammed shut, announcing Nic's brother Ethan had returned home. If Nic was caught lying down, he would somehow end up with Ethan's chores before he could leave the house. Nic rolled over and slowly dragged himself to his feet as Ethan's footsteps approached. Nic lifted the box when Ethan kicked open Nic's door and said, "Oh good, your room is finished. Dad said he wanted to talk to you, and that you need to help him take down the pictures in the hall."

"That's not my job, it's yours," Nic replied.

"Not anymore. And talking goes both ways, so grow up and start talking to Dad again. It's not his fault we're moving."

Before Nic could argue, Ethan was gone.

Nic stood in the middle of his desolate room and then staggered forward, weighed down by the box filled with his childhood memories. He passed through the doorway, leaving behind only his desk, bed, and an empty dresser. It didn't matter, though, because he would never come back.

Once downstairs, Nic set his box down by the front door and wrote his name on it. He found his dad in the middle of the hall, with most of the pictures already packed up. Nic joined his father as he stared at a photo of his own childhood friends, who were around twelve at the time, the same age as Nic, Tate, and Sophia.

Just like his dad, Nic was light skinned, blue eyed, and had curly brown hair that was impossible to control. In the photo his dad held, his dad had knobby, grass-stained knees, which no doubt came from him leading his friends on dirty adventures, something that Nic was guilty of as well.

This particular photo was taken the afternoon that Sophia's dad, Mr. Day, had emigrated from Seoul to the United States. Just like Sophia, Mr. Day was tall for his age, with a round face and wide eyes that helped express his highly curious nature.

The scrawny boy in the middle of the photo, Tate's dad, had dark skin and chubby cheeks. Despite having both Nic's dad and Sophia's dad in a headlock, everyone was grinning widely.

This photo was the one that marked the day his dad's lifelong friendship began. The three boys had been such good friends that they managed to move to the same neighborhood as adults so they could hang out.

Just like their fathers, Nic thought that he would be inseparable with their kids, Sophia and Tate, through adulthood. Now their friendship would be cut short, all because Nic was moving away.

Nic's dad placed the picture in a box and started to take down some more. "I think it's good that you get to see Sophia and Tate one last time before we go."

Nic shook his head and said, "Yeah," which broke his weeklong silence without portraying his frustration. To make sure his point was heard, Nic added, grumbling, "We could always find a house here in town." This was a touchy subject with them, but Nic didn't care. They had to move; that was not an option. The whole neighborhood was being bought out by the California High-Speed Rail Authority. They had to move, but they didn't have to leave Sunland; that was his dad's choice, and that was why Nic had stopped talking to him in the first place.

His dad stopped and stared at Nic. His face flushed in anger, but instead of losing his cool, he calmly replied, "You know, Nic, sometimes you have to choose a new path in life and make the best of it. This is an opportunity for us, and in the long run, we'll be better off."

Nic shook his head, and asked, "Do you really think your life would've been better off if your parents moved you away from Mr. Kerr and Mr. Day when you were a kid?"

"It's already done. We're moving."

Nic began to protest, but his response was cut off before it started when a loud revving engine indicated a truck had pulled up outside. Nic looked away and then pulled the last picture from the wall, avoiding his dad's eye contact.

Nic handed the picture to his dad as his mom came in through the garage. With her home, Nic could finally leave. "I finished my room, Mom. Can I go?"

His mom glanced at his dad. She crossed her arms, her lips pursed to the side, indicating that she was considering how to reply. She could probably tell that Nic was being *difficult*, but instead of questioning what happened, she thankfully let it go. "What about dinner?"

"I'm not hungry. I had a sandwich about an hour ago."

"Okay," she said, holding the door to the garage open. "Be back here tomorrow morning by nine. We'll need to be on the road by eleven."

"You know," his dad said, "you *could* stay and help finish packing."

"I would rather just live at Tate's house for now on." Nic was still angry and added before he could stop himself, "If you actually cared about how I felt, then you wouldn't be so happy to ruin my life by leaving."

Nic turned, flung his backpack over his shoulder, and fled into the garage. Half expecting his parents would stop him for his outburst, Nic didn't look back. He ran to his bike on the driveway and sped away.

Nic's street was one of a few scheduled for demolition in order to make room for the high-speed rail. Most of the neighbors had already moved away, leaving only a handful of homes with people in them. People in the news were okay with the eviction, reporting that a couple of houses can't stand in the way of humanity's next big achievement. Nic didn't care if humanity was better off in the long run; he just wanted to stay in his home.

As Nic passed by his living room window, he could see his mom rubbing his dad's back, comforting him. Telling them that they didn't care about him came out more hurtful than Nic had expected, and he would probably be in trouble later. If he was lucky, they would cut him some slack because the move was, as they say, *hard on him*. He shook his head and then pedaled down his empty street toward Tate's house.

Nic hadn't even ridden his bike a block from his home when explosions thundered across the neighborhood. He caught a glow from above, tilted his head to the sky, and then hit his brakes hard, sending his bike to a skidding stop.

High above the city, a black saucer-shaped aircraft fell through the air. It spiraled down toward the center of town, but at the last second, it pulled out of its fall and flew in Nic's direction.

A gigantic crystal burst through the clouds behind it, with a dozen violet spikes pointed at the saucer. The crystal had no business flying through the air. Yet it flew.

Electric-blue flashes lit up the sky as missiles fired from the crystal and then slammed into the saucer. In return, the saucer fired an emerald-green beam that bathed the atmosphere in an

eerie glow. The beam went wide but hooked around to track the crystal's every move. An invisible field stalled the beam, but in a flash, it pierced the crystal's defenses and hit it with enough force to burn a hole clear through the other side.

Nic stood slack-jawed as both aircraft approached. The saucer shimmered, and then disappeared as it passed overhead. Despite it turning invisible, thick exhaust billowed in its wake, showing a clear path to the hills behind McGroarty Park. The saucer flickered back into view as it skipped off a distant hilltop and then vanished once more before crashing out of sight.

Explosions erupted from the crystal ship, and it plummeted to the ground not far from where the saucer came down. The crystal crashed with a blast that sent plumes of fire and smoke high into the air.

As the rumbling in the sky faded, the howls of the neighborhood dogs took over.

Nic spun around to look at his house, but nobody had come outside. He stared back at the hills, attempting to judge the distance to where the aircraft crashed. If he hurried, he could make it before sundown. He was not far from Tate's house, and it was only a couple of blocks farther to McGroarty Park. If Nic was lucky, Sophia would already be there, and they could all leave as soon as he arrived.

Ignoring the handful of neighbors who came out to investigate the sound, Nic raced his bike uphill toward Tate's house. Hours until sundown, the sun's summer heat sapped away

Nic's energy. But with the promise of one last adventure with his friends, he pushed through his growing exhaustion.

With a block to go, Nic passed under thick trees that lined the street and hid the unique smoke patterns that still hung in the sky. He rounded the street corner and spotted Tate's house. Sophia's bike lay on the sidewalk in front of it, at the bottom of the steps leading up to the front door.

Sophia had just reached Tate's door when Nic's bike crashed on top of hers, causing her to spin around in alarm. Nic raced up the steps two at a time, gasping for air as he went.

Sophia eyed him suspiciously as he approached. Her honey-brown hair was kept tucked under a tan baseball cap, hiding her face, which Nic knew all too well. Her face was round and a bit plain, but her large, curious eyes radiated intelligence. She smiled, but waited for Nic to reach her before asking, "You okay?"

Opening his mouth to respond, Nic instead took in a couple more breaths. He ran his fingers through his shaggy brown hair in a vain attempt to keep his hair out of his eyes. No matter what he tried, he always appeared as if he just got out of bed.

Sophia stared back at Nic, eyebrows raised, and waited.

"I saw something ... two aircraft ... blew each other out of the sky. They were ..." He took a deep breath and put his hand on Sophia's shoulder. "I don't know what they were, but we should go find out. I know where they landed."

"Really!" Sophia said. "Can we actually get there? Let's get Tate." She rang the doorbell and then slowly turned back, frowning. "Wait. Did that actually happen, or are you trying to trick me again?"

"No, it really happened. I can prove it." Nic pointed to the sky behind him.

Sophia squinted toward the sky, but when Nic spun around to point her in the right direction, his view was blocked. If there were any remnants of the aircraft battle, they were now hidden behind the tall trees that lined Tate's street.

Sophia cocked her head to the side. "You expected me to believe that you saw flying aircraft that you can't identify?" Her cheeks flushed before she added, "I'm embarrassed to say that you had me fooled for a second."

"No, I'm serious. It happened." Nic waited for Sophia's usual optimism to return, but sighed when she turned back to the front door as someone approached.

The door swung open with Tate's mom, Mrs. Booker, standing in the doorway. She was a short Black woman with braided dark-brown hair, and she always wore a bright smile. "Oh, hey Nic. Are you all ready for the big move tomorrow?"

"Yeah," Nic replied. In the excitement, he had somehow forgotten about his move. The question snapped him back to reality, and he added in a tone meant for his dad, "The house is almost ready to be knocked down."

Mrs. Booker frowned. "Well, I hope our families can still get together in the future. I'll have to plan something with your parents."

Nic knew she was just being nice. He would see their family again but accepted that once he moved out of Sunland, things would change forever. "Thank you. I'll look forward to seeing you again too."

Mrs. Booker stepped aside, allowing them to come in. "Well, have fun tonight. Tate's up in his room. And hello to you too, Sophia."

Sophia responded with a pleasant smile and an awkward wave as both Nic and Sophia dashed inside.

Without bothering to knock, Nic flung open Tate's door and as always was bombarded with aviation memorabilia. Posters of various aircraft hung on the walls, and model planes lined his countertops like planes on an aircraft carrier.

Tate's obsession with flying started with his dad, who was a pilot. Even before Tate's dad died of cancer, his only desire was to become a pilot like his father. As a way to help cope with his death, Nic and Sophia helped build the frame for the flight simulator rig that Tate sat in.

The rig itself was made out of plywood, which was painted to match the design of an F-22 from the outside. It even had a dome that covered the top half, though it rarely left its place on the floor, which Tate used as a laundry hamper. The rig started with just a frame and his desk. Over time, though, Tate managed to add a second screen, flight joystick, and various additional gauges that had no other purpose but to look cool.

Tate wasn't very tall and was easily hidden behind his gaming chair. He didn't turn back and probably didn't notice their arrival, being too enraptured by his flight path.

Nic approached, cautious of disturbing Tate as he began to land. Sophia leaned forward to point out something on the screen and startled Tate. He flinched, jerking the controls to the side, sending the plane toward the ground. It wasn't much, but enough that if Tate hadn't logged so many hours in the game, he would have crashed. He tugged the joystick back to the other side and typed some commands on his keyboard, managing to avert the crash.

With the plane safely on the ground, Tate slowly spun in their direction. "Another successful landing." His face was plastered with an ever-present smirk. His curly black hair was cut short on top and faded around the sides. Despite his slouching,

Tate was always well-dressed, now with a black-and-white-striped shirt tucked into his jeans. "It's about time you two got here."

"I had to work on my summer camp project," Sophia said.

"Do you realize that the purpose of summer is *not* to have to do any of that stuff?"

"I get to build things," Sophia said. "Like robots. Next week, I get to put my robot in an arena and fight it against others."

"That actually sounds all right," Tate said. "Anyway, you're here. I finished making the Dungeons and Dragons campaign an hour ago, and it will be *epic*."

Nic cleared his throat, anticipating Tate's reluctance. "Tate, we're leaving."

Tate's left eyebrow arched as he said, "What about our game? We won't have enough time to finish the campaign if we go anywhere first."

"We have to check out something I saw in the hills, just beyond McGroarty Park."

Rather than standing, Tate sank deeper into his seat and asked Sophia, "What's this about?"

Sophia only shrugged.

Tate side-eyed Nic, smirk fading.

"I'll tell you on the way," Nic said, "but we should go."

"Is this really what you want to do for your last night?" Tate said, shaking his head. "Remember the last time you dragged us into the hills on a treasure hunt?"

"It's called geocaching, and lots of people do it. Don't forget, we found the cache filled with treasure."

"Nic, the treasure was a bunch of erasers shaped like animals. The people that left it there did it because they didn't want them."

"I still have mine," Sophia said as she picked up a model jet and began playing with the moveable parts, one of which came off.

"Yes, Tate," Nic said. "This *is* what I want to do for my last day. So, let's go."

Tate frowned, but he dragged himself to his feet. He took the model jet from Sophia and put it back in its spot. "This is a decoration. I just finished putting this one together yesterday. You know, you really don't have to touch everything."

"Sorry, but it's new. That's why I was looking at it," Sophia replied.

Tate rolled his eyes and then turned to Nic. "Before we go, you have to tell me what we're actually doing."

Nic cleared his throat, bracing for Tate's disbelief. "Two aircraft crashed in the hills, and we're going to go find them!"

"Not just any aircraft, UFOs," Sophia said, staring at Tate, probably to see if he was in on what she now thought was a joke.

Tate's smirk faded into a grimace, but he remained silent.

Sophia asked, "Did you really not know about this?"

Tate didn't move.

Nic sighed but added defensively, "I didn't say UFO. I said I didn't know what they were."

"You said they were flying objects you couldn't identify. You know that's the definition of UFOs, right?"

"Okay, they were UFOs. And they crashed in our neighborhood. Don't you want to go check them out?"

"You know," Tate said, "I want to be a pilot. But I don't think I want to see a plane wreck."

"I'm telling you, they weren't planes," Nic said. "Besides, it's one last adventure before I leave. Come on, we have to go."

Tate stared blankly in front of him with his mouth parted. He blinked and then glanced up at Nic, frowning again. "Fine. But let's hurry. If we're quick, we might have time to play some of the D&D campaign when we get back."

Tate left his room without bothering to shut off his flight simulator.

They passed Tate's mom at the bottom of the stairs. "Oh, are you leaving?" she asked.

"Yeah," Tate replied. "Nic wanted to check something out at the park."

"All right, I'll be gone when you return. I'm picking up your sisters from camp in about an hour."

"Ugh," Tate groaned. "My summer of peace and quiet has come to an end."

"Now, don't start before they're even home."

"All right, sorry." Tate hugged his mom and asked, "Do you think I could have Dad's old bomber jacket?"

"Uh, sure. It's hot outside. Do you even need it?"

"I'll be okay."

"All right, help yourself. It's in the garage."

"Yeah, on the top shelf," Tate said, leaving for the garage. "Bye, Mom."

Nic followed Tate and simultaneously with Sophia said, "Bye, Mrs. Booker."

When they stepped into the garage, Tate had stopped to stare up at a storage bin on an upper shelf. Grabbing a toolbox, he dragged it under the bin he wanted, scraping the floor as he went and causing everyone to cringe. Tate stood on the toolbox, but was still a couple of inches too short. He was the oldest of the three of them by almost six months, but was the shortest by half a foot. "Sophia, grab that for me, would you?"

Sophia reached up and pulled down the bin, setting it in front of Tate.

Tate popped off the lid to the bin and dug through it, pulling out an old sage-green jacket. Tate put on the oversized jacket and attempted to straighten out the creases caused by it being in the bin for so long. He fixed the collar and then patted the lone aviator patch that Nic guessed came from Tate's dad's time in the air force.

"Why are you going to take that with you now?" Sophia asked. "It's one of the hottest days of the year."

"My mom said I could wear it, so I'm wearing it." Tate turned to Nic and stared at him with arched eyebrows. "If we go searching for whatever you *think* you saw, this is just going to turn into a boring hike."

"What I *think* I saw was two spaceships shoot each other down. And if we hurry, we can be the first ones to find them. It *will* be worth it."

"How do you know they were spaceships?" Tate asked.

"Because, they looked like spaceships," Nic answered. "One was a giant flying crystal, and the other was a flying saucer with a cloaking device. It disappeared in the middle of the sky."

Tate turned to Sophia, who returned Tate's skeptical look. "You know, Camp Pendleton is a little south of here. I bet they are testing some new drone designs."

"They were not drones."

Tate shook his head but pushed his bike out of the garage. It rolled down the driveway, wobbling before crashing. He picked up a flashlight and stuffed it in his backpack, which he threw across his back as Nic and Sophia grabbed their bikes from the sidewalk.

Tate hopped onto his bike and stopped next to them. "Cloaking device? You probably just lost track of it."

"You'll see, Tate."

Sophia took off first, pedaling up the street, followed by Nic and Tate. The whirring echoes of helicopter blades pulsed through the air. Two military helicopters flew overhead and began circling the hills in front of them.

"See? Let's hurry!" Nic yelled. "They're searching, but they don't know where to look. I do. We can still get there first."

# CHAPTER 2
# SPACESHIPS

They coasted into McGroarty Park and stopped next to the tennis courts. An open gate across the street led into the Arts Center and to the only nearby trails that led into the hills, but it was blocked by the police. An officer stood next to his car, diverting traffic.

"We're too late," Sophia said. "They're never going to let us pass."

"It doesn't hurt to ask," Nic replied.

"You go," Sophia said. "You might have seen something after all, but I'm still not buying it. I mean aliens, really?"

Nic turned to see if Tate was coming, but he averted his eyes before saying, "This is your adventure, man."

Nic shrugged and then rode over to the officer. Before Nic could ask, he was being waved away. Nic continued, stopping when the officer raised his hand and said, "That's far enough."

"Can we get up to the Arts Center?" Nic asked.

"No. There is a fire up there. You should head home in case the fire makes it down to any houses and you have to be evacuated."

Nic stared up the hill, but no smoke could be seen. If a fire did start from one of the crashes, he was close enough to tell that it wasn't likely it was still going. He shrugged to the officer and said, "Okay, thank you," before coasting back down to where Sophia and Tate were waiting.

"Well?" Sophia asked.

"There's a fire up there," Nic said skeptically.

"Possible, but where are the fire department helicopters?" Sophia asked. "Normally, they're all over the place during a fire."

"Obviously, that's their cover story," Tate replied. "We tried, Nic."

"We're not done," Nic said, shaking his head. "I know another way in."

"But what if we get caught?" Sophia asked.

"We'll be okay." Nic pointed to the other side of the park, past the officer guarding the gate. Three months ago, Nic had gone on a hike with his brother, returning after the gates were closed. There was an exit in the chain-link fence. "You can peel back the fence over there. We'll duck through when the officer isn't looking." Nic was still pointing at the hidden entrance when the officer spotted them. Nic ran his fingers through his hair in a feeble attempt to hide their intentions.

The officer continued to watch them as Nic started for the playground. He led Tate and Sophia down to the jungle gym, where they ditched their bikes underneath the structure. When he looked back at the officer, he was ushering people out of the Arts Center down the road.

"Now's our chance. Let's go," Nic whispered and then dashed across the street. The others were lagging behind him, but they still followed. They crossed the street and ran up to the fence before Nic heard a shout from behind.

"Stay out of the hills, kids!"

Nic ignored the warning as the officer headed their way. He peeled back on the chain-link fence enough for Tate to squeeze through. Sophia hesitated. She stared back at the officer, who was now running their way from the park side. If they went through, the officer would be too big to follow them.

"Go, Sophia!" Nic shouted.

Tate reached back and took Sophia's hand. "We're only going to get in trouble if they catch us. Let's go."

Sophia climbed through and held the fence open for Nic. He scrambled to the other side, brushed his pants clean, and then bolted uphill after the others. They no longer needed any prompting to run, and when the fence rattled behind them, Nic didn't look back but did run harder.

They ran until they reached the trail. They didn't stop, just slowed enough to catch their breath. The trail was steep, but it passed through enough trees to hide them on their trek up the hill.

"Well, we made it," Sophia said. "Now what, Nic?"

"Just follow me. The first spacecraft shouldn't be too far," Nic replied and then continued up the hill at a pace just short of running.

Nic periodically glanced over his shoulder until the park was completely lost from view. Once it was, he slowed down to a little more than a walk.

Tate caught up to him, leaving Sophia trailing behind.

"What makes you think aliens would come here?" Tate asked. "Nothing happens here."

"I don't know," Nic replied. "That movie *E.T.* was filmed in this valley. Maybe *E.T.* was based on a true story, and the alien came back to visit his old friends."

"That's a bit of a stretch."

"Well, we'll find out soon enough."

Sophia hustled forward. "Do you think the aliens are friendly? I mean, I still think you two could be trying to pull one over on me, but if you're not …"

"Probably not friendly," Nic replied. "They shot each other down, remember? So at least one of them must be hostile."

Their trail's switchback headed in the wrong direction, making Nic lead them off trail. The ground beneath them was loose, and more than once Nic felt his feet slide out from under him—not enough to slow them down, though.

The path they took now led through tall trees farther up the hill, until they reached a peak that would give them a better view. They reached the top as the sun began its descent behind the hillside's tallest peaks. In one direction, barely visible through the leaves, a black helicopter circled the distant hills, close to where Nic thought the saucer spaceship might have crashed. There were some houses being built on that side, but most of the land was undeveloped.

Sophia had stopped next to a tree to watch the helicopter and catch her breath. Nic joined her, thinking that they should have already found the first spacecraft.

Behind them, Tate cleared his throat. "I think that might be it." He was pointing past the next ridge to an unseen valley with faint traces of smoke rising into the air.

"We found it!" Nic shouted with a laugh. "That has to be where the crystal one went down. I'm sure of it."

With renewed energy, they all ran toward the smoke. Before

they could peer into the valley to see what made the smoke, distant indistinct voices stopped them in their tracks.

Tate grabbed the others. "Did you hear that?"

"Yeah," Sophia said. "I don't think we're the first ones here."

They crawled the rest of the way until they could peer into the valley. Only fifty feet below them, a smoldering hunk of crystal the size of a small house was embedded into the ground. Shards of black obsidian glass stabbed into the earth like tombstones, while smaller pieces were scattered in every direction. A stench of rotten eggs wafted past them, and an unnatural fog seeped from the crystal across the ground, giving Nic the impression they were looking upon a misty graveyard.

A dozen soldiers with assault rifles were sifting through the debris. Two more stood next to the core crystalline structure: a bald man still wearing sunglasses and a tall woman on a phone.

"Aha! That's it, guys," Nic whispered. "I told you it was a spaceship."

"Could that thing really fly?" Tate asked. "I guess it could be a next-gen military aircraft."

"Give it up, Tate. It's from another world."

Movement below ended their conversation. Four soldiers carried a stretcher out of the wreckage, which held a humanoid shape far too large to be human. They set it down next to the woman and bald man, but because of the terrain, Nic could no longer see it. He glanced around to see if there was a spot to gain a better vantage point. The only place he found was twenty feet from where they set down the stretcher, with part of the spaceship to use as cover. He turned to a grinning Tate, who asked, "Do you think we can get closer?"

Nic nodded and then inched his way forward, when Sophia

grabbed his leg. "Do you really think that is a good idea? They could see us if we got any closer."

"Come on, Sophia," Nic replied. "It's an alien. It's why we're here."

"We saw the spaceship, Nic," Sophia replied. "*That's* why we're here. Whoever that is, is dead."

Nic glanced around. Half a dozen soldiers were spread out below and might be able to see him if he climbed down, but for now they were too focused on spaceship debris, giving Nic a chance to go. "Then don't come down." Nic kicked his leg free and scrambled down the hill to where the stretcher was in sight.

Nic stopped behind a large crystal spike that stabbed into the ground. Tate was on Nic's right, and they both peeked over the crystal like it was a fallen tree. The military woman tucked her radio into a vest pocket as Sophia glanced over the crystal next to Nic, wide-eyed. Nic knew that when it came down to it, Sophia would come along too. She was worried about getting caught, but her curious nature would always get the best of her.

The bald man knelt next to the stretcher and took a deep breath before pulling back the tarp. He unveiled a dreadful crea-ture resembling a massive humanoid reptile, twice the size of a human.

Its skin was pickle green, with large, sunken eyes so black that they seemed to absorb darkness. Its nose was no more than a bump with oversized but closed nostrils. Its wide, snarling mouth parted enough to reveal a row of skinny teeth that belonged inside a shark. Instead of hair, uneven rows of short, stubby horns spread from its scalp down to its thick, muscular neck.

"Look at that," Nic whispered.

Sophia shuffled at Nic's side but couldn't contain her amazement. "Totally," she said softly and then added, "I want horns."

Nic glanced at Sophia to see if she was serious, chuckled, and then returned his attention to the scene, wanting to see more. Nic's eyes widened as the bald man dragged the tarp down to the creature's waist. It wore a tattered, half-burned maroon shirt that opened enough to show its body underneath. Its torso was mangled in the crash as if ravaged by wild animals, with a mossy-green sludgy substance leaking from its wounds down to the ground.

A wave of queasiness washed over Nic, but it couldn't dull his growing excitement. "I knew it—"

The soldier closest to them spun around, causing Nic to duck down, pulling Tate and Sophia with him.

The military woman spoke, "Take this thing over to the field, and don't touch it. The helicopter's due to arrive in ten minutes.

Sophia peeked around the side and then whispered, "They're leaving, except for the lady and bald man."

Sophia inched closer to get another look, and Nic scooted next to her. The creature was being carried away by four soldiers, once again shrouded by the tarp. Even covered, Nic couldn't shake the image of its parted mouth frozen in a scowl.

The woman and the bald man who stayed behind had begun examining spaceship parts that were gathered around them.

"Okay," Sophia said quietly, "you're right about the aliens, but I think it is time we go."

Before they could move, a deep voice called out from the woman's radio, "Eagle 01, Eagle 01, this is Fox 03, over."

She took out her radio and replied, "Fox 03, this is Eagle 01, proceed."

Hoping the momentary distraction would allow them to escape, Nic took a step back up the hill.

"Eagle 01, this is Fox 03. Local police reported three children on their way to your location from McGroarty Park. Over."

Nic froze, and then flattened himself on the ground.

"Fox 03, this is Eagle 01, affirmative. Over."

"Fox 03. Out."

As soon as the call was over, Nic looked up enough to see the woman had returned to examining something black and sludgy that had to have come from the spaceship. The bald man had walked away and was now gesturing to a pair of soldiers. The pair saluted and then headed straight toward Nic and the others, causing Nic to entrench himself deeper into their hiding spot behind the crystal.

The crunching of footsteps approached but didn't slow as the dim shadow of the soldiers rushed past them up the hill, back to where Nic and the others had come from.

"We need to follow them," Sophia said, checking to see if they were clear to go.

Nic glanced around the wreckage. The woman that remained was facing away, joining the only remaining soldiers who didn't go and search for them. The bald man headed off in the same direction as the alien on the stretcher.

When Nic turned back to say it was safe to go, Sophia was already halfway up the hill. Tate was sneaking behind her, and now Nic rushed after them at a distance.

Sophia and Tate lay down where they first discovered the spaceship, waiting for Nic. They watched the crystal spaceship and the remaining soldiers below. Nic turned to face where the saucer had crashed. The easiest way to the other spaceship was up the hill. They would reach another trail eventually and be able to take it close to the area where the invisible ship had crashed.

"Maybe we should head back home," Sophia said, "instead of finding the other spaceship."

"Go home and do what?" Nic asked. "What could possibly compete with this? We can't go back. Our only choice is to keep going forward."

"And if they have the next one locked down too?" she asked.

"And if they don't?" Nic replied, surprised that Sophia actually wanted to head back. "We should leave here, or one of the soldiers could spot us, but we can't go home."

"Imagine what we could find at the next spaceship, Sophia," Tate said. "We should hurry, though."

Ignoring Sophia's protests, Nic crept away until the crystal spaceship was no longer in sight, and then sprinted up the hill, away from the alien wreckage. "It won't be too far, I promise."

---

Shadows from the setting sun stretched across the landscape. They finally reached the other side of the hills and stopped when the trail branched in two directions. Nic scanned the valley below them for any clue of the second spaceship's whereabouts. "It has to be around here somewhere."

Tate crossed his arms and stared back along the trail they came from. They had been searching for a while now, and neither of the others wanted to stay anymore. Once they got away from the military, Sophia was happy to explore. Tate had voiced his reluctance to continue, and his willingness to search was fading with the sun. It wouldn't be long before he tried to convince them to go home again. Time ticked away, and if they didn't find a clue, even Sophia would get tired of wandering around aimlessly.

"All right, Nic," Tate said. "We've looked long enough. We're done here."

"Yeah," Sophia added. "Maybe it's time we head home."

"Shouldn't it be my choice? It's my last day." Nic wasn't ready to leave. When he got home, he had to move. They had more time, not much, but still more time. "No, we're going to keep looking until we can't see anything. If it gets too dark, you brought a flashlight, and we can just take the fire road home."

"No, Nic," Tate said. "It's my turn to pick."

Sophia waited, clearly wanting to say more. She was ready to leave, but as long as Nic refused to go, she would keep searching. When Tate stepped in front of Nic, Sophia shrugged and then wandered off, happy to avoid the first signs of their brewing conflict.

"We're not going to take the fire road," Tate said. "The fire road is barely connected to town; it's why like ten people live back here. It would be much quicker to just walk home the way we came."

"Then that's what we'll do," Nic replied.

Tate stood in front of Nic, glaring at him. "We are done searching. We could have gone home after seeing an alien and its spaceship and still have had time to hang out. Instead, we've wasted what's left of daylight, searching for something that we'll never find. If it was up to you, by the time we left, it'd be so late that when we finally did make it home, the only thing we could do is go to sleep."

"And?" Nic replied. "So what if that's all we do? We are

searching for a spaceship, and that is worth doing, no matter how little time we have left." Nic moved away from Tate and stared across the hillside. He peered down into the hidden valley below, hopeful for any sign of the crash. They had reached the side of the valley that just started construction, with only a couple of homes built.

Tate stepped next to him, and Nic turned away, trying to cut off any further objections before they started. He was hoping to buy himself enough time to continue searching in what was left of the sunset's light.

Sophia had continued up the path of the steepest hill, or what was left of it. The route she took should have continued uphill past where Sophia knelt, but in front of her, roughly twenty feet of the ridgeline was missing. "I think I found something," she called back.

"That's it!" Nic shouted. "That's where it hit!"

Nic raced off the trail toward Sophia through waist-high thorny bushes that tugged on his pants, slowing him. Now that they found this spot, it was obvious that the spaceship hit there. The dirt around him was loose, muddy in places, like it was plowed by a tractor. The plants around him were uprooted and buried under a landslide. It was like something scooped out an entire section of the hill, creating a gully filled with small trees that were smashed, severed, or uprooted completely.

Nic peered down into the valley below, hopeful for any sign of the crash. He searched with renewed hope. Scrubby trees, brush, and boulders filled the rest of the valley, without seeming out of place. The only evidence of something being off was that the top halves of dozens of trees were scattered across a flat patch of ground hundreds of feet away. Besides the severed trees, the hillside below had no other sign of disturbance and no sign of the spaceship.

When Tate finally caught up, Nic said, "It must have bounced here first and then landed downhill."

"I don't see anything, Nic," Tate said. "Even if it hit here, there is nothing below us except a couple of fallen trees."

Dusk approached, and the last rays of light began to fade, along with Nic's vision below.

Tate shook his head. "It's not here. Why do you think this is where it crashed, Nic?"

"Because what else could have destroyed this hill? Something big hit here and headed that way. How else did the tops of those trees end up so far downhill?"

"But nothing's here," Tate said as he leaned over the ridge. He opened his mouth to say more, but stopped.

"If it didn't land here, then where is it?" Nic asked under his breath. Taking a step back, Nic crossed his arms and sighed. "I don't know. Maybe the spaceship escaped after all."

Behind Sophia, dozens of trees were collapsed into piles of stumps, broken branches, and wood chips. Sophia leaned against a severed tree, the top half missing, scattered far below. "Hey, Tate, what are you looking at?"

Tate squinted, staring below them. "What? Oh, I thought I saw something moving into that house under construction down there. It looked ... *weird*."

"Define *weird*," Sophia said, frowning.

"I don't know. It was too blurry to make out. Whatever it was, it's heading this way now." Tate ducked away from the edge. "We should hide."

"Is it an alien?" Sophia asked, straining to make out what approached.

Something hustled up the hill toward them, shrouded in an ivory cloak. It didn't resemble the hulking form of the alien at the crystal spaceship. Nic grabbed Sophia and pulled her behind the branches of a toppled tree, which allowed them to keep an eye on what approached. "Whatever it is, it wasn't there a minute ago, but I think it's human."

Tate lay down behind a fallen tree as the cloaked figure scrambled into view.

As it drew closer, the figure became clear. It was human. Despite the hood still being up, eyes shone through like bright-blue beacons of light reflecting the fading sun. Unruly strands of black hair fell from the cloak's hood as they set a backpack on the ground and removed a flask for a drink.

Upon pulling the hood down, the figure appeared to be a woman around Nic's mom's age, but that was not quite right. She was not old, but not young either. The longer she stood there surveying the hillside, the less Nic was sure of her age.

Her bronze skin made her look like she might have spent some time in the sun, but like her age, Nic couldn't make out her ethnicity. Nothing about her made Nic think she *wasn't* human, but why would she be flying a spaceship, and especially when it appeared the military knew nothing about her.

Sophia nudged Nic and whispered, "She looks human. Maybe we should talk to her."

"What could we say? Have you seen a spaceship?"

"Maybe. If it's hers, think of what she could tell us."

"Think of what she *won't* tell us," Nic said. He didn't want to risk her stopping them. "I doubt she'd want to explain to a bunch of strange kids why she was flying a spaceship. As long as she doesn't spot us, she'll be gone in a minute, and we could go find her ship. Now, shush."

A broad smile crept across the woman's lips, causing Nic to wonder what she could possibly smile about after crashing her ship. She knelt in a patch of mud, grabbing a leaf, and then twirled the stem between her fingertips. Sighing, she examined the gully carved out by the saucer spaceship. As she stood, mud fell away from her cloak, leaving it as pristine as when she arrived. She put on her backpack and slowly headed their direction, causing Nic's heart to thump like a drum with each of her steps.

Before she had a chance to spot them, a squirrel ran across the path in front of her. The woman shrieked with delight and turned away to follow the squirrel until it dove under an uprooted tree. She stared at the tree with soulless dull-gray eyes, which transformed back into a beautiful blue when she blinked. But as Nic saw them transform, he saw something else too. The blue eyes had various lines that encircled the pupil, moving independently to the iris. While Nic wasn't close enough to be certain, he was certain that they were not natural.

Catching what Nic did, Sophia whispered, "Her eyes aren't normal."

Smiling, the woman flung the cloak hood back over her head and then roamed along the trail toward the city.

It wasn't long before she was lost from view. Once she was, Nic joined Tate searching downhill with renewed hope of finding the spaceship. "Tate, where did you say the lady came from?"

"You see that house being built," Tate said, pointing to the only house down the hill under construction. "It only has frames for a couple walls. She walked from it straight up here."

"Then that's where we start," Sophia said, stepping forward. She stumbled down the hill past the landslide created by the spaceship. Sophia turned toward the spot Tate indicated and took off as fast as she could go.

With more caution, Nic chased after her. He reached the house under construction as Sophia ran through what made up the house's wooden frames.

Nic stopped when Tate halted abruptly in front of him, spotting a pair of dirty footprints on the house's foundation not made by Sophia.

"Over here!" Tate shouted. "This is where she stepped up." He shined his flashlight on the footprints, following their trail away from the house.

"Let's follow the tracks and see what we can find," Nic said. "Remember, this spaceship was cloaked, so even though we can't see it, it could still be here."

Tate closely tracked the footprints as Sophia ran ahead to the field that would soon be this house's neighbor.

Nic stuck with Tate, searching for a sign of the spaceship's landing, but didn't see anything out of place.

Sophia headed up a little hill and then faded from view as if she had stepped into a deep fog. "Wait, Sophia! Where'd you go?"

"I see it," Sophia bellowed. "It's right in front of me."

A flood of relief rushed over Nic, and a renewed excitement pushed him forward to where Sophia faded away. He reached the fog that took her, and continued with his arms extended as if he were trying to find his way in the dark. Tate joined him, and they marched together toward Sophia's voice.

With each step, the field in front of them faded, replaced by a large blurry object. It was like the spaceship was surrounded in a bubble sphere that hid it from view. Once inside, though, it was all clear. Nic turned back to the hillside they came from, but it was still in focus.

"This has to be the cloaking device I told you about," Nic said, grinning.

Tate rubbed his eyes. "Either that or I need glasses."

Nic's hands shook in anticipation when a black object as long as a school bus came into view. The saucer rested at an angle, half buried in the ground. A single piece of landing gear extended in a failed attempt to hold the ship upright.

They had found the second spaceship.

# CHAPTER 3

# TIME TRAVEL

Nic prowled around the spaceship, examining it with each step. Its metallic outer hull was midnight black, while ash-colored dents and scratches marred its entire surface. Sophia lingered on the ramp until Nic approached and then made her way to the door barring their entrance.

Stopping at a fist-sized hole next to the ramp, Nic peered inside a large, dark room. Tate had stuck his flashlight in another hole to try to see what was inside, but from Nic's vantage point, he could only see open space. He continued up to the entrance but couldn't help thinking that they were walking into a trap.

Tate followed Nic, stopping to examine a twisted scrap of the hull.

"There is a hole at the bottom of the door," Sophia said. She scrambled the rest of the way up the ramp, running her hand along the side of the ship, keeping balance on the tilted walkway. The door was bent at the bottom, and its frame twisted, leaving a gap almost big enough to fit through. She lay down on the ramp, peering inside until Nic and Tate reached her.

"Can you squeeze in, Sophia?" Nic asked.

Sophia reached one arm inside and scooted forward, unable to wiggle past her shoulder. "It's not big enough."

Tate tugged on the door, which rattled slightly. "The door is loose. Maybe we can open it."

Sophia stood up, leaving room for Nic to take a quick peek. He knelt down and stuck his head through the door, but couldn't make out more than faint outlines.

"What are you waiting for, Nic?" Tate asked.

Nic braced his feet and grabbed the door with his hands. They pulled, but it wouldn't budge.

"Maybe if we all pull at the same time," Sophia said.

"Okay," Nic replied. "Now!" They yanked on the door, which slid open an inch with a jerk. "One more time." Nic strained as the door slid halfway open, enough that they could now easily fit inside without using the hole at the bottom.

"Perfect," Tate said. "Sophia, you go in first."

"Sure," she replied, but her eyes narrowed at Tate before asking, "Wait, why?"

"He probably thinks you're going to trip an alarm," Nic replied.

"Well, if you're too scared," Sophia said.

"I'm not scared. I just thought you'd want to go first," Tate said unconvincingly.

Sophia shrugged, took Tate's flashlight, and then went inside, disappearing into the darkness.

Nic followed and then stepped to the side to make room for Tate. Sophia shined the flashlight around, revealing a large spherical room in disarray. Broken pieces of the ship spread across the rounded floor, but it was too dim to see where from.

A single chair in the center remained untouched by the disaster, like a lone house surviving a tornado.

Nic squinted, searching next to the door for a switch, but could only make out a few faint outlines and nothing that could possibly turn on the lights.

Tate scrambled inside next to him and tossed his backpack aside. He shuffled toward Sophia, sending metal fragments clattering to the center of the floor. "Give me the flashlight, Sophia. We have to find something to turn the power on."

Before the flashlight exchanged hands, panels in the ceiling bathed the room in light.

Tate glanced around, dumbfounded.

With the lights on, Nic got a good look around. He stood on the raised walkway circling the thirty-foot-wide spherical room. Nic now understood that the lone chair in the center was designed to have empty space surrounding it.

The opposite side of the room, behind a railing and against the wall, looked like the spaceship's control system that had turned on with the power. Images that reported damage done to the ship displayed on a large broken viewscreen in the middle. The images were partially visible because almost half the screen had fallen, scattering glass across the floor.

Below the viewscreen was a small monitor, but it was not powered on. At each side of the control system, two separate workstations faced a series of controls, but with no screen above them. A single door farther to the right most likely would lead to the rest of the ship.

"Why did the lights come on?" Nic asked.

"The lights are on. Who cares how?" Tate asked, staring at the center of the room. "Check out the pilot's chair." He tossed his flashlight on top of his backpack and then leapt off the walkway toward the central chair, stumbling on the curved floor.

"Watch your step," Tate called back. "The floor isn't level."

"Yeah, I figured that out," Sophia replied.

"Oh," Tate said. "And Sophia! Don't touch anything until we've checked this place out."

Sophia shook her head and then followed Tate to the center of the spherical room. "Do you mean like the pilot's chair?"

"*Please*," he replied while taking a seat. "We all know you're the one who will end up touching something you shouldn't. Just don't push some self-destruct button, and I won't fire any laser blasts."

Nic joined the others as two black rods floated out from under the chair, rising to a spot just above Tate's head. The rods had grooves that could comfortably fit the human hand, and small red buttons poked out in the spot where fingers and thumbs could rest. Tate reached up and grabbed them, arms dangling as if he was riding a Harley-Davidson motorcycle.

Sophia pointed to a button just under the seat and asked, "Should I push it?"

"I got it," Tate said, reaching down and pushing the button and then reaching back up to the rods.

Nic and Sophia fell back as a loud pop came from the bottom of the chair. The leg holding the chair in place detached, blending into the floor, but instead of the chair falling, it hovered in place. The rods that Tate held oozed around his wrists like putty until they fit his hands like gloves. Straps zipped around Tate of their own accord, and then the chair rose into the room.

"Can you stop it?" Nic asked.

Tate managed to pull his right hand free and tried pushing the button under the seat again, but the chair continued to rise until it was in the direct center of the spherical room. Tate's chair stopped, and then they were bathed in darkness.

Shadows in the distance sharpened into the familiar landscape of the hills, and Nic could even make out the house under construction across the way. Nic was outside, but at the same time, he couldn't have left the ship. His heart skipped a beat as he glanced down. Besides the fact that Nic stood in the same spot as before, he now appeared to be floating a couple of feet above the field that the spaceship landed in.

Tate's chair reclined, facing the sky.

Nic lost his balance and took a step forward, falling onto the floor disoriented. "Hey, Tate! Can you turn this thing off yet?"

"Yeah! I think I got it."

The light returned, and the chair began lowering to the floor.

When Nic's eyes focused again, he could no longer see outside.

"See, Tate?" Sophia said. "That's exactly what you get when you mess around with things you don't understand."

"We're lucky nothing happened, Sophia," Tate said, "but I'm still going to see if I can figure out how to fly this thing."

"Wait until I'm on the walkway," Nic said, heading to the door at the back. "I want to see if we can find out what happened here."

Nic had to step over pieces from the shattered viewscreen that had been blasted by whatever pierced the ship's hull. Its parts were mixed together with rubble that fell from the ceiling, walls, various scraps of metal, as well as tiny clear tubes and circuitry.

Sophia ran with him, and a crunch from the debris on the floor accompanied each step they took. They stopped on the walkway behind the rail and turned back to Tate.

With both of them out of the center of the room, Tate's chair rose. It stopped, and Tate was plunged into a sphere of darkness once again. For Nic, the light shone down all around him, but the space around the chair remained in shadows. It was a visible representation of night and day.

Nic stuck out his hand into the sphere, and his hand disappeared, enveloped by black smoke. In the sphere's center, the faint outline of Tate in the chair reclined, pointing him toward the sky.

Sophia stood under the viewscreen that displayed images of the ship's damage. Though only half the screen was visible, most of the ship was still displayed. Every part that was on screen flashed in various shades of red. Nic couldn't imagine the saucer would ever fly again. One of the parts turned black as the ship's engines revved, and Nic wondered if it was something that Tate was doing. "What are you up to, Tate?"

"I was just trying to see if we could lift this thing off the ground," Tate replied. His chair was now lowering to the floor, and he was clearly visible again. "Don't worry, nothing happened. I think some of the controls are missing. It was like I didn't have all the options needed to fly."

"Or everything you need to fly is broken," Sophia said, pointing to the screens above them. "And what happened to not pushing anything?"

"I could've pushed more buttons," Tate replied. "I bet one of the triggers on the handles would fire a weapon. Besides, I only touched what wouldn't cause a problem."

Sophia shrugged and then headed to the workstations on the right side, stepping over the debris as she went, when Nic noticed movement near her foot.

"Don't move, Sophia!" Nic yelled.

Sophia froze, stopping on a metal plate. Her face winced as her eyes turned to face Nic.

Nic stared at her feet, trying to find what moved. When Sophia sighed and then turned to face him, he saw it again.

"Funny, Nic," Sophia said.

"No, I'm serious." Nic approached her. "There is something by your foot. What *is* that?"

A spider, with a body as big as Nic's hand, lay pinned under the metal plate Sophia stood on. Nic inched forward, staring at it. "It's a huge tarantula."

Sophia stepped back, releasing it from what held it down, but it didn't run. Nic leaned in, examining it up close. It was missing two of its limbs, and the tip of one broken leg tapped against the floor, making a soft click of metal on metal. It would twitch periodically, but made no attempt to stand on its feet.

"It's a robotic tarantula," Nic said. He picked up a piece of metal the length of a pencil, hooked it under an outstretched broken limb, and lifted the spider off the ground.

"Well, don't pick it up!" Sophia said.

"It's okay," Nic replied. "I don't think it's working." He reached out and brushed off crumbled pieces of debris. He set the huge tarantula on his open palm, letting its legs hang from his hands like drapes.

"*Great,*" Tate said. "Spiders from outer space."

"It's not from outer space," Nic said. "This spaceship is clearly a human design."

"How do you figure?" Tate asked. "You saw the cockpit, Nic. The chair floats in the air, and you can see through walls. I mean, the thing was invisible. This is way beyond anything humans can make."

"That's true, but even though the cockpit is super advanced, it wouldn't fit that alien. Besides, the robot is a tarantula and not a crazy outer-space amoeba thing."

Sophia leaned in and poked the tarantula, which twitched again in response. "Also," she added, "the lights turned on when you said *power on*."

"That's right," Nic said. "Tate, you said you wanted to look for something to turn the *power on*, and then the lights came on. We just didn't realize why; well, I guess Sophia did."

"But if this is a human ship," Tate said skeptically, "why is it so advanced?"

Nic didn't know and didn't respond. He held the tarantula on his palm at eye level when it twitched again and then sprang to life. It leapt from Nic's hand, causing him to fall back onto the walkway, legs spread. The tarantula landed between his legs and crept toward him.

Nic scurried back in a backward crab walk, with the tarantula in pursuit. "Smash it, Sophia!"

Sophia removed her backpack and slammed it down on top of the spider.

The tarantula squeezed out and continued on its path. Nic stumbled, shaking in horror as the tarantula skittered around him, passing his face.

It climbed up the wall to a hole big enough to stick three fingers in and stopped. Leg after leg entered the hole until only its body remained. It burned red hot before filling the damaged hull, leaving behind a silver splotch.

Nic took a deep breath. He stood, and then slid his finger across the warm surface that used to be the spider. "It's flat."

Sophia pointed to half a dozen similar silver blemishes marking the surfaces of the room. "The spider has to be what the ship uses to make repairs."

"Well, if it is human design," Tate said, heading to the workstation to the right of the viewscreen, "let's figure out why the ship is so advanced." He took a seat, managing to turn on a three-dimensional screen in front of him.

Sophia took a closer look at the monitor below the viewscreen and the various controls in front of her.

Nic headed for the workstation on the left when Sophia ducked down to a loose panel. She pulled it open, showing the inner workings of the ship, drawing all three of them to it like moths to a light.

It appeared to be a power source of some sort. Whatever it was, it wasn't that big. It was the size of Nic's hand if he spread out his fingers, but only an inch thick. Or a six-legged starfish, if it was made out of metal glowing arms, a perpetually moving orb in the center, and enough wires to be tangled for a lifetime if just one fell out of place.

The orb in the middle, while only an inch wide, appeared semi-transparent, but instead of seeing through to the other side, Nic swore he was looking into a vast empty chamber.

"If we unplugged it," Sophia said, "we could probably take it out."

"No, Sophia!" Tate shouted, kneeling to take a look. "Why would we ever want to do that? Just let it be. It could be powering the cloaking device, for all we know."

"Relax, Tate," Sophia said. "I wasn't going to pull it out. I just said we probably *could*."

Tate closed the panel, sneering at Sophia, and then headed back to his workstation. Nic left Sophia to examine the device's controls. He headed to the left workstation and took a seat on a mesh-fabric chair that reminded him of one in his dad's office that he wasn't allowed to sit in. He sank into it and found it even more comfortable than his father's.

The desk surrounded him in a semicircle, which came alive as Nic ran his hand across its smooth surface. An image of a keyboard appeared, along with a projection of an empty screen that followed the curve of the desk. The keyboard wasn't from an unknown alien language; it was similar to the keyboard Nic used at home. This one had many more keys though, which Nic recognized but was unsure what they could mean.

The keyboard keys lowered as his fingers passed over them, yet the cold, smooth table below his fingertips gave Nic the chills. He pressed the power button, causing a list to appear on the projected screen in the space in front of him.

*Diagnostic Test*
*Earth*
*Teratas*
*Fleet*
*Mission Log*

Nic reached up and poked at *Teratas*. His fingers passed through it, but the image in front of him changed to the familiar shape of the crystal spaceship. A line above it named the ship *Terata space fighter*. On its side were a list of features, from acceleration to weapons payload, all in values Nic was unfamiliar with.

Nic selected a golden arrow next to the spaceship. The image changed to a spiky crystal ball labeled *Terata drone*. Its features indicated it was the size of a small car but unmanned. He cycled through more ships: *Terata transport, Terata warship,* before finding one labeled *Terata command ship*. It reminded Nic of a giant saguaro cactus covered with limbs that folded in on themselves.

"Guys," Nic said, "that alien spaceship isn't the only one."

"Where are the other ones?" Sophia asked. She now stood in front of a small alcove containing a panel with a variety of switches. She reached out and flipped one.

"Stop pushing everything, Sophia!" Tate said. "We have no clue what they could do."

Sophia stopped and stared at Tate with a lopsided sneer. "How else are we going to learn?"

"Really, Sophia? Remember, we want to avoid pushing a self-destruct button."

Sophia flipped the next switch with a smile. "Yeah, Tate. But another could activate the ship's artificial intelligence program. You never know."

"Sophia, the term *curiosity killed the cat* describes people like you."

"Meow," Sophia replied, flipping another switch, which turned on a monitor above the weird power source. "See, Tate?"

Nic backed up a screen and then selected *Mission Log*. A list of videos displayed with the strange woman from the hill pictured next to each one. "Guys, I found something."

Tate headed his way, passing by Sophia as she sat in front of a computer with a pair of clocks above it.

"That's the alien lady, right?" Tate asked as he made his way to Nic.

"The human lady, yes. She left these videos. Maybe they explain what happened," Nic said. "Sophia, come here."

"What?" Sophia asked, still focusing on the images in front of her. "Uh, yeah. I'll be there in a minute."

Tate turned back to the screen in front of them and said to Nic, "Play the last video."

Before Nic selected anything, the video started, due to Tate's command. A three-dimensional image of the mysterious woman from the hill sat in the pilot's chair. She wore a navy-blue shirt partially tucked into black slacks. Her frazzled black hair stuck out at odd angles, and puffy red eyes indicated she might have been crying.

*This is Nadezda Wright. The date is ... the date is July 9, 2022. I successfully deployed the disruptor and disabled the command ship's shields, but ... they didn't stay down. So... I fled here. I was followed by a space fighter, which I managed to shoot down before also crashing on Earth. The local authorities found the space fighter but were unable to find me. Cloaking is operational for now, but ... my ship will never fly again. I'm going to use current Earth technology for repairs rather than risk being spotted ... another time. Printers are down, so I will return after finding food in town.*

The video ended, leaving Nic with more questions than answers. "She attacked a command ship."

"Yeah, and she is going to use *Earth technology*," Tate said, adding air quotes for emphasis. "That means she isn't from Earth, right?"

"No, Tate," Nic said. "The ship is a human spaceship. She's human."

"But Nic," Tate said, "what if that lady was sent to infiltrate human society? She might not be the same as the other freak, but she could still be an alien. I mean, look at this place."

Nic shook his head, glancing past Tate to Sophia. In front of her, the screen displayed the spaceship with two clocks and a big green button labeled *Start*. Sophia stared intently at her controls.

"Hey, Sophia!" Nic said. "Come here."

Sophia, ignorant of Nic's comment, reached forward and pressed the button labeled *Start*.

"Sophia," Tate said, "what did you just push?"

Sophia froze, and then stammered, "G-guys. Uh, you were right, Tate. I probably shouldn't have pushed that. I just wanted to see if ..."

A woman's robotic voice began a countdown.

"*Ten.*"

"Sophia!" Tate yelled. "Was that the self-destruct button?"

"*Nine.*"

Sophia sprinted for the exit, yelling, "Run!"

"*Eight.*"

"*Seven.*"

"*Six.*"

Sophia leapt outside through the door, followed by Tate.

Nic jumped outside. His shoe caught on the damaged door-frame, and he fell face first onto the ramp.

"*Five.*"

"*Four.*"

Nic scrambled to his feet. He raced down the ramp to Sophia and Tate, who were already on the ground outside, curled into balls, bracing for an explosion. Nic dove between them, landing hard enough to knock the wind out of him, but still heard a faint, "*One,*" from the spaceship.

*Thump!*

No explosion came. Nic groaned as he stood, and then turned to find the spaceship was gone. All that was left was the depression in the ground that it had created.

"What happened to it?" Tate yelled.

Nic rubbed his nose. "Maybe it's cloaked." He plodded back and reached out, half expecting to touch the spaceship's hull, but his hand passed through empty space.

Tate turned on Sophia, his hands clenched tightly into fists. "You always do this. What happened to not touching anything?"

"I'm sorry," Sophia said, her face reddening. "It's just, I think I figured out what was going on. And I didn't want anyone to think it was a stupid idea, so I wanted to prove it first."

"But if you figured it out, Sophia, you should have just said," Tate said, exasperated.

Nic returned to the others and stood next to Sophia, staring back to where the ship should be. "What did you figure out?"

"Well," Sophia replied, "the ship was made by humans, but everything was more advanced than we have. What if—I mean, floating chairs, seeing through walls, and invisibility are all things people might be able to do in the future. What if—"

"Wait," Tate said, "are you telling me you thought the spaceship was a time machine? That power source you found was actually a time machine?"

"Well, yeah," she replied. "It certainly looks that way now, doesn't it?"

"If it was, why would you send it away? We should have stayed inside." Tate grabbed a rock and threw it through where the spaceship had been.

Nic stood in silence, unable to comprehend the possibilities. If it was a time machine, they could have gone anywhere. If it was a time machine, that lady, Nadezda, must have come from the future. "Sophia, where did you send it?"

*Thump!*

Nic turned back to the ship, expecting it to be gone, but it had returned. It was no longer embedded in the ground as it was before, but was still at an angle due to the uneven ground that it rested on.

"A minute later," Sophia said grinning.

Tate's jaw dropped. "Sophia, you're a genius!" He ran to the ship, followed by Sophia, and then Nic.

Once inside, Sophia sprinted back to the time machine controls. "So, are you sure we should do this? I mean, maybe it isn't a good idea after all."

"What do you mean?" Nic asked. "We have a chance to see the future! How can we not take it?"

"It's just, that lady was fighting aliens. What if she needs the time machine?"

"It's a time machine," Nic said. "We can go *whenever* we want, and when we return, it'll be like we never left. What could possibly go wrong?"

Tate rubbed the back of his neck. "Which way should we go? Honestly, I would rather see what happens in the future."

Sophia's frown deepened, indicating that she still didn't think they should go. "What if we went home and then came back after getting some real supplies. All we have now is what we brought for the sleepover."

"No," Tate replied. "If we leave, then that Nadezda lady will come back. It's now or never."

"I guess we really won't get a second chance at this," Sophia said reluctantly. Her brows raised, staring at Nic. "Well?"

"What?" Nic asked.

"You're the leader, man," Tate said.

Nic groaned. "I'm not the leader." When they continued to stare at him, Nic added, "To be safe, we should go a short distance to start. That way we will be familiar with whenever we go. Maybe just a year into the future, the first time."

"Nothing will have changed in a year," Tate said. "We need to go far enough that we will notice a difference."

"Yeah," Sophia said, "but we don't want to see any of those aliens."

"Fifty years then," Nic said.

"Thanks, boss," Tate said with a smile.

Sophia made adjustments to the device. The second clock now read 2072, July 9, 19:48:47. "Are we ready?"

"Yes," Tate said.

They were already at a slight angle because of the way the ship rested on the ground. Nic grabbed the table, expecting a bumpy ride. "Ready?"

Sophia pushed the button.

The robotic voice once again began to count down. "*Ten.*" As the countdown continued, Nic heard a whistle created by the wind blowing through the ship's holes, indistinct sounds of nature, as well as an irregular hoot of an owl outside. When they arrive in a new time, the owl would be gone, maybe replaced by its descendants. Nic could find his family in the new time, and he would even be an adult by then. He couldn't imagine what else could change in the next fifty years. Technology would advance, of course, but would everything else change for the better?

"*Three.*"

"*Two.*"

"*One.*"

Nic winced from pressure building in his ears, like they were about to pop from elevation change. He raised his hands, covering his temples.

*Thump!*

## CHAPTER 4
# THE FUTURE

*Fifty years later*
*July 9, 2072*

The entire spaceship dropped away from beneath Nic's feet. His stomach lurched into his chest, and he gasped, anticipating a hard fall. The ship didn't drop far but still landed with a crash. He was able to steady himself on the workstation in front of him, but was knocked off his feet by a tumbling Tate.

Nic lay on the floor, realizing that the ship's drop came from it being at an angle when they left and being on level ground now.

While he lay, he waited for the pressure that built up in his ears to fade away. It didn't hurt, but the ship sounded weird. Then he realized that the pressure that built up in his ears was already gone; it was just the sound, or change of sound, that he found so unnerving. The wind had ceased blowing, and he could no longer make out any outside critters through the spaceship's holes. The only thing he heard now was the faint sound of a stream. It was clear that they had moved without Nic having to look outside.

Tate rubbed his arm and groaned, "Did we make it?"

"I think so," Sophia said. "This says we're in 2072."

"Well," Nic said, getting back on his feet, "let's check out the future."

Nic started for the entrance, but before he got there, the lights inside the spaceship flickered and then extinguished.

"Hey, ship, power on! Lights!" Tate yelled, but they remained in the dark.

The spaceship was dimly lit by streams of light that shone through the dozens of holes in the damaged hull and the light coming through the doorway, but it was no brighter than a room lit by candlelight. Nic inched his way across the room to try to peek outside. Once he reached the doorway, he felt the flashlight that Tate tossed onto his backpack. He handed it to Sophia and said, "Go back to the time machine controls and try to get us home."

"What happened?" Tate asked, following Sophia through the darkened ship. "Did we make it or not?"

Nic ducked down at the doorway entrance and then peeked outside.

The spaceship barely moved, but everything outside had changed. Nic couldn't help feeling that he fell asleep and then woke up in a nightmare he created.

When they left, an open field surrounded them, but now Nic thought they might be in the middle of a forest. He searched for the outside lights, finding them attached to walls that were hidden by variety of plants. Bushes and small trees flourished, while vines climbed up walls to the glass topped pergola above them. They time traveled into the middle of an atrium, not a forest.

On the atrium floor, a small path led to a long wooden bench, on which sat three figures too backlit to reveal their features.

"Can you send us back, Sophia?" Nic asked.

Tate stood over Sophia, shaking his dimly lit head. "We just got here. Besides, we can return home at any time. It's not like anyone knew we were coming."

"Tate," Nic said, "look outside. They *did* know we were coming and have known for fifty years."

"You don't know that for sure, Nic."

"Okay, Tate," Nic said, and then added sarcastically, "I suppose those three people on the bench are casually waiting for a bus."

Leaving Sophia behind, Tate headed to the door, stopping next to Nic. His eyes squinted and then darted around, searching the atrium.

One of the figures remained seated, but the other two stood. The smaller of the two turned down the path and actually skipped out of sight.

"I changed my mind," Tate said. "I think they did know we were coming. Sophia, get us out of here."

"Sorry, but there is no power. I can't turn it on."

"You're supposed to be the smart one. Figure it out."

A woman's honeyed voice called to them, "I killed the power. You might as well come out."

"What do we do, Nic?" Sophia asked from across the room.

"Why are you asking me?" Nic asked. "I don't know what to do."

"You're our fearless leader, man. Lead us out of this," Tate said. He turned back to Sophia and yelled, "Keep trying, Sophia, or this will be the shortest trip ever."

"Well, I wouldn't say the shortest. It lasted fifty years," Sophia replied.

"You know what I mean."

Sophia stood next to the time machine controls and shrugged. She left it to join Nic and Tate at the door. She crouched and peered into the atrium.

Nic felt like an animal in a zoo, caged in and being watched by their keeper. "I'm going out there. If we can't go back now, we can still see what's going on in this time. We'll find a way back later."

Nic headed outside and approached the strangers.

A skinny old woman leaned into her cane. When she turned back to the boy, still seated on the bench, the light caught her face just right, portraying a far younger version of herself. Her eyes confirmed Nic's suspicion, as the odd lines encircling the pupil continued even though her eyes remained in place. It was Nadezda from the spaceship's video. Though now, she had wrinkles, and her short hair had grayed enough that black strands were a rarity. She reminded him of his grandma, and he half expected her to pinch his cheek or offer them a plate of cookies. She remained silent, though, now staring at the ship's entrance.

Nic turned back to the ship. Sophia and Tate were on the ramp now and hustling to join him. Behind Nadezda, a boy rose from his seat. Nic watched him, stunned as each mechanical step of the pale boy revealed that he—or it—was actually a robot. It wore jeans and a polo shirt but had a plastic face like a mannequin in a department store, except for its glass eyes.

Tate stopped next to Nic, but Sophia continued until she was inches from the robot's face, and stared deep into its eyes.

The robot took a step back and said in an electronic voice, "Wow there, Sophia. You are so close that I can smell your breath."

"You can smell?" Sophia asked, taking a step back but still leaning forward.

"No. That was my attempt at humor. I was trying to imply that you are too close, that is all." It held up its hand. "I am pleased to meet you."

Sophia grabbed its hand and shook it up and down. She turned back to Nic and Tate and said, "I'm shaking hands with a robot."

Tate motioned to Nadezda, who was staring at Sophia. Her eyebrows rose as a grin spread across her face.

Sophia let go of the robot and took a step back next to Nic. "Just being friendly. You should try it sometime, Tate."

Tate shook his head.

To take attention off of the others bickering, Nic stepped forward. His mouth opened, but he struggled to find what to say, and remained quiet.

Nadezda cleared her throat. "It's so nice to finally meet the three of you."

Nic was surprised by her tone. If she was actually happy to meet them, then maybe they shouldn't be worried.

"We can talk more pleasantly inside," Nadezda said with her smile fading. "I'll let you know what it will take to get home."

Nadezda saying *what it will take to get home* left Nic questioning if something went wrong. He turned back to the time machine and relaxed, knowing he could get back as easily as he arrived.

With a nod from Nadezda, the robot started down the path. Its head swiveled slowly to its side, and then it spoke in its electronic voice, "This way, please. You do not want to see what we use to guard the atrium; it is ferocious."

Tate spun around and stared into the shadows cast by the spaceship.

Nadezda's smile returned. "He's only joking. He's actually the atrium's caretaker."

Nic chuckled, while Sophia still eyed the robot in fascination. They entered a living room decorated for the past, despite being fifty years in the future. Nadezda hobbled over to a chair, and Sophia followed the robot until it backed into an empty corner of the room. Its foot stopped on a metal plate that reminded Nic of a Roomba's docking station.

Nic watched Tate head to a rosewood couch upholstered in a moss-green fabric, the hardwood floor creaking with each step. Tate sat, slouching into the couch, resting his head on his hand. On the wall in front of him hung a map of the world from the early eighteenth century.

Even without the robot docked in the corner, it was clear they were in the future. Behind the couch, a canvas painting of a young Nadezda at a party moved like a video stuck in a loop. On the floor at its side, a ten-foot circular platform had no apparent purpose until Nic noticed a small headset hooked next to the wall, resembling a virtual reality system.

Nic crossed the room to sit next to Tate, and a large bay window caught his eye. Outside, a row of residential houses stood where, to him, an hour before lay a single house still under construction. The time machine had created an entire neighborhood with the click of a button.

Hooking her cane onto her chair, Nadezda studied Sophia as she examined the canvas painting. Nadezda hummed a soft tune that Nic couldn't make out and smiled the same way she did when she followed the squirrel fifty years ago. Her expression hadn't changed, but Nic still struggled with the fact that the old lady in front of them was the same person they saw roughly an hour ago.

Tate had kicked his foot over the arm rest of the couch and stared at the old world map on the wall, while Sophia took her seat.

The door at Nic's side cracked open with a creak. Nic glanced over, noticing a light-brown eye staring back at him. One that Nic thought was quite catching but didn't have the futuristic lines like Nadezda. With a blink, the eye was gone behind the slowly closing door.

"Well," Nadezda said, "I've rehearsed this in my head, but now that you are here, I'm not sure where I should start." She straightened her back and then rested her hands in her lap.

"How did you know when we would arrive?" Tate asked.

"I didn't," Nadezda replied. "I have waited in this atrium on July 9, between 7 and 9 p.m. every year since you left. I would have been notified if you arrived when I wasn't here, but it was much more likely that you would pick a specific number of years to time travel. It wasn't so bad, though. Every year I would stay home and celebrate the anniversary of my arrival on Earth."

"What happened when you realized your spaceship was gone?" Sophia asked.

"It was my first time here. It was wonderful—the plants,

the animals, and even the air lacked the metallic odor that was so common on the colony ship I grew up on. So, with me stranded in your time, I made the best of it. I have lived a long, happy, and productive life." Nadezda paused, smiling.

Tate shrugged, leg still dangling over the armrest. "Well, we found your spaceship. You can't blame us for trying to find out what it could do."

"Yes, Tate," Nadezda replied. "You're right, and I don't blame you. I should have been more careful."

"We did borrow the spaceship," Nic said. "But we really were going to return it."

Nadezda nodded. "It wouldn't have been a big deal if you *borrowed* the spaceship, but that would mean that I would have gotten it back. However, you took it, with the time machine, and that is where the problem really lies."

"What does it matter that we *took* the time machine?" Tate asked. "It's back, and you can take it *whenever* you want."

Nadezda chuckled. "Oh, no. My time traveling days are behind me. I might have if you had returned after ten years, or even twenty, but I'm too old now to go gallivanting through time."

Everyone silently waited for her to continue, with the only sounds coming from the next room where Nic had caught someone spying on them earlier. Nic sighed and ran his fingers through his hair. He understood that Nadezda lived her life on Earth, but he didn't understand why. Why was she stranded in their time? They could go back right now, so what was he missing?

"So," Nadezda continued, "I don't know how much you figured out when you were on my ship, but in the future, humans are at war. Trapped in the past, I did the only thing I could do to help. I used my knowledge of the future to advance human technology in the past. Now, I know you want to get home and return the time machine to my younger self. But, *if* you don't make it home, then hopefully my time on Earth will have made a difference."

Sophia glanced at Nic but didn't say anything.

Tate planted both feet in front of him and sat at the edge of his seat, serious for the first time since they arrived. "What do you mean, *if* we don't make it home?"

"This might be difficult for you to hear," Nadezda replied, motioning for Tate to relax. He scooted back as Nadezda cleared her throat. It was only a moment, but seconds seemed to stretch on for an eternity.

"Well, sending you home is not that simple. The time machine we developed only travels into the future—"

"What!" Tate yelled, standing. "If your time machine only goes to the future, then we'll never see our families again!"

# CHAPTER 5

# EARTH'S FUTURE

"You can't go back in time using just my time machine," Nadezda said, motioning for Tate to take his seat again. Once he did, she continued. "However, nature provides us with a way to travel into the past, by the use of wormholes. In order to travel into the past, you must find a temporal wormhole capable of sending you to any time before 2022. Then, the time machine developed in my time could be used to travel into the future, to your future and back home."

"So, wait," Tate said. "Did you use your time machine or a wormhole to get to our time?" Tate asked.

"I suppose I should start from the beginning," Nadezda replied, putting her hands together. "Before I was born, in the year 2243, an alien race called the Terata attacked, causing the extinction of human life on Earth." She paused to let what she said sink in.

Nic's heart skipped, struggling to beat again. His breath caught in his chest as he stared at Nadezda. Human life would *not* survive! Nadezda could be the only person who could change that, and she was stranded in the past. All humanity could be lost because they took her time machine.

Nadezda sighed and then continued, "Before Earth's capture, three interstellar colony ships escaped. My ship, the *Pinta*, began researching a way to defeat the Terata. The *Pinta* scientists came up with a device that could overload the Terata command ship's shield, thus allowing us to finally take them out. However, the scientists were too late. The only way the new weapon would be effective is if it was used when the Teratas first attacked. So, they switched their research to time travel."

"That couldn't have been easy," Sophia said.

"No," Nadezda replied, "but humans had discovered a wormhole in the past, not knowing what it was at the time. So, with that research, the *Pinta* scientists were not starting from scratch. By the time I was born, our scientists had figured out how to time travel into the future, but still couldn't travel into the past unless they used a naturally occurring temporal wormhole. We found one, halfway between Venus and Earth. I was chosen for the mission and was supposed to be joined by others, but the Teratas had found us. In the mad rush to escape them, I was the only one to survive the trip through the wormhole."

Nadezda's eyes dashed around the room, as if remembering a scene as it unfolded, some horror of the past she could never forget. Her eyes welled up with tears, but she continued, "I passed through the wormhole and ended up in a small city over Sweden in the mid-1940s."

"Wait," Tate said. "Why, if you went through a wormhole near Venus, did you end up on Earth?"

"I wasn't sure," she replied, wiping her tears. She smiled

and then continued, "I have theories, but it's impossible to be certain. Just know that for your purposes, most wormholes, incoming and outgoing, are found within Earth's atmosphere."

A buzzer blared in the next room, causing Nic to turn his head. He glimpsed a girl eyeing them once again through the crack in the door, but she stepped out of view just before the alarm stopped.

"Since I arrived in the past," Nadezda continued, "I used the time machine to send me to when the Terata attacked in the future, the year 2243. I used the weapon to bring down the Terata shields. However, the shields didn't stay down. The Terata continued their attack and forced me to flee through a wormhole I found in space. When I passed through this wormhole, I appeared twenty thousand feet above your city, being chased by a Terata space fighter. I stopped it, and crashed, and then you know the rest."

Nadezda waited for them with eyebrows raised, clearly expecting questions. Tate's usual smirk was hidden under a pout. He scratched his cheek and said, "You said that you don't want to time travel anymore. Are you actually going to let us take the time machine and try to get home?"

"Yes," Nadezda replied. "I want you to make it back. I did what I could to advance technology in my time on Earth, but I unfortunately don't think it will make a difference in the long run. If you three return my time machine to the me of 2022, then I, from that time, will have the best chance to defeat the Terata."

"So," Sophia said, "how do we even find a wormhole?"

"The time machine is programed to stop as soon as a wormhole into the past is detected and point you in the right direction. Your time to pass through the wormhole will be limited, though. In our research, wormholes are temporary, lasting as little as a couple of hours to as long as a week. Most wormholes will be too small to pass through, but the time machine is also designed to expand the wormhole enough for a small spaceship."

"But you said that your spaceship was broken," Sophia said. "How could we even make it to a wormhole without flying to one?"

"It's true, my spaceship won't help you. Cars don't fly yet, but they will soon. They might be your easiest option at first, but no matter what, you will have to find something that flies."

Nic didn't know how to acquire anything that flew but was more worried about the time machine itself. "Does the time machine even work without your spaceship?"

Nadezda smiled. "As far as the time machine goes, I can easily remove it from my spaceship. And I can make it portable enough that you can either just send yourselves or pick a vehicle to send through time."

Nic imagined a car would be easiest, but it was nice to know that they could use anything.

"How many chances will we have?" Tate asked.

"It's hard to know for sure, but there should be a couple wormholes between now and the Terata War. If you don't make it home before the Terata War, then the wormhole will be on the other side of the Teratas, in space, and you will be stuck in a time when humanity is lost. So, make sure you are successful before that." Nadezda sighed and then added, "It is your choice. Either travel into the future in search of wormholes or stay here in my time."

Nadezda wanted them to go and was giving them a choice, but Nic felt sick at the possibility of not making it home. Now that Nic no longer had to move, he knew that he couldn't stay. It seemed to Nic that the time machine did all the hard work; all they had to do was go through the wormhole, and then use the time machine again to get home.

"We have to try," Nic said, and then added in a cracking voice that betrayed any sense of confidence, "We *will* make it home."

Tate nodded, his smirk returning. He would be the last one to admit they were in over their heads, a fault that Nic was sure would never change. In a way, Nic wished he had the same outlook, but doubts were starting to creep in. Before his doubts took hold of him, someone burst through the kitchen door.

A beautiful girl, roughly Nic's age, strolled into the room, balancing in her right hand a tray with a porcelain teapot and matching cups. Nic recognized her as the same brown-eyed girl he had glimpsed through the doorway. Apart from their eye color, this girl reminded Nic of a youthful Nadezda. She was bronze skinned, with frizzy black hair pulled into a ponytail. Her eyes danced between them as she set the tray on the coffee table. She poured tea into each cup and began passing them out.

"Thank you, Zoe," Nadezda said, accepting a cup.

Nic stared into Zoe's eyes with raised eyebrows until she handed him a cup. She handed cups to Sophia and Tate before taking the last cup and sitting in the chair next to Nadezda. "It's so nice to meet all of you."

"Uh, yeah. Thank you for the tea," Tate said, setting his cup on the coffee table. He turned to Nadezda. "Should she be in here while we talk?"

"My granddaughter knows what happened," Nadezda replied.

"Well, you guys are different than I imagined from those old news stories you were in," Zoe said with a smile. "This is *so* surreal."

"We were in the news?" Nic asked. "What did people say about us?"

"About what you would expect," Zoe replied. "You were lost children, and your parents were worried about you."

A pang of regret hit Nic at the mention of their parents. He was sorry about the way things ended with them and would do anything to just be home. Not that he was ready to move, but he missed his family already, even his brother.

A buzz came from a watch attached to Nadezda's wrist; she glanced down to a message waiting for her. She stood and said as she left the room, "I must answer this. I'll be back in a minute."

"So," Zoe said, unable to keep the sheer glee from her voice. She sat, resting her elbows on her knees, leaning forward with a wide grin. "What was it like?"

"What?" Nic asked.

"Traveling through time, obviously."

"I got a terrible pain around my ears, and then we were here," Nic said. "All the pain's gone."

"The landing was a little rough too," Sophia added.

"Oh, how wonderful," Zoe said.

The happiness that she felt for their arrival gnawed at Nic. They were stuck here, may never see their families again, and she acted like it was the first day of summer vacation.

"Wonderful?" Tate spat. "That's an awful thing to say. What is so wonderful about not being able to go home?"

Zoe stammered, "I-I'm sorry. Well. I mean. It's terrible that you are here, but you traveled through time, and that's amazing." Her cheeks flushed when everyone remained quiet.

Nadezda returned but did not sit down. "It's getting late, and I have to take a short trip tomorrow after the three of you go."

"Already?" Zoe asked. "You were supposed to be home for the rest of summer."

"Well," Nadezda replied, "with the spaceship here, I need to make arrangements for it. I'll have someone come by tomorrow to check in on you."

"Don't bother," Zoe said, dejected. "I'm just going to stay next door with Romona."

Nadezda nodded to Zoe and then addressed the rest of them. "I need to remove the time machine from the spaceship. It will take a little time to make it portable, but I'll finish before morning. You three can stay in my house tonight. Make sure to get some rest and eat if you're hungry. After all, you have a big day ahead of you tomorrow."

# CHAPTER 6
# A NEW START

Nic startled awake when Zoe knocked on the door the next morning. She peeked her head inside and said, "Come get breakfast. Sophia is already downstairs talking to Grandma about how to work the time machine." Before Nic could say a word, Zoe was gone.

Rather than getting up, Nic rolled to his side and thought about his family. He couldn't imagine what his parents went through when he never returned home. Even his older brother, Ethan, would miss him, not that they hung out since he started high school.

Heavy breathing from the next bed signaled that Tate was still asleep.

Nic stood up from his twin bed and stared outside at the neighborhood. His bed behind him beeped, and when he turned, the sheets flattened. As if done by a ghost, the bed cover crept up to the pillows, forming a perfectly made bed.

Nic pulled on his shirt from yesterday and then left the room, leaving Tate still sleeping behind him. He made his way downstairs and stopped at the base of the steps to admire a picture of a much younger Nadezda. He stood there entranced, lost in how much younger she was only yesterday.

Thinking of Nadezda as an old lady made Nic wonder what happened to his parents. The thought of how worried they must have been made him feel sick to his stomach. They never found out what became of him, and unless he made it home, they never would. He still didn't understand why they had to move away, but now he would do anything just to be able to tell them that he was okay.

Nic didn't realize when Zoe arrived. She stood next to him; her hair was pulled back into a ponytail that had a purple high-light on the side that she added since last night. She smiled and said, "It's an exciting day! I feel like I have been waiting for this my entire life." She took his arm and pulled him into the kitchen. "Come on. I'll show you how the kitchen works."

Nic chuckled at not knowing how a kitchen works and then realized that things probably changed a lot since his time. He entered the kitchen, underwhelmed. It wasn't very big, with a short wall of closed cabinets and a nine-paneled display case of various plants and herbs. The only counter available was at the center island, which had enough room for only one person to do any prep work for a meal.

The kitchen was also open to a rather large dining area, which was where Sophia sat in a separate breakfast nook talking to Nadezda. Sophia, like Nic, wore the same clothes as yesterday. She hunched over a large three-inch-thick tablet with a wide grin on her face, listening intently to Nadezda.

The tablet was enclosed in a protective case. It had to be the time machine, but Nic thought it would be bigger, given the size of the time-travel device and all the wires that surrounded it on the spaceship.

Sophia's eyes brightened when she noticed Nic. "It's about time you got up. Nadezda is teaching me how to use the time machine." She held up the bulky tablet and waved it back and forth, and then set it down. "Hurry up and get something to eat so you can join us."

Zoe pulled Nic over to the kitchen island, where the first thing Nic noticed was that in the center display case, surrounded by various plants and herbs, was a terrarium filled with grasshoppers.

Nic frowned at the grasshoppers. "Why do you have pet insects in the kitchen?"

"Why, those aren't pets," Zoe replied, laughing. "They're food."

A grasshopper crawled across a twig, causing Nic to cringe at the mere thought of eating it. "Well, you'll never catch me eating one."

Zoe chuckled again and then said, "You don't have to." She pulled a tablet out of a hidden panel on the counter, which currently held a recipe for a berry smoothie. She backed up a screen and selected breakfast, and then told Nic, "Just pick something you want, and it will be made for you."

Nic stared at the monitor and then picked the first thing that sounded good, which was a waffle. A prompt asked if he wanted any mix-ins, which made Nic glance over to Nadezda, who wasn't paying any attention to him. With the choice being his, Nic selected chocolate chips and sprinkles. The screen displayed the recipe, listing each of the ingredient and where they were in the kitchen. When he clicked start, a timer popped up with two minutes. "That's amazing."

"Oh, yeah," Zoe replied. "It scans the food available in the kitchen, and the monitor displays recipes that can be made from those ingredients. You can pick a recipe and set a time for the food to be ready, and the kitchen will prepare everything. Pretty advanced, huh? Compared to what you're used to anyway."

"So, it will make anything you want?" Nic asked.

"Anything that can be made with the ingredients we have at home," Zoe replied. "If you run low on anything, then an order is placed at the store, and food is delivered to the fridge outside, which is connected to the kitchen."

Tate lumbered in with his jacket draped over his arm and his shirt on backward. He yawned and then rubbed his eyes before joining Nic and Zoe. He noticed his shirt, which he promptly spun around, before grabbing the monitor. "Oh, is this a menu?"

By the time Nic's breakfast was ready, Tate had ordered a breakfast burrito. Nic took his waffle out and set it on a plate but didn't bother with a fork.

Leaving Tate behind, Nic and Zoe joined the others at the breakfast nook.

As Nic sat next to Sophia, Zoe remained standing and said, "Well, I'm leaving now. I'll finish packing their car on my way out."

Nadezda got up to say goodbye and was nearly knocked over by Zoe's sudden embrace. Nadezda stood up straight and said, "I'll be back before you know, dear."

Zoe backed up, bit her lip, and then gave Nadezda another quick hug, before leaving with a trembling lip. Nic thought that their goodbye was a little odd, but Nadezda leaving meant that Zoe was on her own because of Nadezda's broken promises. Since Nadezda was going to send someone to check on her, and

Zoe seemed familiar with this protocol, Zoe being on her own had to be fairly common.

When Nic sat down, Nadezda continued, "Security is already set up for the three of you. When you turn on the screen, you will have to let it run a facial-recognition scan and verify your fingerprints. But as you are already holding it, and looking at the screen, you probably won't even notice these safety precautions. After the scans, at the password prompt, enter *1-2-3-4*. You'll need to change it, obviously, because if someone gets their hands on the time machine, that will be the first password they'll try."

Nadezda stared down at the time machine and then nodded. "I believe that's everything. Do you have any questions, Sophia?"

"No, I think I got it. I'm ready." Sophia grabbed the time machine and held it up to Nic and Tate. "Let me show you how it works, guys."

"Can you explain this on the way?" Tate asked, donning his flight jacket.

Sophia shrugged and then shut off the time machine, stuffing it in her backpack. "Well, I'm ready. Do we have to time travel right away? I wouldn't mind exploring a little while we're here in this time."

"It would be best if you did your exploring as you went," Nadezda replied. "While you are time traveling, you don't want to change something that will affect you in the future. A little change now might make things harder for you in another time. It's best to get it right the first time."

"Makes sense," Sophia replied and then hustled outside, Tate following with burrito in hand.

Nic watched them skip down the dirt path through a

window as Nadezda got up from her seat. Nic left with her, heading for the car in silence.

The car didn't look like a car from their time, but it also didn't have a sleek design you would expect from a futuristic car. It only had one door and a hatchback trunk, but it was big enough to be spacious inside.

The car was mostly a tinted cube of glass, with a blue bumper that encircled its base. Because of its boxlike look, Nic imagined that instead of driving, they would be shipped from place to place.

Sophia sat on the dirt, examining one of the car's wheels. Instead of the normal black rubber tire that Nic expected, these tires were big, blue, and spherical. If Nic had seen one off of the car, he would have thought that it was an oversized handball.

Tate had climbed inside the car but joined Nic when Nadezda approached, clearing her throat. She pulled three watches out of her pocket and handed one to Nic, Tate, and Sophia. She pulled on the watch that she wore around her wrist until it came off in the size of a six-inch ruler. She then tugged on its sides until it stretched into a five-by-seven-inch tablet.

"This dataPad technology is pretty standard today. However, I was able to modify them with tech from my time, allowing them to continue to be functional even in the future. I also made changes necessary for a time traveler. It is, of course, used as a personal identification card. But now, *whenever* you go, your dataPad will display your age and your adjusted birth date. That way, if you are scanned, you will appear to be twelve, not born in early 2010s. In addition to your ID card, the dataPad serves as a tablet and coin wallet." She pushed the edges together, returning it to the size of a watch, and then slapped it around her wrist.

"Did you say wallet?" Tate asked, searching through the functions in its tablet form. "Like, you're giving us money. How much?"

"You have enough for some purchases, but I wouldn't go overboard. Just be thrifty, and you'll have enough."

Nic expanded his dataPad, twisting it with light pressure. A strap on the back allowed him to attach it to his wrist and remain in tablet form. When he got to the home screen, it displayed four icons labeled: Adaptive Navigational GPS, Internet, Personal Data, and Scan & Display.

"Thank you so much for everything," Sophia said, shrinking her dataPad and then strapping it to her wrist. She gave a Nadezda a quick hug and then pulled out the time machine.

Nic pushed the ends of his dataPad together, returning it to its watch form with its screen now displaying a clock that read 9:36 a.m. "Thank you, Nadezda. We'll get your time machine back to you in 2022."

"You'll be fine," Nadezda said, smiling. She patted Nic's back as he turned to the car, and then added, "Just remember to get something that flies when you get to your new time."

"Thanks," Tate said and then climbed into the driver's seat. Nic watched him tug on the steering wheel embedded into the dashboard before leaning outside to ask, "What about the car? I can't get the steering wheel out. How am I supposed to drive?"

"The steering wheel comes out in an emergency. *You* don't need to drive anyway; cars drive themselves nowadays. Just wave your dataPad over the ignition sensor, type in where you want to go, and the car will take you there. Should the need arrive to manually drive, your modified dataPads are able to unlock the controls. With those, you would have been able to start my spaceship, if it was working. However, I would wait to override the autodrive system until that is needed."

Tate's hands slid from the steering wheel, disappointment that he wasn't about to drive evident in his groan as he scooted over. Nic got a good look at the car's interior. There were two swivel lounge chairs in the front and an L-shaped couch and a table in the back. There was room on the couch for another person, but the rest of the couch was taken by an oddly shaped tarp that covered their backpacks, tent, food, water, and whatever else Nadezda told Zoe to pack for them. Sophia got in second and found her seat on the couch.

Nic got in, shut the door behind him, and sat in the now-pointless driver's seat. He considered checking under the tarp to see what they got, but he decided to wait. The car was hastily packed and would be more spacious after repacking, but they would have to figure out what they needed.

Nic and Tate spun their seats around until they all sat facing each other. Sophia set the time machine in her lap and then selected the size icon. The device projected a three-dimensional image, which enclosed a twenty-foot sphere around them. Sophia manipulated the field until it engulfed only the car in a turquoise light. "It's ready."

"Okay, Sophia," Tate said, "how far into the future are we going this time?"

"I'll let you know when we get there," Sophia replied. "Any last words?"

"Yeah," Tate said. "Don't act like this is a death sentence."

"Well, speaking of death sentences," Nic said, "do either of you know how long before we need to worry about the Terata War?"

"No," Sophia replied, "but we don't have to worry about it

yet. Nadezda did say that a wormhole was being studied between now and her time. So, we have at least one try. Probably a couple though.”

“Okay, then,” Nic said, “we need to name the time machine.”

“Why?” Tate asked.

“Because we can’t talk about *our time machine* around other people.”

“What if it stands for something,” Tate replied smirking. “How about, Stuck Here in Time?”

“That’s not quite what I’m going for,” Nic replied, chuckling. “We’ll think of a name later. Oh, I can’t wait to see the future. Let’s go.”

Nic took one last look around. It was the first time he’d been outside since the neighborhood was just plots of land. Nadezda stood on the dirt driveway in front of the garage. Her house behind her was a really big, white, two-story home, with windows and a balcony on one side. It was exceptionally plain from the outside, possibly to accommodate the rather large atrium on the inside, which now held a spaceship. The yard was in dire need of care, with overgrown plants and weeds all around. Nadezda clearly chose to prioritize whatever work she had over any sort of yard maintenance.

Across the street were a couple of fenced-off plots of land with no houses. A trail ran between them, and it seemed like this land would be hard to sell. Both plots weren’t very deep, so the houses that would probably be there in a new time would have to be long and skinny.

Sophia counted, “Five. Four.”

“Why are you counting?” Tate asked.

"Well, the counter was attached to the ship, so we don't have it anymore."

"What is the point of the counter being removed if you're going to count anyway?"

Sophia shrugged. "It's for effect."

The tarp from the back of the car flew off of their gear. Nic, Sophia, and Tate jumped as Zoe reached for the time machine. "What are you guys waiting for? Let's go already!"

"What are you—" Nic said.

"How did—" Tate said.

"When did—" Sophia said.

A faint pressure built up in Nic's ears, not as painful as last time, and then the world outside the car vanished into a cloak of darkness.

*Thump!*

CHAPTER 7

# THE JOURNEY BEGINS

*Thirty-three years later*
*September 15, 2105*

The world flashed back into view. In a blink, Nadezda's house appeared as if it were the model of a before-and-after home renovation. The new owners painted it a dark gray, added a room, and fixed the yard so trees lined a newly paved cobblestone pathway. While the changes improved the house's curb appeal, the new driveway was over a foot lower in the new time, making the car reappear in the air.

The car fell, causing Nic's stomach to rise into his chest. He screamed, and a chorus of screams echoed from the others. The car smashed to the ground, deploying the airbags, which slapped Nic hard enough to make his ears ring.

Once the car settled, Nic rubbed his head and then ran his fingers through his hair. Sophia lifted her head, wincing. Tate pinched the deflated airbag in front of him until it slipped out of his fingers, automatically getting sucked back into the recesses of the car.

"Is everyone okay?" Nic asked.

Sophia nodded.

"I'm fine," Tate said, laughing. "You crashed, Nic. I'm driving next time."

"It's not like I could steer," Nic replied. "At least now we know why Nadezda said that time travel should be done while flying."

The three of them twisted around to stare at Zoe. She gazed outside with a bright smile. "Never been better."

Sophia chuckled and then stared down at the time machine. It lit up Sophia's smiling face as she hunched over it. "It is two forty-five in the afternoon in the year 2105."

Zoe clapped her hands together and shrieked. "We traveled thirty-three years." She tossed a backpack aside and went outside.

Nic left the car and stepped into a swarm of butterflies as they fluttered by.

Zoe spun around, stopping to face across the street. "Oh, and look, they made the lots across the street into a park. It seems impossible for so much to change in such a short time."

The same butterflies passed in front of Zoe as she stood, arms out, eyes closed, and taking a deep breath.

Tate left the car and faced her. "Well?"

"Well, what?" Zoe asked with a shrug.

"What are you doing here?" Tate asked.

"I wanted to come, obviously. It was about time you guys left too. I was getting a little cramped under the tarp."

"What I mean is, you're not one of us. Why would you come along?"

"You're ruining the moment," Zoe said, her shoulders slumping and bright smile fading. "I'm here for the time travel. This is an opportunity of a lifetime." Her smile returned as she waved her arm toward the park across the street. "How else could I see for myself what happens in the future?"

"Live your life," Tate replied.

"No," Zoe said. "Grandma has been telling me stories for years, but to actually travel through time? It's an opportunity I couldn't let slip by." She crossed her arms and looked away from them up to Nadezda's house.

Nic liked Zoe, but everyone else was torn away from their families when Nic led them to the time machine. He couldn't understand how Zoe would be able to leave her family behind, but she did and was only able to because of Nic's actions that trapped them in the future. It was his fault they weren't home now, and he felt responsible for everyone now, including Zoe. "Well, it doesn't matter, Tate. There is nowhere she can go now but with us."

"What about your family, Zoe?" Tate asked.

Zoe sighed and then replied, "Grandma's always working to save the future of humanity. She'll miss me, but I know she'll understand why I had to do this."

Sophia set the time machine in the car and grabbed the tarp from the back seat. "We should probably move everything to the trunk, so we have more room for the ride."

"Right." Zoe headed to the car. "We should've realized the driveway could change. I wonder what else has changed. Oh, this is so exciting!" Her eyes narrowed as she scrutinized Nadezda's old house. "I wonder what happened to her after we left."

"You could look her up," Nic replied.

Zoe stared down at her dataPad, briefly considering it. "It's thirty-three years later, and I would probably only find her obituary. It doesn't matter, because I'm going to see her again."

Thinking about Nadezda, Nic's own parents came to mind. They would have been well over a hundred years old in this time. If Nic never time traveled, he would probably have already been dead too. If he did have family in this time, it would have been his brother's kids, or their kids. He might even have a great-grandniece or -nephew his age. The thought made him feel separated from the world. The only ones on the planet like him were Tate, Sophia, and now Zoe.

Nic's head hung low, and he spotted a speck of yellow peeking out from the edge of his shoe. He lifted it and groaned. "Oh man. I stepped on a butterfly."

"Ha," Zoe said. "You just started time traveling, and you're already stepping on butterflies."

"What do you mean by that?" Nic asked.

"You know," Zoe replied. "The butterfly effect."

Nic looked around to see Tate scratching his head and Sophia shrugging.

"The butterfly effect," Zoe repeated. "By making a little change in the past, you can alter the future forever. Like stepping on a butterfly in the time of dinosaurs, and then humans never existing."

"You're weird, Zoe," Tate said, but added when Zoe began to frown, "but I'll play along. Good one, Nic, you killed off the dinosaurs."

Nic shook his head. "I can't kill off something from the past by stepping on something in the future. Time travel doesn't work in reverse, Tate."

"Especially for us," Sophia said cheerfully.

"Then we will never find out what you killed off." Tate

glanced at Zoe and smiled. "Haven't scientists from your time perfected cloning dinosaurs yet?"

"Not dinosaurs. DNA breaks down completely after a couple million years. Scientists were able to clone a woolly mammoth, though. Well, sort of. Nic can kill them off again if he wants to." She skipped to the car and pulled out a backpack.

Nic hobbled to the edge of the driveway and scraped the butterfly off his shoe. When he returned to the car, he helped Sophia fold the tarp as Tate moved a couple of Nalgene bottles into each of their bags. Zoe knelt next to the car, sorting through their bags, putting some food and water in the car for the ride.

Nic stuffed the tarp into the trunk and then imagined falling farther the next time they time traveled. "You know, falling when we arrive in another time could be a real problem."

"We'll be fine as long as the terrain doesn't change," Sophia said as she shut the trunk. They returned to the car; Tate and Nic sat in the two front lounge chairs, while Sophia and Zoe spread out on the couch.

"Before I send us through time," Sophia said. "We have to set where we are going to leave from. When we left 2072 I set our location to an exact position from Earth, think of it like GPS. When we returned to a new time, we were in the exact same position. However, the new homeowners had lowered the driveway when it was paved over. So, we fell the difference in height between the old driveway and the new one."

"If you set where we leave from," Tate said, "Can you set where we return to?"

"No," Sophia replied. "We have to return to the exact same spot. We can change what we are traveling in relation to, like from Earth to say the Moon, but why would we do that unless we were there?"

"The only other thing that needs to be changed is what we are traveling in. It could be a car, a spaceship, or we could even just send ourselves." She leaned forward, putting the time machine on her lap. It displayed the car outlined with a blue glow.

"The important thing here," Zoe said, "is that we can time travel in anything we want. Like a police box."

"Why a police box?" Sophia asked.

"You know, like in *Doctor Who*," Zoe replied. "We've already taken a car, it wasn't quite a DeLorean from *Back to the Future*, but we might as well travel in a police box too."

Silence left Sophia shifting in her seat. "I haven't actually seen *Doctor Who*."

Zoe gasped. "That's sacrilegious for a time traveler."

"I haven't seen it either, or *Back to the Future*," Tate said. "Maybe, if we thought we were going to be time travelers, we would have."

"But they're classics," Zoe replied. Her mouth hung open, in clear disbelief.

Nic didn't want to admit that he hadn't seen them either and decided to change the subject. "Where are we going, Sophia?"

The time machine resting on Sophia's lap now displayed a three-dimensional image of Earth, with two red dots near the West Coast of the United States. Sophia zoomed in on the two locations, until the map that displayed was similar to a two-dimensional one you would find on Google Maps. One red dot centered in Sunland, California. The second dot flashed near the California-Nevada border. "It says the wormhole is 220 miles away, and it will be there for just under two days."

"Just two days?" Nic asked. "How long has the wormhole been there?"

"It arrived when we did," Sophia replied. "That's how the time machine knew when we could return."

Tate leaned over and pointed to the second dot. "That's in Las Vegas." He faced the steering wheel still lodged inside the dashboard. He ran his fingers across the it, searching for a way to start the car.

"Well, let's get going," Sophia said. "I know we just ate breakfast, but it's going to be dinnertime by the time we get there."

Tate fumbled with the steering wheel until Zoe said with a sigh, "Use your dataPad as a key, remember."

The car started when Tate swiped his dataPad across the ignition. "Thanks, Zoe. You're not useless after all." He opened his dataPad and typed. When he stopped, the car crept out of the driveway and turned onto the street.

Zoe sneered at Tate and then turned to Sophia. "Is he always like this?"

"You'll get used to him," Sophia replied. "He's kind of like an old computer you have to hit before it works."

Zoe's head tilted quizzically. "Why would you hit your computer?"

"Forget about it, Future Girl," Tate replied. "It's something before your time." Tate returned his hands to the steering wheel, despite not actually being able to drive.

"Don't worry, I'll fix him." Nic reached across to Tate and lightly slapped him on the side of his head. "Shut up, Tate." Nic turned back to Zoe and offered a toothy smile.

"Hey," Tate said, "don't distract the driver."

Zoe laughed as the car rolled onto the next street. It weaved its way through the city of Sunland until they reached the freeway. The car eased onto the freeway, increasing speed until the speedometer read 100 mph.

Traffic was much lighter than Nic expected, with only a handful of other cars on the road. Most of the ones around them had an Uber or PickUup decal on their side. Those cars were a little taller and longer than theirs, and even more of a boxed shape, but with windows tinted so much that he couldn't see inside them.

The reason behind the emptiness of the freeway was clear when Nic glanced up, gasping in disbelief as a line of cars zoomed by fifty feet above them. "Look up, guys. There are flying cars!"

They plastered their faces against the windows, prompting a laugh from Zoe. She opened her dataPad and swiped through current events. Her laugh didn't bother Nic, but he turned back to the flying cars, not sitting quite as close to the window.

The cities they passed included run-down buildings mixed with prosperous futuristic communities. An apartment complex on the side of the road loomed over them. Sophia pointed to it. "Look at that."

The forty-story complex was covered in plants. It was rectangular at the base, but each rectangular story was rotated slightly, giving the building a spiral shape. Since each floor was staggered, every balcony had room for a large fruit tree, which made Nic think of it as a vertical orchard.

Nic opened his dataPad to the identify app. He held his dataPad out until the oddly shaped building centered his screen and displayed *Sunnyside EcoVillage.*

*Established in 2085, Sunnyside EcoVillage provides luxury all-inclusive homes at an affordable price. No vacancy. Contact home office for placement on its waitlist.*

Sophia stared at the building, eyes wide and mouth gaping.

"It looks like a resort," Nic said, mirroring Sophia's goofy expression.

"Well, I'm not that impressed with a building filled with trees." Tate pointed to the cars zooming past far above the freeway. "But we did finally get flying cars."

"Flying cars have been around for a while," Zoe said. "In the past, they were considered too dangerous for regular use until flight became fully automated, which clearly it has."

"Speaking of the past," Nic said, "once we make it through the wormhole, we will be in the past, right?"

"Yes," Sophia said. "The time machine can locate both past and future wormholes, but Nadezda set it up for us to only find the ones that go into the past."

"Perfect," Nic said. "That means we can travel to any time between where the wormhole takes us and home."

"How far back will the wormhole take us?" Tate asked.

"I don't think she mentioned that," Sophia replied.

"I know," Zoe said. "It could be a hundred years. It could be thousands. Before they could expand the wormholes wide enough to pass through, the scientists on the *Pinta* found one that went ten thousand years. It depends on the wormhole. If it took us to, let's say, the year 1000 BC, we could make stops as we travel forward again. So, what touristy time in the past would everyone want to see before going home? Personally, I want to see Greece in its glory days."

Sophia answered next. "I would love to see the pharaohs in ancient Egypt. Although, I think that was around five thousand years ago. Oh, and maybe we could find early-edition comics. Can you imagine coming back home with dozens of first-edition Superman comics?"

"I would like to see Medieval England," Nic said. "Maybe visit a working castle, if we can find one."

"In 1903," Tate said while straitening his dad's flight jacket, "the Wright Brothers flew their first plane in Kitty Hawk, North Carolina. We can watch it happen."

"I guess it will depend on what time we end up in, and how easy it is to get around," Zoe said. "Grandma said it took her a while before she understood which of her technologies stood out in your time. It's just fifty years, but could you imagine driving this car in your time?"

Nic grinned as he pictured the four of them pulling up to his house in a literal car of the future. With his family moving, though, his imagination turned to one of his family already gone, living out their lives, never to see Nic again. Behind him, Nic caught a glimpse of Sophia pulling up a picture on her dataPad of a news article about them missing. She sat motionless, staring at a zoomed-in portion of her parents.

Nic stared out the window and thought about his last memory of his family, and by the sudden drop in mood around him, he knew the others were doing the same. Nic had acted out ever since he found out they would move. He cringed, thinking back to the last thing he said to his parents. "Before we left, I told my parents, 'If you actually cared about how I felt, then you wouldn't be so happy to ruin my life by leaving.'"

Zoe leaned forward, resting her hand on Nic's. It was warm to the touch, and he found it comforting. "Moving away from everything you know is a tough choice for anyone. I know, I just did it. I'm sure your parents were sad about moving too." When Nic looked at her doubtfully, Zoe continued, "What I mean is, they understand what you were leaving behind and know why you said that. I'm sure all will be forgiven by the time you get home. They are your family, after all."

Nic never thought his parents were sad about leaving, because they were always acting cheerful about it. Now, he wondered if they were just pretending, and didn't want to show him their own disappointment. He groaned when he thought back to how hurtful he was over the past couple weeks. He was still angry with them but missed them dearly.

Zoe took her hand away and pulled a necklace out from under her shirt. She clicked it open and projected a small photograph of Nadezda. "Grandma's life's work was always fighting the Terata. The only way to do that in the past was to advance technology, and that took a lot of her time. Don't get me wrong, I love her, but she didn't always have time for me. Since my parents passed, I've been by myself more than I would like to admit. I always kind of felt like neither of us was in the right time. I really just want to find a place where *I* belong."

"Well, when my dad died," Tate said, "my mom put on a brave face, but I know the whole thing wrecked her. We have to make it back, because I can't be the one to put her through losing family again."

They sat in silence for some time, dwelling in memories of the family that they hoped they would find again. Nic spent the rest of the trip silently staring out the window, hoping to have a chance to tell his family he was sorry.

In the time it took to get there, the car acted like their home. Without anyplace to stick trash or anyone who cared, the car, which started out as clean, had transformed into one covered in crumbs and littered with wrappers and discarded drinks.

It was late afternoon when they reached Vegas, forty-five hours before the wormhole would close. The car left Las Vegas Boulevard and soon stopped at the side of the road.

"Where's the wormhole, Sophia?" Tate asked.

Nic spun around and stared at the two-dimensional map showing the wormhole was just across the street. Sophia pointed to the building there and said, "It's in the parking garage. We made it!"

The parking garage was filled, but not busy; one car had pulled in when they arrived, and it parked in the first spot inside the garage. Moments later, three cars left the garage, leaving through the exit at the street right next to them. The three driverless cars passed by, going to pick up whoever had just called for them.

Zoe pointed at the logo on the cars. "Oh, look. They're Lyfts. It's on the building too. Lyft is a driving service from my time. People use it and companies like it for transportation. That way, they don't have to buy cars."

"Yeah," Tate said. "We've heard of Lyft, Future Girl. It was in our time too."

"But I thought you didn't have self-driving cars," Zoe replied.

"We didn't," Sophia said. "People drove them."

"Oh," Zoe said, sinking in her seat, and then began searching her dataPad.

"It shouldn't be too hard to get home then," Nic said. "Nadezda said to explore on the way. That's now, right?"

"Yes," Tate replied. "So, how long will the wormhole be there, Sophia?"

"We have a little less than two days."

"Perfect!" Nic said. "Then let's explore the future before we go to the past."

# CHAPTER 8

# IMPLANTS REQUIRED

They were a couple of miles from the wormhole when they arrived at a hotel. They had no plans to stay, but it did have shops to explore and places to eat. Unlike the main entrance to the casino, which had Circus Circus written in bright neon lights, the entrance they stopped in front of only had double doors. The path leading up to the doors was lined by large trees carved out to look like a tunnel.

Instead of parking, Nic was surprised when they rolled to a stop at a curb. Zoe leapt out. "Let's go."

"Why aren't we parking?" Tate asked, climbing out of the car.

Nic closed the door and stepped next to Zoe. He turned to watch the now-empty car drive off. "I guess this is valet parking." The car didn't go far. Nic stared in amazement as the car drove itself to a small outdoor lot that he didn't even see at first. None of the cars in that lot seemed to have a Lyft, Uber, or PickUup decal on their side, and Nic thought it might have been because those few in the lot were personally owned cars. The rental cars with the company logos on the side were all parking in a garage at the corner of the block.

Zoe stood with her arms crossed and eyebrows raised.

"What?" Nic asked. "We're still new to this."

Zoe started toward the food court entrance. "The car drove all the way to Vegas, and you didn't realize it could park without us?"

"Nope," Tate said, following Zoe.

A woman in a flowery hat passed them on her way to a Lyft car at the curb. A quad-copter flew after her, with a bag strapped underneath. The whole side of the car opened with hinges on the roof, allowing Nic to glimpse the inside of *modern* cars.

Inside this car was plain, similar to their own, with seating and a table that reminded Nic of a booth in a restaurant. The woman sat down in the back, and her quad-copter landed on the table in the middle. She began sorting through the purchases she made as the door shut. The car drove off, leaving behind two more Lyft cars that waited by the curb, possibly for other people who had called for a pickup but had not yet come outside.

They walked toward the entrance, passing through a large tunnel carved out of trees. An older man in a straw hat and suspenders was working on clearing out the pathway but left enough branches along the sides that his job wasn't really done, despite him walking away. Even in the future, when it was time to leave, your job was done.

The entrance doors swung out before they could reach for the handles, allowing them to step inside a huge open-air courtyard. Above them, a network of quad-copters buzzed, moving as deftly as bees. They swooped and dodged, staying above their owners who navigated the food court below.

The food court itself was not very large, but still a little bigger than Nic's school cafeteria. If seen from one of the quadcopters above, it would have been in the shape of an old wagon wheel with a small section in the middle for food, and seats all around the outside circle.

"It's time for lunch," Sophia said, glancing down at her dataPad. "Well, technically dinnertime, but we should try some future food either way."

Despite driving for three hours, Nic felt like he just woke up. It was weird to start the day just a few hours ago and it already be dinnertime.

Zoe shrugged. "I guess I could eat. Why don't we grab a booth over there after we pick out our lunches?"

They headed through the seating area on the way to get food, passing a couple in a booth eating a salad topped with fried bugs. Nic winced, but he continued, his stomach churning as he examined the choices for food. "Half of the food here is an insect of some kind."

"Of course," Zoe said. "I forgot, when you grew up, insects weren't considered food here yet. It was always more common in other countries, and finally was accepted twenty or so years after you left. If you're really that picky, then stick with grasshoppers, crickets, or ants."

"You eat ants?" Tate asked.

"They're pretty good, though they can be a little spicy. You get used to them pretty quick."

"I think I'll try some bugs," Sophia said.

A burger stand caught Nic's eye and gave a less exotic choice for food. "Well, you'll definitely *not* catch me eating a bug."

Tate chuckled.

"Well, it's your loss if you don't try anything new," Zoe said, and then headed to a taco stand, followed by Sophia.

Nic grabbed a plain burger and some barbeque flavored potato chips from a company that he didn't recognize. There was no cashier, and Nic wasn't sure where to pay for his food. He saw Zoe leave for a seat, and went to go ask her, but almost dropped his tray when his dataPad buzzed. A warning had popped up on the screen saying he was leaving without paying. A second message asked if he would pay for it now, which he checked yes.

After paying for his burger, Nic found Sophia and Zoe at a table, eating tacos. Nic joined them as Tate returned with two burgers and a bag of candy, which he offered. "Does anyone want some chocolate?"

Zoe shook her head at first but then smiled at Tate. "I think I will." She took one, popping it in her mouth. "My favorite."

The lumpy chocolate reminded Nic of chocolate-covered nuts. He took two pieces, biting into one with a crunch. The chocolate melted in his mouth, mixing with an odd peanut flavor with a hint of chicken.

Sophia studied a piece she took, her eyes squinted and then she frowned. "Tate, what kind of chocolate is this?"

"Only the finest chocolate-covered crickets I could find," Tate replied. "And Nic, I guess we got to see you eat a bug after all."

Nic coughed. "Aw, that's why it's so crunchy." He pulled a piece out of his mouth. "Is this a leg?"

"You should see your face," Zoe said, laughing.

Sophia shrugged, tossing the chocolate into her mouth. After finishing, she added, "Not bad."

Nic held the second piece of chocolate in front of him, making out a cricket beneath the chocolate coating. He flicked it at Tate, but it soared over him, landing on the floor. A foot-tall robot came out of the bottom of the trash can. It drove over the chocolate, collecting it, and then retreated underneath the trash can.

"Well, that's cool," Sophia said.

Nic noticed a couple at the next table sneering at Tate when he tossed more crickets onto the floor for the trash robot. Their eyes had the same technology enhancement as Nadezda, but with lines spinning around the pupil. When Nic glanced around, every eye he could see had the same upgrade. The couple had returned to their conversation in subdued voices, glancing periodically in their direction.

"Stop throwing trash on the floor, Tate," Nic said.

"Yeah," Sophia said. "People are looking at us funny."

"Naw," Tate replied, tossing another cricket. "They were looking at us funny before I started feeding the robot."

Nic hadn't noticed any extra looks earlier. "We are unattended minors, and one of us is misbehaving, thanks to you, Tate. We should be keeping a low profile here."

"Who cares?" Tate said. "Minors aren't allowed in the gambling part of a casino. We're in the mall."

"We don't need another reason to stick out," Zoe said.

"Fine," Tate said, shrugging. He placed the bag of chocolate crickets onto his tray to throw away. Sophia snagged them and tucked them into her backpack. "I'll save those for later. We shouldn't throw away good chocolate."

Nic glanced around the food court; it felt like the neighboring couple was not the only ones talking about them in whispers. Besides throwing pieces of chocolate insects on the floor, Nic couldn't figure out why they stood out so much.

Nic hadn't given their appearance that much attention. Their clothes could be dated, but Nic didn't have the fashion sense to see how. The whole food court had a variety of hairstyles, some with spikes or large hoops and others colored in every shade of the rainbow. Some people in this time had puffy sleeves that you could find on a play actor, but nothing that Nic thought would be completely out of place in his own time. Some of the people could still pass as someone straight out of the 2020s without a second thought.

Zoe left the table to drop her plate in the trash. Tate laid his plate on the floor for the robot, which promptly picked it up.

They left the food court, passing stores for dream analysis and holographic design. Sophia ran into a store called Electronics Today, which held a variety of high-tech quad-copters and various other gadgets. Nic followed, finding Sophia holding up a round disk and excitedly saying, "Jetpacks."

Nic shrugged, hoping he would never use one. While flying around could be fun, Nic was worried about the falling part.

They spread out in the store, but Nic didn't linger too long. He left Sophia at an adult-sized onesie massager, passed a chuckling Tate while he read about fart-filtering underwear, and then Zoe, whose mouth was gaping at a hot-pink skateboard with no wheels.

A man's deep voice came from the back of the store. "I never got a notification that you came in. I'll be with you in a moment."

"Okay, thank you," Nic replied, but he was already eager to find the arcade. He left the store with Tate before the man came out to help them. Zoe came out next, followed by Sophia. They continued past random shops, including one with a single eye above the doorway that followed them as they passed. Zoe pointed inside. "We should check out that implant store later. We can learn about out the latest technology."

"What are implants?" Tate asked.

"In its most basic form," Zoe replied, "implants are small chips that are installed in your head for the purpose of modifying neurotransmitters in the nervous system, which can be used to boost your sight, hearing, thought process, or even help fight diseases and boost all aspects of your immune system."

"That's a thing?" Tate asked.

"Yep," Zoe replied. "In my time, though, it was only for the rich. Now it looks like it's as common as a dataPad."

"Look," Sophia said, pointing to the next store. "Let's go to Pod World first. It's the arcade."

The neon-blue sign Pod World flashed on and off as they approached. They stepped inside and then stopped. Dozens of spheres, twenty feet wide, spread throughout the vast room. Dim lights shone down on them from above, while a wispy fog drifted over the floor. The whole setting gave Nic the impression that they had stepped inside an alien spacecraft filled with giant eggs.

Nic roamed between the alien-like pods until he stood in front of one labeled Mech Wars. A screen above it showed a humongous robot stomping through the remains of a city. The silhouette of the person inside the pod waved their arms, which were mirrored precisely by the robot in the game. He turned to the others and said, "Well, anyone want to try one?"

"I'll go first," Zoe said, ducking into a game pod called A Race through Space. She entered the pod and sat in a chair similar to the seat on Nadezda's spaceship, with a pair of joysticks replacing the armrests. A moment later, Zoe said, "Nothing's happening."

"The game has to be activated somehow," Nic said. "Try your dataPad."

"Here it is," Zoe said. "I got a message asking me to insert a coin." She flinched as straps from the chair fastened her in place, and the chair rose to the center of the pod.

The door slid shut, and the monitor above it turned on, setting Zoe in a spaceship in the middle of a dozen other ships. A countdown began at ten and reached zero while Zoe fiddled with the controls. The other spaceships blasted out of sight while Zoe's ship puttered forward and then launched out of bounds at the first curve. Her spaceship respawned in the middle of the track. She repeatedly shot out of bounds without turning, until *Time's Up* displayed on the screen.

Zoe left the pod and shrugged. "It was too difficult. I think this is meant to be played only if you have an implant installed. I was able to use some controls on the dataPad instead, but not enough to fly around."

Tate laughed. He straightened out his father's oversized flight jacket, patted the air force flight patch, and said smugly, "Or maybe, you're just not that good. Watch how it's done." He strode past Zoe and then hopped into the game's pod. Straps wrapped around him, and the door shut.

Sophia turned to Zoe. "Don't mind him. He plays flight simulators more often than Nic jumps blindly into things he doesn't understand."

"But not as often as Sophia wanders off," Nic replied, cheeks burning. Zoe looked at Nic grinning, which brought an unintentional smile to his lips.

The race started with Tate's spaceship motionless, and then

he shot out of bounds even quicker than Zoe, which prompted a shriek of laughter from her.

Tate shouted, "I heard that!"

When Tate's spaceship reset, the ship rotated upside-down, and then flew out of bounds again. When the race finished, Tate peeked his head out of the pod and said, "You guys should move on. I'll be here for a while."

Nic smiled at Zoe and then spun around, looking for Sophia. Instead, he found a woman on the other side of the arcade in a Pod World shirt, staring at him as if he had just broken a game pod. He looked away, but when he glanced back, she was heading his direction.

Zoe grabbed Nic's arm and pulled him through the arcade to where Sophia was waving them over. She stood in front of a cluster of game pods under a sign saying The Goblin King's Treasure. Sophia was already inside a pod when they got to her. Zoe hopped into one, and Nic entered a third.

By the name of the game and the fact that it was multi-player, Nic knew that this would be a futuristic Dungeons & Dragons game, and he was ready. He considered going back to Tate to tell him what Sophia found but knew that he wouldn't leave the spaceship simulator yet.

Nic stood in the middle of the game pod and waited for something to happen. He turned back and saw the strange woman at the A Race through Space game. She was scratching her head while peering around game pods, clearly searching for something, hopefully not them. Nic was hoping the door would close before she spotted him and then remembered to check his dataPad. It displayed a message:

*Insert Coin to Play. (Yes / No)*

Nic selected *yes*, which shut the door and caused the floor to rise in a circle around him as if he were standing in the center of a large bowl. When the floor stopped rising, straps wrapped around him of their own accord, keeping him from leaving. A new message on his dataPad asked him to choose a character, and Nic went with a default Warrior, which started the game.

Nic looked down and saw that from somewhere within the game pod, a large broadsword and a shield were projected into his hands. The walls and ceiling around him morphed into a room made of stone. Torches hung on the walls, and he heard the sound of banging in the dungeon behind him.

Staring down at the curved floor, Nic wondered how to move around while standing in the bowl. He didn't have any real controls available to him, so he did the only thing he could: he tried to take a step. When Nic's foot slid back to the middle of the bowl, he realized that the bowl was the method for moving around in the game.

With another step, he understood there was a big problem—his character only lunged forward and then returned to its place. He needed to figure out how to move forward, or the game wouldn't work for him. Then it hit him—without the implant, there was no way to navigate the game. He was stuck where he was, at the beginning.

The sound of knocking on the wall behind him sped up, and Nic did the only thing he was capable of doing and spun around to see if the knocking was something coming to battle. In front of him, a wizard in gray robes and a large pointy hat continuously ran into a wall, each time making the familiar knocking sound.

Nic laughed but didn't know what to try next. When the wizard disappeared, Nic guessed that either Sophia or Zoe had just given up on the game. Without knowing how to move forward, Nic groaned in disappointment and held up his dataPad to find out how to leave. The dataPad showed additional controls, but Nic knew instantly that it wouldn't work.

Zoe was waiting for Nic when he left the pod. "It's a shame," she said. "I think if we had implants, it would've worked. Did you see where Sophia went?"

"No, but she wanders off all the time," Nic said, looking around. "Although, before we got in the game, there was a lady that seemed to be interested in us."

"What do you mean?"

"She looked right at me, and I think she was coming to see us when you pulled me away to this game. I haven't seen her since, though."

"That's odd," Zoe said. "Maybe we should get going."

Tate was still in the spaceship simulator, so they decided to find Sophia first. She hadn't gone far and was watching a video above a game pod of someone sprinting and leaping across the moon's surface. Nic glanced around, but thankfully, there was still no sight of the lady from before.

"Sophia," Zoe said, "we need to get going. Let's get Tate."

"Okay," Sophia said, frowning, and headed back to the spaceship simulator with a skip in her step.

They stood outside the simulator as Tate actually crossed the finish line. Nic glanced around again, spotting the strange lady turning in their direction, and with Zoe in her sight. He took Zoe's hand and pulled her out of the lady's view, just as Tate exited the spaceship simulator.

"Well, I finished the race," Tate said. "Wait." He smirked, pointing down at Nic still holding Zoe's hand. "So, you two are holding hands now?"

Nic and Zoe both dropped each other's hand. Nic ran his fingers through his hair in an attempt to hide his discomfort. When he turned to Zoe, she stared back at him. Her cheeks flushed a rosy color before she averted her eyes. Sophia stood to the side, arched her eyebrows, and smiled at them both.

Tate laughed and then said, "Oh, don't worry."

"Um," Nic said, cutting Tate off before he could get started trying to embarrass him, "there is some lady looking for us, and we need to go."

"What did you do?" Tate asked.

"Nothing, I swear," Nic replied defensively. "Let's just go. We can hide out in another store or just head back to the car while we figure out what is going on."

Zoe peeked back toward where Nic had spotted the lady and then rushed toward the exit. "Let's go!"

# CHAPTER 9
# OUT OF REACH

Nic left Pod World trailing behind the others. Without implants, Nic wasn't able play any games. He still didn't understand why, though. Zoe said before that an implant was used to modify the nervous system, but how did that allow someone to select an option in a video game. He hustled forward, catching up to the others. "Zoe, I think it would be best if we understood exactly how implants work, seeing how they seem to be required to do anything here. If they just made us smarter, then why are they needed to play games?"

"It's the same thing as when someone has lost a limb," Zoe replied. "People get mechanical replacements that work just as effectively as the real thing. That's why someone with a mechanical hand can continue to play a guitar just as well as before they had lost a hand."

"Well," Tate said, "robotic limb replacements were never that effective in our time."

"Oh. Well, then think of it like this," Zoe continued. "Grandma had not only the brain implant, but also an eye implant, like the people in this time. Those two implants connect in a way that allowed her to essentially have a personal computer in her head. The brain implant does the processing, and the eye implant displays a personal screen. When playing those games, there was a link between the game and the implant that would allow you to manipulate controls as if you had lost a limb."

"So," Sophia said, "that makes people cyborgs."

"Look, that's the implant store. Should we check it out?" Tate asked.

"I don't know," Sophia replied. "Maybe we should just head to the car."

Nic was still undecided on whether they should stay or go when Tate replied, "We'll be quick." Rubbing his hands together and smiling, he added, "Maybe we could get implants installed while we're there. If we did, when we got home, we could store test answers in our heads, and our teachers would never find anything because it would all be hidden."

"Well, you're right. Our teacher definitely wouldn't find anything in your head," Nic quipped.

Sophia and Zoe chuckled, stepping into the store first. It was like they were in the biology section of a children's museum, complete with a projected human body advertising organ repair, which Zoe headed for. Tate frowned at Nic but skipped past, stopping at each exhibit long enough to touch every display. Sophia went to a section about hormone regulators in the nervous system, similar to what was available in Zoe's time. The only other people in the store were at the back. A clerk facing away from them, and a middle-aged woman with gray eyes glancing about the room.

In this store, they were able to upgrade the human body just as easily as upgrading a new phone. Nic joined Zoe as she selected biological organ replacement, and then liver, prompting an advertisement to appear.

*Regenerative cellular technology has allowed humankind to shape the health and wellness of our bodies. With our new liver formula, you will get the needed cellular components injected into your organ to repair any damage that has occurred in your lifetime. Talk to your doctor about the new liver repair system today.*

With the idea of organ failure being literally a thing of the past, Nic wondered how long people actually lived in this time. When Zoe clicked over to heart restoration, Nic took another look around the store, spotting that the only other customer had just finished checking out and was leaving the store. She glared at Nic as he pretended not to notice her. She paused long enough for him to feel uncomfortable and eventually said to the clerk as she headed for the exit, "It would do you good to take care of the rubbish you have in this store."

Nic glanced around at the clean room and then chuckled about how crazy this lady was for thinking it was filled with trash. Then he noticed it wasn't the store she was looking at; it was Nic and his friends. Whatever they had done in this time, they definitely should've left already. The lady left the store, scowling at Tate as he tugged on the artificial eyeball, which sprang back to the exhibit, tethered in place.

With the lady's comment, the clerk at the back of the store had turned around to face them, wide-eyed, seeing them for the first time. He fumbled with a device he held, dropping it to the floor. Instead of picking it up, he stared at Sophia, and then Nic and Zoe in disgust. Tate squeezed an artificial eyeball between his fingertips like it was a toy made out of putty. The clerk's eyes scrunched together, and his mouth opened enough to show teeth, making Nic feel as welcomed as he would be if he were greeted by a snarling dog. "How do people come into an implant store without an implant?"

Before anyone could respond, Sophia silently hustled out of the store.

"So what if we don't have implants?" Zoe asked. "Is that a problem?"

"Obviously," the clerk replied. "It's against the law. Everyone is required to have an implant, even *simple* folk like you."

It all made sense. People were giving them funny looks when they ate. The lady in the arcade was searching for them. They were actually breaking the law. Nic was surprised that they hadn't been captured yet, but thought that maybe people didn't want to get involved in arresting children.

"Sorry, man," Tate said, "but our parents are hippies. We can't have implants until we're eighteen."

"Look, kid, I know that you are *simple*," he replied, "but even you would know that your parents can't stop you from getting an implant."

"Uh," Tate said. "It's a religious thing."

"That's enough," he replied. "Leave, or I will contact security."

"We were leaving anyway," Nic said with a mock smile. "Thank you for your hospitality."

Zoe shrugged at Nic and then left in a hurry to join Sophia.

Nic and Tate left the store too, with the clerk continuing to stare at them with dull gray eyes. The last thing Nic heard him say as he passed out of earshot was a single word, "Security."

Sophia was pacing just outside the store when they left. Zoe hustled away, leading them back in the direction of the food court. Nic glanced back when the store was almost out of sight. Nobody was following them outside.

"He called for security," Nic said. "Do we run?"

"Yeah," Zoe replied, and they took off.

It was pretty much a straight shot back to the food court. They only passed a family and a couple on the way, but they were able to continue running, with a little more than funny looks.

They made it to the Electronics Today store, which was just around the corner from the food court.

"Can we catch our breath?" Sophia asked, panting.

"Sure," Zoe replied, but continued forward at a brisk pace.

She raised her arm, displaying her dataPad in tablet form. "So, the implant law is to keep track of people. With that clerk's eye implants, he would've been able to identify us just by looking at us. I think he thought we were criminals."

Tate grimaced. "I don't know how I feel about people knowing who I am just by looking at me."

"It's basic info," Zoe said. "Used in case of emergency and to deter crime."

"Sounds like a real-life Sims game," Sophia said.

"I'm not sure what that is, but the profile that displays is your standard online bio."

"I don't have an online bio," Tate said.

"You do if you ever used social media. Look, it doesn't really matter if you have a profile or not. To him, we're breaking the law."

"Well, I still don't get why he called me *simple*."

"He was calling you an idiot," Zoe said dryly. "If it makes you feel better, he was calling all of us idiots because we don't have implants."

"How do you know that, Zoe?"

Zoe studied Tate's face and then pointed to her dataPad. "I literally just looked it up. On second thought, maybe he was only talking about you."

Sophia chuckled and then asked, "If it's against the law to *not* have implants, then do you think they would arrest us?"

"If they took us in," Tate said. "Then we'll have an insanely difficult time getting to the wormhole before it closes."

"Well, we're heading to the car now," Nic said. "We need to get through the wormhole while it's still easy to do."

They turned the next corner and found the food court now in sight. It was still dinnertime here, but it was getting a little late. As they approached the seating area, Nic could see that there were more people around than ever, and none of them gave more than an awkward glance.

Ahead of them, Zoe looked around so much that if Nic didn't know her, he might think she was lost. The locket she wore around her neck was in her hand, which she was clicking open and closed repeatedly, without looking inside. Her eyes darted to each person they passed, and she spent enough time looking behind them that Nic didn't feel like he needed to.

Hustling forward, Nic joined Zoe. Once he did, she only glanced back one more time before saying, "Don't be alarmed, but we're being followed."

Nic, Tate, and Sophia turned at once. Two large men in

security uniforms were strutting toward them a hundred feet away.

When Nic returned his gaze to Zoe, she rolled her eyes. "Let's try not to make it obvious that we're onto them."

Nic led them through the seating area, picking the most crowded path, in hopes that they would lose the security on the way. Before, people didn't pay any attention until they passed, but now everyone around had stopped what they were doing and were staring long before they were seen. Despite the crowd, the security guards seemed to know right where they were and broke into a run as the exit came into view.

Dropping all pretense of blending in, they sprinted for the doors. They made it outside as shouts from the guards followed. "Stop there!"

Nic held the door open for the others and then spotted a thick branch. He grabbed it, as Zoe shoved the doors shut behind them. Together, they wedged the branch between the doors, knowing it wouldn't hold for long but would hopefully delay the guards long enough to escape.

Nic made his way down the tree-lined exit, racing after Zoe. The sun had gone down since they arrived, but there was enough light to see that Tate and Sophia were about to reach the car.

Nic turned back around about halfway to the car to check on the guards, who were still at the doors. One of them had squeezed through the poorly barricaded doors and yanked the branch clear, allowing the guards' chase to start up again. Nic reached their car and jumped inside.

Tate entered the route to the wormhole, and the car's lights flipped on as it slowly rolled on its way, with the two guards catching up. The car stopped once they reached the street and wouldn't go any farther. Tate hit the dashboard. "Why did the car stop?"

"Maybe the guards could stop it somehow," Nic replied. "Hey, Zoe. Didn't Nadezda say we could override the driving system?"

"Yeah," Zoe replied, "but I don't know if that includes when the police have already stopped it."

"You won't know until you try," Nic said. "Tate, let Zoe take over."

Tate scrambled into the back seat as Zoe scooted over. She pressed her dataPad to the ignition and then began swiping through different controls.

With Tate pushing his way to the back seat, Nic climbed halfway into the front. A bang on the door caused him to fall to the floor. He scampered back, buckled in, and stared out the window at a guard shouting, "Get out!"

"Done," Zoe said. The steering wheel popped out in front of her. "Where do I go?" She sat on the edge of her seat, less from the excitement of the moment and more from the fact it was the only way to reach the pedals and still see out of the windshield.

"It's not far," Sophia replied. "Down Las Vegas Boulevard, to the left."

They turned and then sped down the street, heading straight for the headlights of oncoming traffic. Zoe swerved around a car, missing it by inches.

"You're going the wrong way!" Tate yelled.

Zoe veered from side to side as cars approached. "You said go left!" She stopped trying to avoid the cars coming at them and sped forward, but they didn't crash. The oncoming cars separated like Moses parting the Red Sea. The autopilot in the oncoming cars engaged in time to avoid an accident.

Nic turned around to watch the cars file in behind them like a zipper. He breathed a sigh of relief but then grimaced when a police car swooped down from the sky. "Guys, we've got a problem. There's a cop right behind us."

"That was fast," Zoe said.

A second police car flew past, landing a hundred yards ahead of them. It released a floating roadblock that extended across the entire road.

"What now?" Tate asked.

"Turn here," Sophia replied.

Their car skidded across the street, slamming into the side of a building, but continued forward. Nic recognized the wormhole's parking garage, the gate still shut tight.

Zoe didn't slow down. She plowed through the entrance and sped into the garage.

"It's above us," Sophia said. "Keep going up."

Zoe drove up the ramp, periodically scraping the side of the car. She passed floor after floor until they reached the roof. "What now, Sophia?"

Sophia swiped through the options on the time machine. "Hold on."

The night sky was lit up by the flashing lights of three police cars hovering above them. Two more police cars blocked the garage exit. Nic glimpsed an officer in the garage fling a hand-sized quad-copter toward them. It flew at them, disappearing from view when it dove under their car.

A loud *clang* preceded the car shutting off.

"What's the deal, Sophia?" Tate asked.

Sophia's shoulders slumped. "This can't be right."

"What's wrong?" Nic asked.

"Well, we're here," Sophia replied, "but the wormhole is

above us. Even if I expand it enough to pass through, we can't reach it."

"How far?" Tate asked.

"Fifty miles or so," Sophia replied, which caused Nic to gasp. He couldn't even imagine where that was. Sophia continued, "When we drove here, we used a map program like Google Maps. When we arrived, I forgot to switch it back to three-dimensional, so I never saw how far up it was."

Three police vehicles circled above. Beyond them, the wormhole remained unseen and out of reach.

"I guess it couldn't be so easy that we would make it back through the first wormhole we found," Nic said. "If we only had gotten something that flew, I think we could've still made it."

A voice boomed from the garage, "Get out of the car with your hands over your heads!"

"Well, we can't stay here anymore," Tate said with a groan. "Send us into the future."

"Do you think the next time we arrive in could be the Terata War?" Sophia asked.

"I don't think so," Zoe replied, "but we are one step closer to it. We won't know what time will be our last chance, unless we end up in the Terata War."

Nic ran his fingers through his hair while he scanned the sky for a glimpse of the wormhole, despite its distance. "So close, yet so far."

"It's ready," Sophia said.

Tate turned to the closest officer approaching the car and waved. "Might as well say goodbye."

Everyone followed Tate's lead. Nic waved, barely noticing the pressure that built in his ears signaling their next trip through time.

*Thump!*

---

*Eight days later*
*September 23, 2105*

At first, Nic thought something went wrong. Although it was a little darker than when they left. Nic searched the sky for the police, but they were gone. Flooded with relief after their close call, Nic chuckled.

"Well, that was fun," Tate said. "When are we, Sophia?"

Sophia fiddled with the controls before saying, "We are a week later. It's still 2105, but now the twenty-third of September."

"Well," Nic said, "that means the local police will still be looking for us. How long do we have?"

"Three weeks," Sophia replied. "But I'm afraid this one is somewhere in space. It's actually pretty far. I'm surprised that it is still in range for the time machine to pick up. I thought Nadezda set it to find ones nearby, but this is in the middle of our solar system."

Leaning to stare at the stars, Tate asked, "Are people exploring the solar system yet? Can we even get there?"

Zoe was already searching her dataPad. "It looks like humans have managed to begin printing a base at Marius Crater on the moon. Oh, and even at Arsia Mons on Mars. But traveling in space is not really a thing for common people."

"So," Sophia said, "then we couldn't stow away with astronauts on a space shuttle."

"Unfortunately, no," Zoe replied. "Plus, we have three

weeks. I know it could be done in Grandma's time, but not now. It's impossible."

"We can't stay here when the local police will still be looking for us," Nic said. "Sophia, just send us to the next time."

"All right," Sophia said. "Here we go."

*Thump!*

# CHAPTER 10
# HYPER-SPEED TRAIN

*Thirty-one years later*
*April 26, 2136*

The sky brightened, and the newly setting sun started its descent over the horizon. They were in a new time. The open, top level of the parking garage remained empty except for two cars, one blocked in by their now-powerless vehicle.

"It's six forty-three at night, thirty-one years later." Sophia rested the time machine in her lap while she typed on the dataPad still attached to her wrist. "It looks like the wormhole has now appeared in Europe and will be there for three days."

"Then to the next wormhole." Zoe held her dataPad over the car's ignition. "It won't start."

"We should get into a new car in this time anyway," Tate said. "One that flies. If we had a flying car five minutes ago, we might have already been in the past."

Zoe stepped outside and crawled under the car. When she stood, she held a fist-sized triangular drone with four propeller blades tucked underneath it. She tossed it aside and tried the ignition again. "And the car's still dead."

Nic glanced around the parking lot, still half expecting a police officer to arrive. A brisk wind blew past as he stepped out of the car. Eager to continue the journey, he followed Tate to the trunk, donned a plain black jacket that Zoe had packed for him, and retrieved his backpack. Their bags had basic supplies, each with a sleeping bag the size of their fist, a toothbrush, a tent that Nic carried, some food bars, and water. They didn't have any change of clothes, but given what they did have, Nic felt as prepared as he could be. He tightened the straps on his backpack and then asked, "How are we going to get to the other side of the world?"

"We can get there with a flying car! Is this really a choice?" Tate asked.

Zoe dug through her bag and pulled out a sleeveless red puffer vest, which she put on. "Let's worry about how to get *there* after we get away from *here*."

Tate snickered. "People in your time have weird taste in clothes, Zoe."

"What do you mean?" Zoe replied. She saw Tate staring at her vest, and then said, "This vest is identical to the one worn by Marty in *Back to the Future*." She looked to Nic for help. Having not seen the movie, he only offered a shrug.

Sophia stepped out of the car, put on her jacket, and then stuffed the time machine in her backpack. "How are we going to avoid people singling us out for not having implants?"

Zoe sighed and then held her arm up and searched through her dataPad. "It's not an issue this time. Fifteen years ago, a law was passed that no longer required everyone to get an implant. Today in 2136, everyone still has an implant, but sometimes people turn them off so they can live what they call *the simple life.*"

"Okay then," Nic said, heading to the lot's exit. "Let's get going. We need to put some distance between us and this car."

They made their way down the stairs. Nic was staring at his dataPad, searching for a flight to Europe but having trouble finding any. "I can't find any flights," Nic said. "I mean anywhere. It's like people don't fly planes anymore."

"Well, what are we going to do?" Sophia asked.

They had reached the bottom of the parking garage and paused momentarily as they figured out what their next move was.

"Hyper-speed train," Zoe replied. "They have trains here with top speeds of just over 3,500 miles an hour, and there is a train station in Vegas."

"Wow!" Sophia said. "We have to go about 5,500 miles to get to Europe; that would take an hour and a half at that speed. Wait, how fast are airplanes, Tate?"

"Around five hundred," Tate answered. "Thirty-five hundred means that trains go much faster than the speed of sound. No wonder people don't fly planes anymore."

"It's been over a hundred years," Sophia said. "There was bound to be technology advancements."

"Yeah, but ..." Tate said, facing Nic. High-speed trains were a sore subject for Nic, as that was the main reason his family had to move, but it looked like they really were the way of the future. Tate continued when Nic didn't return his gaze. "How does a train, of all things, go that fast anyway?"

"Magnets lift them off the ground, eliminating friction," Zoe replied, "and then other magnets push it through tubes that have lowered air resistance."

Tate sneered at Zoe. "Yeah, but shouldn't there be problems with traveling over the speed of sound? And what about the passengers? The G-force alone would crush everyone."

"They speed up slowly, just like an airplane. The real trick is how the train crosses the ocean. That wasn't possible yet in my time."

"Well, how do they do that, Future Girl?" Tate spat.

Zoe winced at the nickname. She lowered her dataPad to glare at Tate. "Look it up, Caveman."

Nic chuckled, but Sophia immediately spoke up. "Don't fight, guys," she said. It looked like she wanted to say more about their bickering, but she just walked away.

Tate called after Sophia, "You don't have to wander off every time there is a disagreement."

"Enough, Tate," Nic said. "It was frustrating for everyone to miss the wormholes, but it will be even harder next time if we aren't getting along."

Sophia was waiting at the gate for the exit when they caught up to her. Before Nic could even consider how to leave the Lyft lot, a car came up from behind, opening the gate. They all rushed out after it, and Nic was pleasantly surprised when it stopped on the street right in front of them.

"I called a car," Sophia said before climbing inside.

They left in their driverless car, arriving ten minutes later at the McCarran Hyper-Speed Train Terminal. Nic stepped out of the car into a crowd and stared up at a cylindrical building.

Instead of lying on the ground like trains should, a dozen trains were parked vertically along the walls of the building. The train passenger cars were smaller than Nic expected, cube shaped, but rounded at the corners.

They followed a horde of people into the terminal. The

majority of the travelers wore business-casual attire, possibly commuting for work. Nobody stopped to buy tickets, and Nic couldn't find where to go if someone needed one.

An elderly man with a shaggy beard stood on a raised platform in the path of the crowd, welcoming people to the train station. His grin widened as any passerby would head his direction but would fade when they went around him without a glance. Instead, the crowd would pass by with their arms outstretched and hands flicking around as if they were shooing away a fly.

Tate laughed, pointing to one of the fly-swatting travelers. He waved his arms in front of him and moaned, *"Brains."*

"They're not zombies," Zoe said. "They're using their implants for computers, Tate. You're not."

Ignoring Zoe, Tate staggered after Sophia and groaned, *"Brains."* Sophia chuckled and then hurried to the bearded greeter.

A smile leapt to the old man's face as they approached. "Greetings! Is there anything I can help you with?"

"We'd like four tickets to ..." Tate said, and then turned to Sophia. "Where are we going?"

"Paris."

"Nice. Nic and Zoe should enjoy that," Tate said, and then faced the greeter again. "Four tickets to Paris, please."

Nic's cheeks heated up as he caught Zoe staring at him.

The old man scratched his beard. "You can purchase your tickets online."

"We weren't sure when we'd arrive," Nic said. "We wanted to buy the tickets once we got here."

"Living the simple life, eh?" he said, smiling.

"Uh, yes," Nic replied.

"How are you going to pay for your tickets?" he asked, snickering. "With cash, I expect." The old man glanced to each of them with a broad smile, expecting a response.

Nic cracked an awkward smile, because the man's grin was contagious. Inside, though, Nic was wondering what they were going to do if they needed cash. "Um. No, we have dataPads."

"I mean *cash*, you know, paper money." The old man's growing chuckle died out when nobody else laughed. "Aw, I'm just kidding. It's a simple-folk joke." He shrugged and then added, "I guess paper money was too far before your time."

They remained silent as people continued to swarm past them, but the thought of cash being before their time caused Nic to snicker behind his hand. Next to him, Tate cackled, which broke Nic's composure. Nic erupted into laughter along with Sophia and Zoe. The man appeared concerned at first but soon blossomed into an infectious belly laugh.

Their laughter was brief, cut off by the fact that more and more people turned their direction. The people who passed only paused long enough to put their arms down as they walked by, but it was enough that Nic hung his head low and waited for the others' now-awkward laughter to dissipate.

Tate held out his dataPad to the still-laughing man, who squinted at it. A red line encircled the iris of his now-gray eyes. "All paid for. The train leaves in twenty-two minutes. If you miss it, you will automatically be added to the next train leaving for Paris. Take the blue-framed elevator to the thirty-second floor. Your trip to Paris takes two hours and forty-seven minutes, including a brief stop in DC."

"Thank you," Nic said, and then followed the others across the station into an empty elevator. It rose rapidly through the floors, and then stopped with a ding.

The doors opened to an empty square room. At its center hung a poster advertising a SpaceX Dragon-class cruiser. At Nic's next step, the poster disappeared and was replaced by a three-dimensional image of a cylindrical space shuttle taking off. Sticking out his hand, the shuttle passed right through it as a cheerful voice announced, "Join the countless explorers who have left Earth behind."

The image of Earth shrank in size, giving the impression that the space shuttle had launched into the sky. "You will orbit Earth, experience the weightlessness of space, and dine on delicacies from all corners of the world."

The shuttle orbited the moon once before landing on it. "You will spend the night at the Aitken Lunar Research Facility and be one of the growing number of people to moonwalk. Book now for the experience of a lifetime."

"Sign me up," Tate said as the advertisement ended.

"Can we?" Sophia asked.

Nic followed Zoe across the room and said to Sophia, "We have to concentrate on getting to the wormhole."

Zoe had already entered their train car when Sophia hustled up to an alcove built into the wall. The top and bottom panels lit up with an electric-blue light as Sophia stuck her hand inside. "I wonder what this is."

Not wanting to miss their train, Nic took Sophia's arm and led her toward the doorway. "We'll figure it out another time."

"We have a couple minutes," Sophia whined but trudged into the train car anyway.

The train compartment that they stepped into was a ten-foot-wide cube. It was wide enough to comfortably seat eight passengers, with an aisle dividing the two sides. A booth on the left side was already filled with four travelers, separated by a wide table. None of them spoke; in fact, all but one stared off into space with gray eyes. The woman who didn't search the internet with her implant was staring out the window that looked over the city of Las Vegas.

Nic stepped across the compartment to the booth on the right and stuffed his backpack into the empty cubby under his seat. He couldn't help staring out the window, which over-looked the city, basking in the sun's fading rays far below. Imagining a fall to the ground, Nic quickly sat across from Zoe and grasped onto his seat's armrests a bit tighter than was necessary.

The local news playing on a screen above them was cut off by a sixty-second countdown for the train's departure.

Sophia slumped into her seat next to Zoe and placed her backpack between her feet. "I guess there wasn't time to look around after all."

"Obviously," Tate said, sitting down next to Nic.

Nic's breath caught in his throat as the train lowered, like a roller coaster getting ready to take off. The train headed down the tracks, and their cabin rotated in order for them to stay level. Attempting to avoid thinking about how high they were, Nic found himself smiling at the purple streak in Zoe's hair. She caught him smiling and grinned as she returned to the news on her dataPad. They descended below ground, where heights were no longer a problem. Nic was able to breathe easily again but unable to stop himself from smiling whenever Zoe glanced his way.

As soon as the train was horizontal, the cars latched together. The window that had just overlooked the city was no longer there, replaced by a doorway that allowed a path down the length of the train.

Nic stooped, peeking over their seats and peered back and forth across the train when it accelerated, causing him to fall back into his seat. The feeling persisted as they continued, the train clearly taking a long time to reach its full speed.

"That was cool," Sophia said.

From the corner of his eye, Nic caught Zoe waving her arms. She pointed up to the screen above them, which had returned to local news. A reporter stood next to *their* abandoned car.

The reporter's handlebar mustache flapped around as he spoke. "On this spot over thirty years ago, a 2070 Honda Escort vanished right before our eyes. The four kids fleeing from the police were never seen or heard from again. Thought to be an elaborate hoax, this mysterious vanishing car has now returned, and the four suspects are once again wanted for questioning. It is unclear if the police are aware of the suspects' true identities, but the global visual recognition network has been updated to notify the police of their whereabouts, so far without any hits."

A picture of the four of them from the shops at Circus Circus displayed on the screen, causing Nic's heart to skip. He glanced over to the other passengers to see if they were watching. Three of them were lost in their implants, searching the internet or whatever they did when their eyes were gray. The fourth one briefly glanced at the news report before returning her stare outside.

The report continued as the image of them transformed from them as kids into them as adults. "The appearance of the suspects from 2105 have been age-progressed through to today, which puts their age around their mid-forties."

Nic sighed deeply and then slumped into his seat.

"The four suspects left the scene early this evening, but

neither implant identification nor the substantial DNA left behind at the scene were enough to identify them. Updates to the story will follow shortly. This is Elwood Champion reporting."

"They're looking for adults," Sophia whispered.

"Yeah," Tate said, not bothering to lower his voice. "It looks like all three of us turn into our parents. Even Zoe looks like Nadezda when we found her. Now we know what we'll all look like when we're old."

Nic said in a hushed tone, "Shut up, Tate."

"I'm just saying—"

"No. Shut up, Tate!" Zoe nodded toward the people in the other booth.

Tate waved his arms, attempting to get the other passengers' attention. "They're all zombies, remember?"

The woman who had been staring outside had turned to Tate with furrowed brow. At first, Nic thought she overheard, but when Tate returned her gaze, the woman asked, "Do I know you from somewhere? I only ask because I swear, I should know you, but without your implants on, I can't see where from."

"Uh, we've never met," Tate replied, grimacing with his hand up to block his face from view.

"Well," she replied, "my mistake." She faced forward again, glancing back once before her eyes glossed over into a shade of gray, lost in her implant.

The cabin's other passengers didn't show any interest in the real world as their gray eyes darted around. The police might be searching for them as adults, but Nic couldn't relax knowing that every person around the world was a potential camera searching for them. Even if their twelve-year-old images weren't in the global visual recognition network, someone could see them and recognize them from a news report.

They made it across the ocean through a submerged transatlantic tunnel. It ran over a hundred feet below the water, like a pliable underwater bridge. Nic had worried about a sea creature crashing into it, but they made it to their destination safely. They arrived at Gare de l'Est Train Station at 7:10 a.m., Central European Time.

Even though they had been awake for what felt like half a day, it was now morning all over again, without ever getting a chance to fall asleep. It was like they just finished a sleepover and didn't bother to change their clothes—not that they had spare clothes to change into.

They had left their train slowly, giving time for other passengers to get ahead. Nic was eager to continue but wished that they could travel while avoiding people at the same time.

"Let's get implants," Sophia blurted out. "It'll save us a lot of trouble, and think how awesome it will be once we get home."

"We could get them," Nic said. "It would be easier to travel, and when we get home, school would be a breeze. But if we get implants, then we might have to tell the people who we are."

"It could be worth it," Tate said.

"Not when we're under investigation," Zoe replied. "Sophia, where are we going?"

A map of Paris displayed on Sophia's dataPad. "We have to go that way toward something called the Carrousel Arc de Triomphe. The wormhole is practically touching it."

"Well, let's get going," Tate said. "I have this weird feeling that every time someone looks at us, you can actually see them trying to figure out who we are."

Nic looked up, not yet realizing what Tate was talking about. When he looked around, most people were on their implants, and none was paying attention to them.

"Most likely, it has to do with their implants," Zoe said. "Our images might be in the database, but they are not flagged to cause an alarm."

The next person Nic passed had their eyes dart around to each of them. Just before passing out of sight, their eyes glossed over, and they began using their implants again.

"Doesn't matter," Tate said. "If we truly had been spotted, we would probably be caught already."

Nic lowered his head and scratched his brow, hiding from another passerby. "We should probably find something to hide our faces, just in case."

"Over there," Sophia said. She took off her cap and tossed it in the trash, and then ran ahead to a shop selling hats by the train platform's exit. By the time Nic reach the shop, Sophia had already purchased a baseball cap for Nic and Tate and a beret for herself and Zoe.

With her beret on, Zoe led them upstairs into an open terminal. Nic didn't notice any of the stares with the cap as he did without one, but since he rarely glanced up to meet someone's eyes, he felt like he might be missing all the suspicious looks.

With a quick glance around to make sure no one would overhear, Nic asked, "How far is the wormhole, Sophia?"

"About a mile and a half," she replied.

"There's no point in walking," Tate said. "Let's call a car."

Zoe stopped and then faced Tate. "It's only a mile and a half. It'll take a half an hour to walk. Taking a car won't save us that much time. This is Paris, and we're walking."

Nic rested his hand on Tate's shoulder. "We'll be walking through Paris, Tate. A little culture will do you wonders."

Nic followed Zoe's gaze to the arched glass ceiling high above them, which allowed the morning sun to light up the room. Nic watched her as she beamed with sheer joy from everything around her and felt himself grinning. She caught his smile and returned with her own. He knew that she was smiling about the world around her and not him, but as they continued to look into each other's eyes, he thought they were sharing a moment

Nic heard Tate chuckling behind them before shouting ahead, "If you two wanted some alone time, you should have just said something."

Both ignored Tate as they skipped down the street to a large, old ornate church. Zoe led Nic across its courtyard and gazed up to the front entrance. Framing the doors was an intricate carving of people standing on ledges at the base and angels that arced over the large, closed doors.

Nic wondered if the church was still in use or if over time it became something to be admired for its history. "Traveling through time really makes you think about the history around us." Nic nodded toward the church. "I wonder when that place was built."

"Let's find out." Zoe held her dataPad in front of them. The screen displayed the Church of Saint-Laurent, with a light glow surrounding it. The caption below the picture read:

*The Saint-Laurent church is located in the 10th Arrondissement of Paris. This church and monastery were originally constructed in the sixth century and was rebuilt in the fourteenth century in the flamboyant style of Gothic architecture, which was popular at the time.*

The caption continued, but Nic noticed Zoe smiling at him and didn't read any further. In front of him, Tate was waving them over like they were in a rush. Nic tried to ignore him but decided it was useless when Tate started jumping up and down. Nic returned Zoe's smile and then said, "The others are waiting."

Zoe put away her dataPad, which now hung loosely around her wrist. They strolled through the city until they reached the park.

"The Arc is right over there, and the wormhole is behind that," Sophia said, pointing to a structure partially hidden by trees.

Tate ran ahead but stopped once the Carrousel Arc de Triomphe came into view.

In front of them stood a sixty-foot-tall marble structure. Tourists wandered around and under its arches, which supported an intricately carved statue of a woman riding in a chariot.

"The wormhole's on the other side," Sophia said. "Let's hurry."

They circled the Arc, finding a building on the other side. It was three stories tall and cylindrical, surrounded by a cobweb of bars, which made up a scaffolding frame. At its base, people in lab coats were entering through a plastic flap used as a temporary doorway.

"It's right where that building is," Sophia said. "Give me a second to find out how high."

"Do you think the people in this time found the wormhole and built that structure to help study it?" Tate asked.

"I think so," Zoe said. "Grandma had mentioned that people were studying a wormhole in the past. And the people from her time used that knowledge to help build the time machine. Is it inside, Sophia?"

"Yes," Sophia replied. "It will be in the center of the building on the top floor."

Nic stepped forward. "Let's go see if we can reach it."

# CHAPTER II
# STUDIED WORMHOLE

A pair of guards circled the makeshift building, halting Nic in his tracks. Unsure if he should proceed, he shrugged to the others.

Tate stepped past them and then turned back. "The worst they can do is to send us away." Something caught Tate's eye behind them, causing Nic to turn back to see what.

A half-dozen people were walking toward the makeshift building. They all wore lab coats, and the two in the back pushed a hovering cart overfilled with some kind of technical equipment.

"Let's follow them," Zoe said. "Maybe the guards will let us enter the building if they think we're the scientists' kids." She headed toward the Seine River, which ran parallel to the park, at a pace that would allow them to cross paths with the technicians heading toward the wormhole.

The woman heading the other group smiled at them but continued forward without pause. Nic waited briefly and then hustled to catch up to the technicians, with Sophia, Tate, and Zoe close behind. They needed to stay close enough that if the guards saw them with the technicians, the guards might think they were together. At the same time, they couldn't be too close that the technicians would realize they were being followed without turning around.

The one in the front was doing most of the talking, speaking in French. Nic couldn't tell what she said but knew that she was excited from the skip in her step and her chuckling whenever she glanced toward the wormhole.

They approached the building's entrance as the guard's gaze lingered on them. Nic's eyes darted around, searching for something to focus on besides the guards. Tate stared into the sky in a poor attempt to appear casual. Sophia's head hung low in front of her, like something on her shoes required all her attention. The only one who didn't seem like they were hiding something was Zoe. Her attention was drawn to the technicians in front of them, no doubt because she earnestly wanted to hear everything they said. It wasn't until that moment that Nic thought that Zoe might actually understand them.

One of the guards waved at the group of technicians, who all waved back. Tate also waved back, which at first Nic thought was a terrible idea, but joined in when the guard seemed to relax a little and continue making their rounds.

Nic held the others back, allowing time for the technicians to get inside without Nic's group right on their heels. The technicians crossed inside, and through the temporary doorway, Nic could see their silhouettes spreading out across the building. The second that the technicians were inside and out of earshot, Nic asked, "Zoe, do you speak French?"

"*Oui. Un peu.*"

"Uh, what?" Tate asked.

"I'll take that as a yes," Nic said. "What were they talking about?"

Zoe answered as the entrance inside the building cleared out, giving them enough space to enter. "It was hard to make out. A drone discovered it early this morning, and they are getting ready for a series of tests. I caught that the *anomalie* is on the top floor, but that's it."

Nic nodded and then opened the plastic flap, stepping forward without being noticed. He crouched at the entrance until they were all inside.

From the inside, the walls around them seemed incomplete, like they modeled the building after a dome-shaped monkey bar structure you could find on a playground. Three of the technicians that they had previously followed joined another group and were climbing a steel spiral staircase to a platform on the top floor. The other three were on the ground floor, facing away and standing at screens projected above their desks.

Thirty feet above Nic, the wormhole slowly rotated. It was a silvery sphere no bigger than an apple, which continually rippled like waves of water. Around it, a twenty-foot-wide circular glass wall prevented anyone from getting too close but still allowed a closer look from the top floor.

The hovering cart that had been pushed in remained full of equipment in front of them.

"You should expand the wormhole," Tate whispered to Sophia. "If it's bigger, we might be able to reach it. It would also give them something better to study. What could possibly go wrong?"

Zoe groaned before replying, "Well, it could collapse the building. They could figure out that we did it and take away the time machine. They could decide it is unstable and move everyone farther away. We could make it through the wormhole, only to fall to our deaths on the other side. Should I go on?"

"Nah, I'm good," Tate said. "You should've been with us when we took the time machine in the first place."

"Maybe you should've used your heads in the first place," Zoe replied.

"Sophia is supposed to think of those things, not me," Tate replied. "Sophia, you have fallen short lately, so Zoe, you're the smart one from now on."

"*Great*," Sophia said, rolling her eyes. "I'm no longer smart, because Tate doesn't use his head." Without giving Tate a chance to respond, Sophia shuffled under the cart and headed to the center of the building to stand directly below the wormhole.

Nic reached out to push the cart aside but accidentally bumped a button that shut off the hover controls. The cart fell to the floor, scattering its contents across the open room. All around them, workers stopped and stared.

"Uh, sorry," Nic said taking a step back and running his fingers through his hair. "We got lost and wanted to check for directions."

A woman asked, glaring at Nic, "What about the guards outside?" She began picking up all the scattered equipment, returning everything to the again-floating cart. "It doesn't matter. You have to leave."

"Okay, we'll go," Nic said. His gaze returned to the wormhole. A mechanical arm swung down from the ceiling and began releasing a steady stream of a clear liquid into it, with no effect.

They were so close, but Nic couldn't see how to get to it. If he hadn't been so insistent on finding Nadezda's spaceship in the first place, they would've been home. He wondered how much these technicians knew about it and added, "What is that thing?"

"We're not sure. That's why we are studying it. Now, you must leave." She took Sophia by the shoulder and ushered them outside.

They didn't speak until they were out of earshot. Sophia was trailing behind everyone, dragging her feet. "I don't think we can reach it."

"Don't give up yet," Nic said, trying to stay positive, but inside knowing it wouldn't be easy. Even if they could get to the wormhole, people in the building would try to stop them.

Despite trying to reassure Sophia, Nic couldn't help but hang his head low as he followed Zoe. They stopped at a bench, where Nic slumped into the seat next to Sophia. They had time to figure out what to do, but they needed to proceed carefully, or they would get into an even worse situation.

"Any ideas?" Nic asked.

Sophia shrugged. "We could lower ourselves down from the roof."

"Yeah," Tate scoffed, "as if we could somehow manage to get onto the roof, and then dangle down like spies."

The light of Zoe's dataPad lit her face as she swiped through an article. She had opened it as soon as they left the building.

"Did you find anything, Zoe?" Nic asked.

"No," Zoe replied, collapsing her dataPad onto her arm. "I was actually looking into the investigation on us in Vegas. There is nothing new yet." She faced the wormhole building. "I think we have to somehow go straight up from underneath it.

Then again, we will have to fall back down once we get to the other side."

"About the falling down on the other side thing," Sophia said, "I think it was a good thing that we missed the first wormhole."

"What do you mean?" Tate asked.

"Well, when we send ourselves into the future with the time machine, we stay in the exact same spot on Earth. The wormhole is different, it will send us to a different time in the past but will also send us to a new location. Nadezda said that the wormhole will return us somewhere near Earth when we come out, but if we made it through in a car that didn't fly, well ..."

"We would have fallen back to Earth," Tate said.

"So," Zoe said, "whatever we do, we have to fly."

With the wormhole being studied so closely, it seemed like they would have to miss this chance to make it through. Nothing was between the wormhole and the ground floor, but Nic felt that climbing up with an audience would be impossible. "I just don't see how this wormhole is going to work for us." He nudged Sophia and said jokingly, "I suppose it's time for jetpacks."

Tate and Sophia jumped up, yelling, "Yeah!"

"I wasn't serious," Nic said. He didn't like heights, and in a jetpack, there would be nothing between him and the ground. Jetpacks were an option, but Nic would definitely prefer to try just about anything else. "I mean, flying to the wormhole isn't the only problem. Even if we could find jetpacks, how are we going to open the wormhole? If it suddenly got to the size of a spaceship, we could collapse the building. We might even cause some of the locals to fall in. And that would be a death sentence for them."

"That's a good point," Sophia replied. "I don't know that I can adjust the size of the wormhole when it is expanded. But we did see jetpacks in a store thirty-one years ago. We know they have them somewhere."

"Then we need to figure out a way to empty the building before we try anything."

"Relax, Nic," Tate said. "We just have to get past the workers and fly through the wormhole, and then we will be home."

"Well," Sophia said, "we'll be in the past, and then we will be able to make it home from there."

"Besides, if we fail somehow, we could always jump farther into the future. Does it hurt to try?"

"In jetpacks, it might," Nic replied.

# CHAPTER 12

# JETPACKS

After finding a quick meal, Nic followed Zoe to a hobby shop. If her dataPad didn't point them where to go, they would have never found the place. Inside, the shop reminded Nic of his parents' attic, with shelves everywhere overflowing with an endless assortment of boxes.

It occurred to Nic that they might be intruding on private property and might need to leave. They pushed forward, gathering around the lone counter in the middle of the room, and waited for a clerk.

"Zoe, are you sure this is the place?" Tate asked.

Before Zoe could respond, her dataPad buzzed.

Tate glared at her. "Did you get a message?"

"I set an alarm to tell me if there were any updates on us back in Vegas."

"Of course, you did."

"What's the update?" Nic asked.

"They know that we took a Lyft to the train terminal." Zoe rubbed her chin as she continued to read the article, and then added, "They're going to change the search parameters to include our current age and appearance. We'll have a couple hours left at most."

"Does it matter?" Tate asked. "We're on the other side of the world."

"Of course, it matters," Zoe replied. "The police databases are all linked globally in order to stop people from fleeing to other countries after a crime. Aren't they in your time?"

The doors from the back room flung open, ending Zoe's question. An older woman in a flowery dress rushed forward, her eyes darting between them with a look of concern.

Before she said anything, Tate blurted out, "Finally. We need four jetpacks. You have those here, right?"

"Hein? Ben, oui," she said, breathing a sigh of relief. "Yes of course. Is everyone okay?"

"Uh, yes. We're fine," Zoe said with her brows knitted together in confusion. "We wanted to buy something."

"Really?" she asked. "You are welcome to, but I'm surprised you came in person, instead of just having it delivered."

"We're living the simple life," Nic said.

"*Quand même.* You're staying offline even for purchases. I'm impressed by your dedication." Her eyes widened. The worry on her face faded into a wide smile as she rested an arm on the counter. "Well, in that case, it's nice to meet my customers for a change. I'm Doraine. You said you're looking for jetpacks?"

There was no apparent organization to the boxes around them, and Nic couldn't guess where to look first. "Yes."

"Rocketman fans, huh? Are you here for the big race?"

"Yes!" Tate answered.

"If time permits," Zoe added.

Doraine's brown eyes glazed over into a dull gray. When her

gaze returned to them, her eyes were once again light brown. "We only have one model in stock here. It's an older model, but should be okay."

The back door swung open, revealing a hovering flatbed cart with four tall, square boxes. "These are the Rocketeer 500s."

The cart stopped in front of them. They each grabbed a box, except for Sophia, whom Nic had lost track of. "Where'd Sophia go?" He spotted her at the end of an aisle, sitting on the floor, reading the description to one of the items in the store. "Come on, Sophia."

"What?" Sophia asked peeking out around a corner. "Oh, sweet. Are those the jetpacks? How do they work?" Sophia took one of the boxes and opened it up.

"You wear it like a backpack," Doraine replied. "When you turn it on, the straps will secure across your torso and the control sleeves will extend down your arms."

Nic imagined shooting into the air, and then flying straight into the ground. "Should we worry about crashing?"

"I think you will find it difficult to crash even if you tried. The jetpack has sensors that take over when you're out of control and steady you for a safe landing. Just go slowly at first and you'll do fine."

Tate handed Doraine his dataPad. "You can put them on my card."

Doraine took his dataPad, a red line encircling her gray eyes. She handed the dataPad back, smiling. "Thank you. If I can help you with anything else, please come back, or order online when you're done with your simple life. Oh, and make sure you are in approved fly zones. Not every park lets you fly."

The bell on the door rang again as they left the store.

Nic held his jetpack above his head, shielding the sunlight. It was a metallic disc half the length of his arm, but from its weight, it could easily have been an oversized frisbee. Nic put it on his back and strapped in. It hung loose, even with the chest strap attached, and made Nic wonder if the jetpack could take off without him. He tightened the straps as much as possible, then flung his backpack over the top of it, concealing the jetpack underneath.

"What are we waiting for?" Tate asked. "Let's go check out the Rocketman thing."

"We really don't have the time," Zoe said.

"But it's a jetpack sport in the future! The wormhole will be here for three days, right? We have plenty of time, and even if someone gets too close to us, we could always jump through time again."

"And lose any chance of making it through this wormhole," Nic said. The weight of their past choices bore down on him. They had found the wormhole in Vegas but didn't take advantage of the extra time they had. He now understood that time travel should be their top priority, or they might never make it home. "We need to go now. The authorities are about to search for us at our current age, and once they do, we won't be able to reach the wormhole."

Tate scowled at Nic.

"Is it worth it if we get caught?" Sophia asked.

"No, but it is definitely worth it if we don't," Tate said with a smirk.

Sophia shook her head. "Tate, if we jump ahead and the next wormhole is during the Terata War, then we're done for."

"Yeah," Nic and Zoe said simultaneously.

Everyone remained quiet until Tate gave in, sighing. "Fine. Do we at least get to try the jetpacks out before we get there?"

"Yeah," Zoe said. "We'll test them out at the park."

---

Instead of turning to the left and heading toward the Arc, they found a patch of grass on the right. The others ran ahead and wasted no time in turning on their jetpacks. Instead of joining them, Nic pulled out the jetpack's instructions on his dataPad, giving it another look. The controls were easy enough: spread out your fingers in order to take flight, move your arms around for stabilizers, and then make a fist to return to the ground.

Before Nic even took off his backpack, Tate was already flying. Sophia and Zoe were close behind. The others soared through the sky like superheroes in an aerial show, with their jetpacks pulsing at their backs.

Nic returned his dataPad to his wrist and took a deep breath in order to calm his nerves. Heights always bothered him, and this time, having the real possibility of crashing to the ground left his hands shaking.

Zoe landed, wide-eyed and grinning. "Come on, Nic."

Nic didn't want to rely on a machine to protect himself from a painful crash, but he couldn't wait any longer, especially in front of Zoe. He switched on his jetpack, causing the straps around his shoulders to tighten, and mechanical sleeves to crawl down his arms like bugs until they reached his fingertips.

Nic closed his eyes, took a breath, and clenched his hands into fists. He slowly spread out his fingers, prompting his jetpack to rumble and Nic to raise to the tips of his toes.

"*Arrêter!*"

Nic returned to his heels and watched as a guard charged their way. "*Qu'est-ce que tu fiches?*"

Tate zipped to the ground next to Nic as Zoe rushed to the guard to see what the problem was. Sophia had joined them by the time Zoe walked their way.

Zoe returned, frowning. "He said we are too close to national monuments. If we are going to fly, we have to do it at a different park."

"Sorry," Nic called out to the guard, picking up his backpack, breathing a sigh of relief over not having to face his fear yet. They headed for the Arc, and the guard followed them at a distance. Nic's shoulders slumped, and he stared at the ground in front of him. He had a chance to fly and didn't even make it off the ground. Now the task of flying the jetpack through the wormhole once again felt impossible.

As they left, Zoe patted Nic on his shoulder. "It really isn't hard. When we get to the wormhole, all you will have to do is fly straight up. Remember what the lady said about the failsafe system. The jetpack has sensors that take over when you're out of control and steady you for a safe landing. When I landed, I tested it, and the jetpack caught me. It'll catch you too."

"I know. I'll be okay," Nic said, trying to convince himself even more than her.

The guard who stopped them from using the jetpacks left before Nic and the others made it to the Arc. This time, the wormhole building had three guards stationed at its entrance, extra security probably because they got inside earlier in the day. They took a seat in the grass away from the Arc, far enough to not draw any attention, but close enough to see if any opportunity to reach the wormhole presented itself. These guards, however, stayed at the doors with no sign of leaving.

Nic stood next to Zoe and noticed her jetpack sticking out past her backpack. He tugged her backpack into a more concealing position and glanced up in time to catch Zoe eyeing him with a smile.

"Well, while we wait," Nic said, "we could name the time machine."

"We're still doing that?" Tate mumbled.

"Obviously. Any ideas?"

"Time Jumper," Zoe said. "It works for jetpacks."

"Time Jumper is perfect!" Nic said. "Now we just need to figure out a way to evacuate the technicians and avoid the guards."

Before they could discuss their options, Zoe's dataPad buzzed. She stared wide-eyed down at an article and then said, "We're too late. They are now using our current age and photos to search for us. Anyone with an implant will know we are being looked for when they see our faces."

Nic hung his head low, hiding it from any passersby.

"Well," Tate said, "does that mean we should go to the next wormhole?"

"What if the next one is harder to get to than this one, or if we find ourselves in the Terata War?" Zoe asked.

Nic didn't know what to say. They found three wormholes; one was too far in space, and the other two were far harder to go through than they imagined. If they continued to find wormholes that they couldn't reach, they would run out of time.

"I might have an idea for this wormhole," Sophia said. "I mean, it could work."

"What is it?" Zoe asked.

"Well," Sophia replied, "they are looking for us now, and there are people studying in that building. If it was a couple hours after midnight, the scientists should be at home, and the guards might have left too."

"But they're looking for us now," Tate said. "We can't wait around anymore."

"We don't have to," Sophia replied. "I can send us forward in the time machine."

"That's right," Zoe said. "Good idea, Sophia."

Sophia blushed, pulling out the time machine and set it up. The Time Jumper displayed a turquoise light that encircled the four of them in a small bubble. "It's ready. Get in close."

Nic glanced around to see if anyone was looking their way. There were a couple of people around the park, but they were all too busy with their own plans to pay attention to a group of kids in the grass. A tour group was circling the Arc but all facing away from them. "It's clear. Let's go," Nic said, leaning in with the others, making sure they were all inside what would be sent to the future.

Sophia started the Time Jumper.

*Thump!*

---

*Fifteen hours later*

Despite it being three o'clock in the morning, there was enough light in the park that they could still see around them. The Arc itself was lit up like a beacon that drew attention from all around, and that light spread all the way to them. The tour group that was there mere seconds ago vanished from sight, having left hours ago. Everyone else that was in the park when they left was gone, except for the guards. One of the guards was tapping another on the shoulder and pointing their direction.

All three guards headed their way. Nic was in the front, and the guards were sizing him up as they approached. Nic considered firing up the jetpack, but with them staring at him, he waited.

One guard, a tall man with a stern expression, stopped directly in front of Nic. "*C'est euh, ces américains.*"

Nic didn't know what he said, but assumed they were recognized. The guard's eyes narrowed, scrutinizing Nic, as if he knew things were about to go awry. A second guard stepped forward and said, "The four of you are wanted for an investigation and will have to come with us."

From the corner of his eye, Nic noticed the others had moved their backpacks to their chests, exposing their jetpacks. Tiny metallic plates inched down Tate's arms, but the guard's stare held Nic in place. Tate nodded to Nic and then crouched for a jump. They were going to make a run for the wormhole, but Nic wasn't ready.

"You have jetpacks," the guard said with pinched brow. "I'll hold on to those for you while ... Hey! Turn that off!"

"It's now or never!" Tate yelled, launching himself over the guards, followed closely by Zoe.

Nic fumbled with his backpack, allowing the guard to grab it. Instead of fighting over his bag, Nic shook off its straps and hopped away. He turned on his jetpack, and the controls trickled down to his palms as Sophia shot out after Tate and Zoe.

To Nic's side, the guard had fallen to the ground, backpack in hand. He tossed the bag behind him and leapt for Nic, snagging his shirt. Nic tried to jump away again but was pulled down to his knees. He thought he was caught until a blur from above crashed into them, knocking all three of them over.

Nic scrambled to his feet, finding Zoe had returned for him. She saved him but didn't stick around. She shouted as she took off again, "Go, Nic!"

Exhaling the last of his breath, Nic spread his fingers, signaling the jetpack to send him into the air. The guard grabbed at him again, but his grip failed.

Finally launching into the sky like a rocket, Nic lost all thoughts about what lay behind him. A blast of air pelted Nic's face as he caught a glimpse of two guards below racing back to the wormhole building.

In front of him, Tate and Sophia flew toward the building. They moved so fast that Nic couldn't imagine them avoiding a collision with the doors. But at the last second, they set down harmlessly. Sophia landed and rushed inside after Tate. Zoe touched down at the door ahead of him and then waited.

They were going to make it. The four of them would be in the building before anyone could stop them. The guards were just too far away. Nic's breath was stuck in his throat, and his heart raced like a hummingbird's as the ground rushed toward him. Every muscle in his body tightened, and he flailed his arms, bracing for impact. Instead of landing, he accidentally fired the jetpack again, launching him away from the door.

Seconds later, his feet touched the ground gently. Nic stood still, surprised to be unharmed. He spun around to the entrance twenty feet away where Zoe stood yelling, "Run!" Nic sprinted to Zoe and passed through the doorway with her, followed by the guards closing in fast. A guard burst through the doorway, grabbing Zoe. Nic turned to help her, but before he could, a second guard came in.

Nic searched for a way out but couldn't find one. If Nic hadn't flown off to the side when he landed, they would have made it.

Tate and Sophia stood in the center of the building with the Time Jumper. Tate raised his hands to his head as Sophia slumped down on the ground in defeat.

Nic raised his hands, surrendering. "We give up."

# CHAPTER 13

# CAPTURED

Tate stood in front of what he thought was a one-way mirror, hands on the glass, trying to see through to the other side. Three hours had passed since they were caught and it was early morning again. They were now stuck inside an interrogation room in a police station. The room's only other feature besides the mirror was a large rectangular table that Nic, Sophia, and Zoe sat around. The center of the table was made of glass, with a keyboard built into one side.

Tate rubbed his wrist, which was missing his dataPad. Despite the fact that he never used to wear a watch, now his wrist felt naked. The others waited patiently at the table, Nic resting his head on his arm, looking up at Tate, Sophia staring sleepily in front of her, and Zoe frowning at the mirror.

Tate knocked on the mirror. "Don't we get to talk to a lawyer or something?" With no response, he stuck his mouth on the mirror and blew a raspberry. He turned around to find Zoe glaring at him.

"What?" Tate asked. "Maybe if we get on their nerves a little, they'll stop ignoring us."

"Or maybe they won't care, and you'll just get on *our* nerves," Zoe quipped. She held a locket at end of her necklace and continually clicked it open and closed.

"I don't have to do anything to get on their nerves. They'll probably just get tired of you clicking your necklace."

Zoe opened her locket, revealing a picture of Nadezda. She stared at it for a moment before clicking it shut and then tucking it under her shirt.

"They'll get to us eventually," Sophia said.

Tate searched for some way to occupy his time when footsteps approached from the hallway outside. The door opened, revealing a short woman with gray hair carrying their backpacks and a beige hand towel. She kicked the door closed behind her with the heel of her foot and then handed the towel to Tate. "Clean the mirror, would you?"

"See, I knew it would get their attention," Tate said, reluctantly taking the towel.

Once Tate began scrubbing the glass, the officer set their packs on the floor and took a seat at the end of the table in front of the keyboard. Clearing her throat, she glanced between them.

When Tate finished, Nic was glancing around the room in an attempt to avoid eye contact. Sophia stared at her hands, and Zoe was glaring at Tate. Nothing was said until Tate returned the towel and sat next to Sophia.

"Hello, kids. I'm Lieutenant Chloe Dupont. I would have come in earlier, but with your investigation in Vegas, and nobody being able to find your parents, it took a longer to get to you. For my part, you will have to explain what you were doing in Paris. After that, you will be turned over to your investigators back in the States."

She dumped the contents of the first backpack onto the table and rummaged through the camping gear they got from Nadezda. She refilled the pack after a quick examination of each item. "You have some old-fashioned stuff here. It's all in good condition but still old-fashioned." She finished the first backpack and emptied the next one, pausing her search to ask, "Why are you in France?"

"We wanted to see Paris," Nic said with a sheepish grin.

Chloe scoffed, returned his smile, adding, "Very well, then what did you want with the anomaly?"

Nobody moved, except Sophia who sank lower in her seat, not looking up. With no response, Chloe continued to sort through their things.

"We were conducting an experiment for our science class," Zoe lied.

"I couldn't find which school you attend. And as I said, I wasn't even able to locate your parents or a caretaker. Could you tell me where they are?"

"It's a little hard to explain," Tate replied, "but we're not supposed to talk about where our parents are."

"What about your implants?" Chloe asked, her jaw clenching, showing the first sign of her growing impatience.

"We are living the simple life," Nic replied.

"Yes, obviously. Really simple," Chloe said, shaking her head. "But you didn't turn off your implants. You've never had them. You know that's a problem, right?"

"It's not against the law," Zoe replied.

"*Yeah*, but. You do know that without implants, we wouldn't be able to find you if you were seriously injured. Besides, without implants, we don't know anything about you."

"We have dataPads," Nic said.

"Yes," Chloe said. She clicked the keyboard in front of her a couple times, causing each of their personal information to appear as a document in front of them. "This is the personal information your dataPad provides. Is the information correct?"

Everyone nodded, and Chloe continued, "Your dataPads aren't working right. We have your names now, but the addresses that they provide have different people living at them. If you had implants, that error could never happen."

The contents of Sophia's backpack scattered across the table. The Time Jumper tumbled out, partially covered by Sophia's jacket.

Chloe brushed aside the jacket and half bag of chocolate crickets to pick up the Time Jumper. "This is interesting. What does it do?"

When everyone remained silent. Chloe handed it over to Nic. As soon as he held it, a password prompt appeared on the screen.

Chloe took it back, and then attached a cord from the table to the Time Jumper. It had to be some sort of technology used to go around password protection. Tate knew that Nadezda set up the time machine to be protected from things like this, using tech from her own time. He could only hope that Chloe couldn't get in. And he laughed out loud in relief when *Password Fail* displayed across the screen.

Tapping her finger on the table, Chloe glared at Nic. "What's the password?"

Even though Sophia used it all this time, Tate never saw the password. However, Nic stared blankly at the Time Jumper, ran his fingers through his hair, and then opened his mouth to speak. Tate could clearly tell that Nic knew the password, so Tate jumped in with an answer, "I don't know," Tate said honestly, and then added a lie. "It's our computer project. We have to hack the password. If you could tell us what the password is with that codebreaker thing, that would be great."

Chloe frowned as she stuffed everything back into Sophia's backpack, the Time Jumper last. "Okay, here's the deal. I know we're not getting the full story out of you, or any story for that matter. But your investigation in Vegas is taking priority. You're being sent home. Once you have your implants installed, all of you and your parents will return for an inquiry about what you were doing at the anomaly."

Nic stared at the pack holding the Time Jumper. "Then, can we have our stuff back?"

"We are keeping the jetpacks. Your parents can collect them, should they want to make the trip." Chloe stood, placing each of the backpacks on the table in front of her. "Please take your things and follow me."

They each picked up their packs and left the interrogation room.

"Where are we going now?" Sophia asked.

Chloe handed back their dataPads as they left the room. "I'm taking you to the train station. You're being sent back to Las Vegas."

---

Tate followed Chloe through the Paris Nord Station, a train station near the one where they had arrived. He knew they wouldn't be in custody long. With the Time Jumper back, they could escape from virtually anywhere in an instant, despite their previous mishap.

Looking back, Tate saw Nic trailing behind the rest of them

at a short distance and in a sour mood. He stared at the ground and mumbled to himself too quietly for Tate to hear. Nic was blaming himself for them being lost in time and missing the wormhole with jetpacks. Once they discovered the time machine, Tate knew Nic never had a choice about starting the trip through time, but he was right about the jetpack debacle. If Nic didn't screw up, they would be on their way home.

The terminal was more crowded now than when they arrived in Paris, but after being taken to a small room away from the crowds, Tate began to feel trapped. The room was open enough to see the people in the terminal pass by, but it would be too difficult to make a run for it. If they were to find a place to time jump from, this might be it, though people would likely be there in the new time.

Chloe pointed at a bench and said, "Have a seat. You will be escorted the rest of the way by a Nord station officer."

Once the four of them were sitting, Chloe stepped away and scanned the terminal. She was far enough away that Tate risked starting a conversation. He leaned into the group and whispered, "Well, it was fun while it lasted. It's clear that we'll need to time jump before we leave France, and we should avoid reappearing inside a vacuum chamber meant for trains. Let's try out the next future while she's not looking."

Chloe's eyes swept across them, but she remained at a distance, still too far away to hear their conversation. When Chloe looked away again, Sophia shook her head and said, "If they caught us on camera, disappearing and then reappearing years later at the exact same spot, then they'll have proof we time traveled. Some people might already suspect it or they wouldn't have searched for us at our current age. If we jump now, we'll just be confirming it for them. At the very least, we should try to jump from somewhere out of sight."

"Do we have to return at the same place?" Tate asked. "Didn't you say when we started that you assign where we time jump from? So, instead of assigning where we jump from as a coordinate on Earth, we can pick, I don't know …" Tate paused a moment and watched a group of people heading to another floor. "An elevator."

"Well, yeah," Sophia replied. "If we are, let's say, ten feet from an elevator, and we assign it as where we are jumping from, when we return, we will be ten feet from that same elevator. That could get us to another floor."

"Wow," Zoe said, "I don't think that could get us out of here, because we can't risk returning when the elevator is between floors. But I'm impressed, Tate."

"Thanks, Future Girl," Tate said. "I am pretty impressive."

Tate saw Zoe's jaw clench. She had just paid him a compliment but was already mad at him again. When she glared at him, he realized she didn't like his nickname for her. He shrugged at her, smirking, which caused her to avert her eyes.

"It gives us something to think about," Nic said. "We could assign us to jump ten feet from someone's bag, or a car. The real problem is not knowing where we will be when we return."

"I think we are getting off topic here," Zoe said. "We will still disappear and reappear out in the open, without knowing what is there when we return. The only way we could do any of these things safely, as in not time jump into a person or a wall, would be to have nothing but empty space around us. So, we really are back to needing to find a place with no cameras that should be vacant, when we leave and arrive."

"Even in the future," Nic said, "they won't have cameras in bathrooms. There might be people in them, though."

"I think that is a risk I can work with," Zoe said, pointing to the restrooms across the station.

Chloe returned, staying close enough to end their conversation. She began pacing in front of them until a man with shaggy hair and a crooked nose approached.

Before the man got a chance to introduce himself, Chloe stepped forward, whispering into his ear. She turned back to them. "Have a safe trip, kids." Before they could reply, she rushed off, disappearing into the crowd.

"My name's Gabe Laurent, and I'll take you—"

"I'm going to use the bathroom before we leave," Sophia said, and then walked away.

"Hold on," Gabe said. "You can wait until we're on the train."

Tate spread his arms, pleading. "Lieutenant Dupont said we could go when we got to the train station."

"Fine. Hurry up," Gabe said, rolling his eyes.

The sign above the bathroom didn't have symbols for men and women. Instead, it had the word *shared* and a diagram of three people. As they entered, a side door had the word *single* and a diagram of one person, with an image of a baby to its side. Sophia opened the single door and held it for the rest of them.

"Hey!" Gabe yelled. "Use the regular bathroom! What's wrong with you?"

Tate locked the door behind them and then joined Sophia in the empty corner of the bathroom. "Can we jump yet?"

Gabe banged on the door and yelled, "Get out here!"

"We have to go now, Sophia," Nic said.

Sophia stood, her smile strained and hands shook, which

made Tate think that she was worried about either getting caught or ending up at the Terata War. "Okay," she said, "Get in close and don't move. I'll get it to surround just us again."

They gathered together, and then the light around them vanished.

*Thump!*

<br>

*Twenty years later*
*October 2, 2156*

Without the flash of darkness that accompanied jumping through time, Nic would've sworn that they didn't go anywhere. Even the pressure in his ears no longer affected him.

Nic stayed back and watched Tate open the door and peer around outside. "He's gone. We probably shouldn't stick around here though."

"What about the Terata, Sophia?" Zoe asked.

"Well, it's morning again, 7:30 a.m., in the year 2156," Sophia replied. "It's been twenty years. We have another try."

The burden of being caught faded, allowing Nic's racing heart to gradually return to normal. He glanced around, examining the spotless bathroom. The toilet was a rounded cube that opened automatically when Nic passed it on his way to the sink. Nic ran his hand under the rectangular faucet, releasing a curtain of soapy water the length of the spout.

"If you don't mind," Zoe said, "I have to use the toilet."

Nic left the bathroom and followed Sophia to a bench as Tate entered the shared bathroom.

Zoe came back first, and Tate returned shortly after her staring at his dataPad, with his nose crinkled in confusion.

"What's wrong, Tate?" Nic asked. "Are we being looked for?"

"Uh, no," Tate said, frowning. "The toilet just sent me a message telling me to limit the amount of zinc in my diet."

They laughed.

"Too much information, Tate," Nic said.

"Hey, you're the one who asked," Tate said, yawning. "You know, with the trip to Vegas, the train, and all the time we spent in Paris, we've been up for most of a day. Maybe we should find a place to sleep."

"Good idea," Nic said. "But we should find out our next stop first. Sophia, where are we heading from here?"

Sophia opened the map on her dataPad and added, "The wormhole appeared southwest of here around 3,800 miles, in the Atlantic by Brazil. Oh, this is not good. It will only be there for fifteen hours."

Zoe's face grew pale as she leaned over the Time Jumper. "We can't take a train; that's in the middle of the Atlantic Ocean. I don't think we can get there in time."

Sophia shrugged. "It will depend on how fast we can travel."

Through the windows at the front of Nord Station, they could see cars soaring high in the sky. Zoe was able to take their first car off autopilot; she could do it with one of these too, allowing them to fly to the wormhole. Even with a flying car, though, getting to the middle of the ocean in a little more than half a day didn't give them much time.

"Well, it's about time we got something that flies," Nic said.

"You mean, besides jetpacks," Tate replied loudly. "Because

jetpacks fly. I can almost excuse your jetpack blunder, since we're finally going to get a flying car. For which *I'm* the pilot."

Nic thought of his failure to reach the wormhole. If only he had gotten through the doors without flying off course, they could have made it. "I'm sorry. I really am, but I thought I was going to crash."

"It had a built-in *will not crash* safety feature, Nic!"

If Tate's brashness didn't force them to go before Nic was ready, they could have made it. But they didn't make it, and the others blamed him. He glanced up to see Tate staring at him. Nic clenched his teeth, wishing Tate would drop the subject.

Travelers passing by were turning in their direction, and Sophia started to walk away. She stopped and faced Tate. "People are looking."

"I don't care," Tate replied, causing Sophia to shake her head before abandoning the conversation. She walked back to the restroom, sat down at an empty bench not far away, and began searching her dataPad.

Tate sneered at Nic and then asked, "What happened to you, man? Back home, you would have been the first to jump, even if you were scared of heights."

"Well, after seeing how rushing into everything has been such a problem for us, I thought we could use a little caution for a change."

"But if we didn't go right when the guards showed up, then we would have missed our chance!"

"It's easy for you to say. I couldn't turn on my jetpack with the guards focusing on me. And by the time I could turn it on, you had already ditched me. *You* left, fully knowing that my jetpack wasn't on, and then blamed me when we ran out of time."

"It's true, Tate," Zoe said, coming to Nic's defense. "I had to go back for him. And why? Because I'm not going to leave my friends behind. Why did you?"

Tate opened his mouth to respond but seemed to consider what they said. He sighed before saying, "I'm sorry, Nic, but that still doesn't excuse you flying off course when you landed. We could've been on our way home right now."

Nic lowered his voice. "I wasn't ready."

"Ahem," Sophia said. "We don't have a lot of time. We missed our chance here in Paris. Let's not miss the next one too."

"Everyone could use a little rest," Zoe said, leading them to the exit. "It might as well be in the car on the way."

Nic followed them, dragging his feet. Despite Tate's hasty leap, Nic knew Tate wasn't to be blamed; he was.

# CHAPTER 14
# FLYING CAR

Fifteen minutes later, they were outside, watching their car pull up to the curb. As they were going to be traveling in it for a long time, Sophia opted for a more luxurious rental when she ordered it. It was the length of a large SUV and a little wider too. Nic waved his hand over a circular spot where the door handle should be, releasing the door with a soft *pop*, which slid into a slot underneath the car.

Sticking his head inside, Nic saw that the car was less like a car and more like a small motorhome. It had four lounge chairs facing a small table in the center and even had a toilet in the back. A high bubble dome covered the top, giving passengers a panoramic view with room to stand. Nic searched for Sophia around them, but she had wandered off, saying she would be back in a minute.

"I've got the pilot's seat," Tate said, diving in and sitting down. He spun his chair around, facing the front of the car. Embedded into the dashboard was a control wheel like one found in a plane. Tate ran his hand along its edges, but he couldn't pull it out.

Zoe laughed, following him in. "You can't even figure out where to input commands. Do you actually think you can fly a car?"

Tate sneered at Zoe and pressed his dataPad against the ignition sensor. "Look, I figured it out." He swiped through various controls on his dataPad, waiting for everyone to get in.

Nic spotted Sophia running to them with two bags filled to the brim with snacks. She hopped in and took a seat next to Tate in the front, leaving Nic to sit in the back with Zoe. With them all inside, the door under the car moved back into place, closing with a sharp click and a seamless seal in the glass dome.

A voice from the car speakers said in a flat tone, *"Destination, please."*

Tate took the Time Jumper from Sophia and entered the coordinates. A moment later, Tate spun around in his seat, hands crossed behind his head.

They drove away from Nord Station and pulled up next to what used to be a freeway but now was in the process of being turned into a park. The car in front of them stopped in a yellow circle, and then rose into the air, joining a line of cars above them.

A few seconds later, they crossed into the same yellow circle and began to rise. Nic peeked to the ground ten stories below. They sped up, and the city began zooming by like they were in a low-flying airplane. When Nic looked at the speedometer, they were cruising at just over three hundred miles an hour.

---

Nic lay reclined in his chair with his eyes closed. The uneasiness that he felt when the car took off had subsided. Thirteen hours into the flight, and none of them was asleep more than an hour or two. Nic opened his eyes and stared across the horizon, which was now filled with the Atlantic Ocean.

"How are we doing on time, Sophia?" Nic asked, breaking the silence.

Sophia lowered her arm, covering her eyes, and took out the Time Jumper. "It's good that we got the car when we did. The wormhole will be gone in another twenty minutes."

"Twenty minutes!" Tate yelled. "I thought it was going to take twenty minutes to get there!"

"Yes, but it's not like we can go any faster. Besides, we should make it with a couple of minutes to spare."

The car was driving by autopilot now, even over the Atlantic Ocean. But it could only fly across designated areas. "Do we know how close the skyway we're on will be to the wormhole?"

"Yeah," Sophia replied. "There is some sort of skyway interchange ahead of us, and it's not far after that. It'll only be a mile or so out of our way."

Zoe was able to drive the car in Vegas, but it wasn't exactly a smooth ride. Nic worried that flying this car would be even harder. "Zoe, are you going to be able to take this car off autopilot like in Vegas?"

"Well, I already made sure I could. The flying part will be challenging. But I think—"

"I'm the pilot, remember?" Tate interrupted. "Since you can take it off autopilot, I assume any of us can fly, so I will."

Zoe huffed. "I am more adept at using this futuristic technology. For me, the flight control concepts are ones that were under development in my time. I know what to expect, and I should be the one to fly."

"As if," Tate replied. "I have definitely logged more time flying back home *and* here in the future. In the arcade, I was able to finish the race, and that showed me just as much about the future *flight control concepts* as you could have seen in your time."

Zoe rolled her eyes. She was about to object again, but Tate continued, "Besides, flying a plane is so much more than knowing what button to push. You have to know how to react to turbulence, and I do. I'm ready."

Tate straightened his dad's flight jacket. He looked down at his father's aviator patch and gave it a pat, and then stared at Nic, waiting.

Nic agreed with Tate but hated being the one forced to decide. He looked at Zoe, but she didn't return his gaze. When Nic turned back to Tate, he was already smirking, knowing that Nic would take his side.

Nic sighed deeply and then said, "I think Tate should fly. I mean, he really would know how to react if something went wrong."

"Thanks, boss," Tate said, spinning around in his seat to face the front of the car, the control wheel still embedded in the dashboard.

Zoe mumbled, clearly disappointed, "Maybe we should've flown from the car to the wormhole using jetpacks."

Tate laughed. "Nic would have ended up in the ocean."

Sophia stood up, putting down the Time Jumper to stare past Tate across the water. She pointed. "Look at that!"

A giant pillar rose out of the ocean, spiraling into the sky. At its base, land surrounded it.

"Maybe it's an island," Nic said.

"But we're in the Atlantic Ocean," Zoe replied.

"It's a city!" Sophia said, leaning against the car's glass dome.

As they passed by it, Nic could make out more details. The pillar was a giant skyscraper, with a walkway that spiraled down from the top of the tower to its base. On the ground surrounding it, there were marble amphitheaters and temples that looked like they belonged in Greece. As they got closer, they could see distant people dressed in tunics strolled through docks, while others in bathing suits filled the beaches.

"I feel like we are in the wrong time," Nic said. "Except for that skyscraper, I mean."

The car turned slightly without slowing and sped away from the city.

Zoe held up her dataPad, taking a picture, and then played her dataPad's description.

*The city of Atlantis. The first city to be built on water through world cooperation has become a beloved tourist spot and hub for scientific discovery. This self-sustaining city was modeled after the architecture of the ancient Greeks, with the Temple of the Gods rising high above and far below the water's surface.*

Silence remained until the city was out of sight.

"Back to the flying issue," Tate said as he opened the driver's manual on his dataPad. "I'm going to learn how to fly this thing."

---

Tate had studied the driver's manual until they arrived. Unfortunately, there were so many controls that he believed implants really were needed—not that he would tell the others that.

It wasn't all bad though. Tate found that his dataPad allowed him to do the same functions as an implant would. However, there were a lot of functions to cycle through: thrusters, stabilizers, tilt controls, air dampeners, and more. The real problem came with Tate needing to swap back and forth among each of those functions all while he kept hold of the control wheel.

When the car slowed and came to a stop two hundred feet above the highest wave, Tate pretended to have everything under control. "All right, guys. It's simple enough. Zoe—"

Tate's dataPad shook, and a message displayed.

*Constable David Miller:*

*"Are you in need of assistance?"*

Looking up, Tate saw everyone else staring at the same message on their dataPads.

"Ignore him," Nic said. "We don't have much time."

"Agreed," Zoe said. "I'll change it to manual controls."

Tate glanced back down and started to close the message when a second one displayed.

*Constable David Miller:*

*"An agent was dispatched to your location and will be there to assist you shortly."*

Tate swiped both messages away and then waited for Zoe to unlock the flight controls.

The control wheel came loose, allowing Tate to take hold of

it. Thrust levers extended in place where a gearshift would have been in a car, and a three-dimensional image of the car and the waves below displayed on the dashboard next to the speedometer and the altimeter.

A dull voice spoke from the car's speakers. *"Autopilot disengaging."*

"All right, Tate. I have complete confidence in you," Zoe said, shrinking her dataPad and wrapping it around her wrist.

Tate turned to Zoe, surprised to find a pleasant smile with no hint of sarcasm. He thought she would fight him about being the pilot until they passed through the wormhole. Tate appreciated Zoe's confidence until he noticed her death grip on her armrest.

Tate didn't want to let the others down but worried that they wouldn't make it. Even with his limited preparation, their flight might come down to the fact that without implants, flight controls were limited.

"All right, let's see what this thing can do." Tate patted his dad's aviator patch and then gripped the control wheel as the car lowered. His dataPad was expanded to tablet size and strapped to his wrist, acting as a mock implant. Every control for the car had a different screen on his dataPad. He swiped through the most important ones while mentally checking off takeoff procedures.

"No pressure, Tate," Sophia said, "but we need to go. The wormhole will close in less than two minutes."

"Two minutes!" Tate twisted the wheel, rotating the car toward the wormhole. He took a deep breath and pushed the thrust controls forward.

They didn't move.

Tate stared at the controls, willing the car forward. He scratched his head as seconds ticked away.

"What's wrong, Tate?" Nic asked.

"Nothing happened, obviously." Tate ran through the controls, searching for what he missed. "Give me a minute."

"We only *have* a minute, Tate," Sophia said.

"Got it," Tate replied, flipping a switch on his dataPad.

The car shot forward, pinning Tate to his seat. He eased back on the thrust and swiped over to the stabilizing controls, but the car seemed to just shut off and began to fall. Tate swiped back to the thrust screen, giving it a little more power until the car once again shot forward. Without the controls provided by implants, Tate couldn't control their speed. He needed more hands.

The only way to keep them going forward was to go at full power. He straightened them out but gave up on slowing down, instead concentrating on stabilizing their flight path.

"Just a little farther," Sophia said. "Fifteen degrees to the left."

Tate searched unsuccessfully for the wormhole. "I don't see it, Sophia."

"Sorry. There. I expanded the wormhole. Do you see it now?"

A floating silvery sphere grew to the size of a house. Its surface rippled like rocks were spattering it from all sides.

"That's it!" Sophia said. "It's to the left."

"I see it," Tate said, correcting their course.

"Slow down!" Nic yelled.

"I can't!" Tate shouted back as a warning flashed on his dataPad.

Turbulence knocked them off course, and Tate overcorrected. They shot past the wormhole as the car rotated onto its side. Tate screamed in frustration, releasing the thrust so he could turn the car around. He pushed the thrust forward again and the now-spinning car shot toward the ocean below.

Tate's stomach lurched into his chest, and they spun two more times before he managed to flatten them out. He slowed their descent, but not enough. They plummeted toward the ocean, prompting a yell from Tate. "Hold on!"

When they hit the water, Tate's seatbelt erupted in a series of airbags that wrapped around him, protecting him from the fall. The airbags retracted back into the belt in time for Tate to see that the car had belly flopped on the ocean but didn't sink. Tate searched the sky for the wormhole and sighed. "Sophia, the wormhole?"

"It's gone."

Tate turned to the others, and their wide eyes stared back. Failure had sunk in, and they slumped into their seats. Now that Tate was the one letting everyone down, he felt terrible about picking on Nic about his jetpack blunder. He turned to Zoe and realized that if she was able to help control the car using her own dataPad, Tate would have had the extra hands that he needed. If they had worked together, they could have made it. Tate shook his head. "Sorry, I wasn't—"

Tate gawked out the window at a wave peaking over them.

"Hold on!" Sophia yelled.

The wave crashed over the car, submerging them long enough to douse the sunlight. The car emerged, but by the time daylight reached them again, a second wave sent them under.

"We're going to sink!" Sophia yelled.

# CHAPTER 15
# ATLANTIS

Zoe imagined sinking to the bottom of the ocean. She stared out the window at a wave cresting above them and gripped her seatbelt, straining to stay rooted in her seat. The car tilted with the slope of the wave, and a chorus of screams rang out as they were swallowed again by the ocean.

Darkness enveloped them as they were plunged under water. Zoe grabbed on to an armrest to steady herself and pulled back in alarm, as the armrest was wet enough it could have been dunked in water, much like their car was being right now. While the gap between the door and the car was seamless before they crashed, now it wasn't. Water poured inside, as if someone had just turned on a bubbling fountain.

A portion of daylight returned as the car breached the surface, still rising and falling at the ocean's will.

"They're trying to contact us!" Tate yelled.

Their car bobbed back to the surface like a buoy but did not rise again. Zoe's dataPad had shaken, probably the same message as Tate's, but she didn't read it. Instead, her vision turned skyward, and to her relief, a car descended toward them from above. A dim emerald mist swirled around the car. Zoe pressed her hand against the dome windshield above them. "I think we're in a tractor beam."

"Sweet," Sophia said, hunching over the time machine, protecting it from splashes of salt water as the car straightened. "Oh, no," she added softly, but as Sophia wasn't looking at the water attempting to swallow them, Zoe thought something else might be wrong. Zoe didn't have time to ask Sophia as the next wave reached out to crush them. Zoe braced for the wave's impact, but instead the car shot into the sky.

"Hold tight! They're bringing us in," Tate said.

They attached to the side of the much larger vehicle with a loud *clank*.

A collective sigh of relief resonated from the others as they continued into the sky. Zoe released the grip on her seatbelt and watched the ocean rush by outside.

"Are we safe?" Tate asked, his shaking hands releasing the control wheel. "I mean, should we jump into the future to avoid being caught?"

"What good would that do?" Zoe asked. "We would be in the future, but the car would be plummeting back toward the water."

"We're stuck until they take us back," Sophia said, and then added with a grimace, "And we took a bit of damage." She held up the Time Jumper, which had a long crack running down the middle of the screen.

"Can we still use it?" Nic asked.

"I think so," Sophia replied, shrugging. "I can still mess with the controls, but we won't know until we try."

"*Great*," Zoe said, "another thing to worry about."

A buzzer shook Zoe's arm, and a message popped onto the

dataPad, inquiring as to their safety. They were safe; at least they didn't have to worry about drowning. Now they only had to be worried about being captured once again.

Before Zoe could start a response, Nic said, "I'll tell them that nobody is hurt."

Zoe glanced around at the others. To her they all looked a little worn out, as if they'd spent the entire day doing yard work at home and finished with a water balloon fight.

Nic chuckled and asked, "We *are* okay, right?"

They were all right. Wet, but all right. So, everyone nodded.

Accepting their temporary safety, Zoe sank into her seat. The recent excitement of almost drowning paired with lack of rest left her drained. They had now been awake for more than twenty-four hours without true sleep, if she didn't include the car's flight to the wormhole, during which none of them could have gotten more than an hour or so of sleep. The others slumped over in their seats, no doubt feeling the same exhaustion.

Twenty minutes later, Zoe found herself gazing upon the city of Atlantis. She felt like they were preparing to dock in a space station rather than a manmade city. The skyscraper was far larger than she originally believed, with the huge building resting at the center of the island. A walkway on its outside wound around the entire building, tapering up to its peak, well over a hundred stories high.

Zoe recognized a replica of the Greek Parthenon as they descended. It sat on a hill overlooking what appeared to be an ancient city. In the shadow of the looming skyscraper next to them, ancient Greek life played out below.

Troupes of actors dressed in ornate ivory and lilac-rimmed togas performed plays on stages. A few others in the peak physical condition of Olympic athletes wore crimson togas and patrolled the city, assisting the crowd. Given the atmosphere, it occurred to Zoe that the togas must be the employee uniforms on the island.

They landed in a courtyard, a crossroads between the bustling marketplace and the skyscraper. It was an open field of grass that could serve as a meeting ground for some kind of large event.

A middle-aged woman stood outside their door with a medical bag in her hand. "My name's Betty." She glanced around inside, her eyes pausing on the floor of the car, where a pool of water hadn't drained. She reached out her hand. "Come on out, dear. We will get you settled and on your way as quick as we can."

Zoe took Betty's hand and exited the car into the saffron hue of the setting sun. The constant hum of waves crashing on the shore provided pleasant background to an extraordinary city.

After everyone got out, Betty gave a quick check to see if anyone was hurt. They were good enough for her liking, so she headed to her car. She turned back smiling at them and said, "I'll be with you in a moment. Welcome to Atlantis."

As soon as she left, a man in a deep-crimson toga approached. He stuck a frisbee-sized box onto their car, which rose a foot off the ground. With no more effort than pushing a baby stroller, he pushed their car into a small garage repair shop.

While they waited for Betty, they were left alone. Despite them being stuck in the future, Zoe found the city to be relaxing. The gentle crashing of waves echoed from every direction, and a light breeze was welcomed after being stuck in their car for hours. In the city down the hill, busy but happy crowds never gave them a second glance. For now, at least, they could take a breath.

The others were staring across the ocean at a line of buoys that somehow appeared to keep the waves at bay. Even after another failure to make it through a wormhole, Zoe wanted to remember this moment. She held out her dataPad to scan their images and surroundings, moved a bit, and then did it again. She sent the image she created to her necklace, which now displayed their three-dimensional image of the four of them overlooking the city.

As the others stood away from her, Tate with his arms around them, Zoe couldn't stop herself from thinking that she still was not one of them. The pleasantness of being on Atlantis faded, and Zoe's smile turned into a frown.

Zoe knew that Nic liked her but was unsure why. Sophia was friendly, but she was friendly with everyone. The excitement that Tate had for their adventure and camaraderie that he shared with the others was never directed at her. The four of them might have gone on a crazy adventure together, but she still felt like an outsider.

Zoe had grown up knowing them, though, first from rumors in town, second from Grandma Nadezda. They, however, didn't even know Zoe existed until a little more than twenty-four hours ago. The fact that she joined them without giving them a choice felt like she had forced their friendship.

As Betty returned, Zoe placed her necklace back under her shirt and joined the others for an update. Zoe caught Nic smiling at her but still couldn't shake the feeling that she felt estranged from their group, and she didn't know how long she could go on pretending that she wasn't bothered by it.

Betty stopped in front of them and announced, "We are going to service the car, and we can go over what was found. Why don't you come back ..." She trailed off, looking at the car in their garage. "Well, it's a little late to start today. We normally shut down the garage by 5:00 p.m. Why don't you come back tomorrow, let's say around noon, so we can go over the car's analysis in detail?"

"What do we do until then?" Nic asked.

Betty laughed. "Do you have plans for your stay?"

"Not yet," Nic replied.

"I can arrange something for you." Betty's eyes flashed to a dull gray as she accessed the internet. "What happened, anyway?"

"The autopilot disengaged on the way here," Tate said.

"Clearly," Betty replied. "Do you know why? We tried to contact you, but I guess you didn't notice without implants. You should make sure you get your alerts in the future."

"We will," Nic said.

"You've been assigned a room in the Amphitrite Wing. I hope you enjoy your stay. This situation with you kids is the weirdest I have ever had. It's making quite the story."

Zoe's eyes darted to the others, but they didn't react. Betty could have told the story of their car crash all over the internet as it unfolded. With so much attention on them, it really was only a matter of time before they were asked questions that they didn't want to answer. At least they weren't recognized yet. If they were, then they would have stepped out of the car greeted by police rather than a random cheerful lady. It felt like it was only a matter of time though before they were linked to Vegas and Paris. Zoe resisted the urge to search for their story, at least until they were alone again.

Betty pointed to a ramp leading into the skyscraper. "Head straight into the Temple of the Gods, and an attendant will take care of you inside."

Nic had seen many impressive structures on the trip so far, but none had an entrance that made him feel like an insignificant ant. Straddling the entryway in front of them was an enormous Greek statue that made Nic feel, even more so then ever, he was in the wrong time. The statue itself belonged in the past, being a figure from Greek mythology, but it also made him think about how little he knew about the time they were in. Nic led the way into the building between its legs.

Tate leered above them when they crossed between its legs. "Don't look up, guys."

"Why?" Sophia asked, glancing up. "There's nothing to see."

"Of course, you'd look."

"Ugh," Sophia groaned. "You're so immature."

The doors opened, revealing a great hallway a hundred yards deep with a ceiling like a cathedral. Windows reflected enough of the sun's rays to spotlight various scenes of mythology in the statues that lined their path. Among them were Greek warriors grasping snakes, holding a lion in a head-lock, and jabbing spears at monstrous creatures.

At the end of the hallway stood a man-sized statue of a Greek god wearing a crimson robe similar to those worn by the people found in the city. They stepped into the hall and walked up the pathway in awe.

Zoe took Nic's arm, pointing to the ceiling. "Look at that mural."

Nic caught her staring at him and smiled. His cheeks flushed as he followed her finger to the ceiling.

Fifty feet above them, a mural depicted Poseidon actually drifting in the ocean. The scenery visibly transformed with the tide. Fish swam in and out of caves as Poseidon's chest rose and fell with the ebb and flow of the water.

Zoe's hand still rested on Nic's arm. Unsure of what to do, he held his arm as rigid as a statue. When she looked back at him, she left her arm hooked around his. They continued down the hall arm in arm, long enough for Nic to relax, despite Tate's snickering behind them.

The statue at the end of the hall moved. Its body remained motionless, except its crimson robes that drifted with a slight breeze. The statue came to life and bowed before them. While seconds ago, Nic couldn't imagine it moving, now he couldn't imagine how he mistook this person for a statue.

The man before them raised from his bow and greeted them in a monotonous voice that Nic would expect to find from a teacher giving a history lesson. "I'm glad to see you enjoy our craftsmanship. You may call me Hermes. I am sorry to hear about your difficulties in your travels."

Hermes waved his hand over Nic's dataPad. "You are in room 4234 on the forty-second floor. You will be charged for your room every day you stay past 11:00 a.m. I can answer any questions you have, or you can ask anyone wearing robes similar to mine."

"Do you have a map?" Sophia asked.

"Yes, ma'am. You can access a map online." When Sophia didn't attempt to open up a map, Hermes added, "Did you want a paper map?"

"Uh, no thanks. I guess we'll use the online one."

"Let us know if you need anything else. Please enjoy your stay."

Zoe let go of Nic's arm and headed for the elevators, followed by the others. Nic turned back to find Hermes facing the hall they entered, eerily motionless once again.

It was 5:30 p.m., Atlantis time, when they dragged themselves into their room, completely exhausted. Nic walked down their short hall, passing a bathroom and two separate bedrooms, each with a pair of twin beds.

The end of the hall had a couch with a wide view of the ocean. Behind the couch was a dining table, which was mostly pointless without a kitchen. The only unusual thing there was a two-foot-wide cube with a clear panel built into the wall. It might be a microwave, but Nic neither cared nor had the energy to figure out exactly what it did.

The last part of their hotel room was a spacious but empty room with no obvious purpose. From the outside, the room's odd shape reminded Nic of a hollowed-out marshmallow, if people were to stand inside of one. It was the color of snow, but with countless speckles of tiny black dots at perfect intervals. Nic dropped his bag and then turned back to the others. "Check out the marshmallow room, guys."

Tate tossed his backpack in one bedroom, and Sophia came out of the other, and they both headed to Nic. Zoe passed by Nic with a brief peek inside the room, before she plodded over to the couch with a pout.

"Why do you think this room is so different?" Sophia asked at the door.

"I don't care right now," Tate said, heading for the bedroom. "Let's figure it out in the morning."

Sophia shrugged and then headed for the bathroom.

Nic made his way to the couch where Zoe was to see if something was wrong. She stared out the window at the waves approaching the city, illuminated by the lights coming from the tower. Nic took a seat next to her, unsure if she wanted to be alone, and waited to see if she would speak first. A little time passed as Nic watched the waves, entranced by the gentle rise and fall of the buoys. He ran his fingers through his hair, and then asked, "Are you doing okay?"

"I'm fine," Zoe replied softly.

"If Tate's bothering you, don't worry, he bothers everyone."

"It's not just him. I'm okay."

The locket around Zoe's neck rested in her hand. She opened and closed it repeatedly with a *click, click, click.* Nic watched her flick it open, projecting a picture of Nadezda in the space above the locket, and then closed it again without looking. "It's just, I don't think I belong here."

"None of us belong here. That's why we have to get back."

"That's not what I mean," Zoe said, turning in her seat to face Nic. "I don't feel like I'm part of your group."

"That's crazy."

"It's not. You guys have a connection with each other that I don't."

"It's true that we've known each other longer ..." Nic paused, searching for the right words. "But we wouldn't have made it out of Vegas without your help." Nic thought back to his mistakes. He reached out and rested his hand on hers. Instead of pulling away, she twisted her hand around, interlocking their fingers. Nic smiled at her and then continued, "You've done more for us than I have. I'm the one who got us lost in time in the first place, and we could've been home by now if I hadn't botched our chance with the jetpacks."

"Even still," Zoe said, "it would have been better if I didn't come at all. I mean, Tate still won't give me a chance."

"Actually, Tate acts the same way with you as he does with his sisters. If anything, I would have expected him to be a little worse. Give him time. He'll warm up to you too." Nic smiled, eyes locking with Zoe's. "We're all glad you're here with us. It wouldn't be the same without you."

"I guess. I wish I could prove I'm one of you."

"You already have. With the jetpacks, you returned for me, and when it comes down to it, all of us would do the same for you." Nic gazed into her eyes, as she gazed back into his. He brushed a purple strand of hair away from her eye and left his hand on her cheek, leaning forward.

"Are you two gonna kiss?" Tate bellowed.

Sophia was behind Tate, with her hand covering her eyes.

Zoe leaned back, and Nic glared at Tate. "What? I'd tell you and Future Girl to get a room, but well, here we are."

"Can you not do that, Tate?" Nic asked. He tried to press down his anger, but the more Tate poked, the madder he got. He glanced at Zoe as she stared across the ocean. Her cheeks flushed, and her arms crossed in front of her. Their moment had passed.

"What?" Tate asked, his smile broadening. "So, no kissing."

Sophia slowly headed for the bedroom, clearly not wanting to be involved in the argument. Like in Vegas in the implant store, as soon as something seemed to get out of hand, Sophia was the first to leave. Nic couldn't blame her, though.

"You're being obnoxious, Tate," Nic growled. Tate was too much, and if he continued, Nic wouldn't be able to hold back. "We'll only make it home if we are all working together, but you are at odds with everyone." Nic thought about Zoe saying that she felt like she wasn't one of them. Tate not calling her by her name was part of that. "And for crying out loud, her name is Zoe, not Future Girl."

The corner of Tate's mouth twisted into a grin. "Correct me if I'm wrong, but—"

Before Nic could respond, a shaking Zoe leapt from the couch. She faced Tate, rage flowing through her like fire. Nic thought she was going to hit him, but instead, a shout burst out. "*You*, of all people, should *never* start a sentence that way!"

"I think," Sophia said, returning to Tate, "that we should call it a day." Sophia kept her head down but grabbed Tate's arm and then dragged him toward the bedrooms. "It's late. See everyone in the morning."

Tate looked down at his arm where Sophia held him. Surprise that Sophia stepped in was clearly visible on Tate's slightly parted lips, but he still allowed her to drag him away.

Still red in the face, Zoe yanked her sleeping bag out of her backpack. "I'm sleeping in the white room."

Nic sat on the couch, glaring at Tate as Sophia dragged him away.

Tate headed for one bedroom as Sophia went to the other. "Hey, Sophia," Tate called out. "It's their first fight. Zoe's making him sleep on the couch."

Nic yelled in unison with Zoe, "Shut up, Tate!"

Nic was alone. Lying on his side, he stuffed a pillow under his head and stared at the crashing waves outside. He focused on the dim beacons of light from distant buoys, trying his hardest to not replay the argument. He had only meant to stay there until he calmed down, but sleep soon overtook him.

## CHAPTER 16
# A WELCOME REPRIEVE

A door slammed shut, which startled Nic out of sleep enough that he jumped to his feet. His first thought, *Where am I?*, was answered as he stared across the ocean. Behind him, Tate and Sophia had just come in through the front door, holding bags. Sophia raised hers and said, "Breakfast is served."

Nic ruffled his morning hair, which was messier than normal, and then eagerly walked around the couch to see what they had to eat.

Zoe popped out of the room she had slept in. "Excellent, let's discuss what we do next in here. This room is a holographic rec room. I mean, it's actually called C.A.V.E., or Customizable Artificial Virtual Environment. But it looks like these are regular rooms in homes nowadays, just like a bathroom or living room."

"Really," Sophia said, rushing inside in front of Nic. "So, can you start a program?"

"I think so, but you need to know what program to start," Zoe replied. "Think of it like a modern-day, well, future-day office that everyone has. You design your environment to your liking and use the room as you like."

Zoe typed away at her dataPad and then beckoned them into the center of the once-empty room, which was now morphing into a grassy field before their eyes. Trees sprouted across an artificial hillside, growing from small seedlings into giant sequoias. They grew high into a sky where clouds drifted far past the treetops. Without the doorway, Nic would have believed they were really outside in a forest.

Sophia stepped up to the base of a full-grown sequoia, and reached out to touch it. Her hand passed straight through the projected scenery. With slight hesitation, she stepped into the tree and was hidden inside the projection. She stuck her head and arms out and flailed them around, and said laughing, "Help, I'm stuck in a tree!"

Tate made his way to the edge of the room, where he leaned against what appeared to be an invisible barrier. He knocked on the wall, which made a hollow sound.

"It looks so real," Nic said moving around to examine the room up close. Even small plants swayed in an imaginary breeze, plants that Nic's hand passed straight through.

Sophia plopped down in the middle of the room and then passed out a burrito to everyone as they gathered around. Nic sat down next to her in a patch of dirt that was really just a hard floor.

Zoe sat down, taking her burrito. "Okay then, what's the plan?"

"They want us to check in with them at noon," Nic said.

"We obviously can't talk to them," Tate said, joining the others in a circle meeting. "If we do, then they'll want to know more than we can say."

"They seem more relaxed here than in Paris," Sophia said. "Maybe we could talk to them?"

Zoe shook her head. "No, there have been enough questions about us already. Did any of you realize that Betty was livestreaming our story when we arrived? I wouldn't be surprised if we are interviewed by a bunch of reporters after our supposed meeting. Our crashing outside Atlantis is a world-wide top-ten trending story right now."

"It would have been nice if we could've kept the car as we jump into the next time," Sophia said. "If we had started with one when we jumped last time, we might have had another try."

"We don't really have a choice. We have to jump before anyone has a chance to question us," Nic said. "We'll just have to pick a place to time jump from and hope we have another chance before the Terata War."

"Let's jump from our room," Sophia said. "We could sit on the bed and take it with us, in case we fall."

"My mom is always telling me not to jump on my bed," Tate said, chuckling. "To think, she could've been talking about time travel this whole time."

"No good," Zoe said. "If we jump from here, anybody staying in the room would see us when we arrive in the new time."

"Then we will have to find a place when we explore the city," Nic said. "What is there to even do here?"

"There are a lot of touristy things like the casino and the CES tours," Zoe said.

"CES tour?" Tate asked.

"It's part of the closed ecological system," Zoe answered. "A self-sufficient environment, meaning they reuse everything, and algae is a big part of that system. We can do a CES tour if you really want to know."

"No," Tate said, "there has got to be something more fun than that."

Sophia stuffed the last piece of her burrito into her mouth and then mumbled with her mouth full, "It looks like the main attraction today is a football game at the Parthenon."

"We don't have time for something like that," Nic said.

"Is that American football or soccer?" Tate asked.

"Soccer, between Manchester United and the Atlantean Hoplites. Oh, and the Atlantean team has robots," Zoe said.

"Do you think they program the robots to fake injuries?" Tate asked.

"It wouldn't be the same game if they didn't," Zoe replied.

Tate opened the bag he brought when he got breakfast with Sophia and held it out. "Anyone want some baklava? It is some kind of Greek treat."

"Sorry, Tate," Nic said, "but I can't trust you. I'll pass."

"Come on, man. No bugs, I promise. In any case, it's got to be better than the algae burrito we're eating."

"My lack of trust in you isn't because of bugs," Nic said, glaring at Tate. Nic opened up the burrito to find algae mixed with bell peppers and what Nic suspected could be insects. He wished he didn't look, because despite its appearance and the possibility of insects, it tasted pretty good.

"Are you still upset about last night?" Tate asked. "Look, I'm sorry."

"Yes, this is about last night. Even after you had gone too far, you wouldn't stop." Nic's irritation was returning, but he decided to keep it contained for now. Nic refolded his burrito and said, "Just remember, Tate—at this rate, we aren't going to make it if we don't work together."

Tate opened his mouth to say something but remained silent.

Zoe glared at Tate but then asked Sophia, "Do you have any more crickets?"

Sophia reached into her backpack and took out what remained of the chocolate-coated crickets. She took one piece of chocolate and then, keeping her head down, she slowly took one of the baklavas from Tate. While the taking of treats seemed like a way for them to take sides in their argument, Sophia taking both was her way of remaining neutral.

"Maybe we should just explore the shops," Zoe said, pulling out a handful of crickets. "We might find a place down there to jump from. Plus, the shops are likely to have some fantastic cheap technology that we couldn't even imagine. I would love to get some souvenirs in case we ever find *someone* capable of flying us through a wormhole."

Tate narrowed his eyes at Zoe. His lip twitched, and Nic could tell that he was biting back a retort. Thankfully, though, he said nothing.

"I'm ready when everyone else is," Sophia said.

Zoe ate her last chocolate cricket as she stood. "I'm done. Let's get going."

"Works for me," Nic said. He hadn't finished yet but stood up too, burrito in hand. "Let's go find where to jump from."

---

Nic strolled through marble columns framing the open-air foyer that surrounded the Agora Market. He lost track of Sophia and

Zoe shortly after they reached the market, but Nic took the time as an opportunity to find a place to time jump from.

The only place Nic found was one of a series of structures at the edge of the market. They had walls made of stone but no ceiling, and the floors had cobblestone pathways resting on top of grass. When Nic peeked inside one of the doorless rooms, he found stage actors preparing for a performance. The rest of the building was empty, with two other individual gardens decorated with benches and flowers, and away from any prying eyes.

"Maybe we can jump from here," Tate said from behind him. Tate still wore his jacket, despite everyone else stuffing theirs in backpacks. The sun was still climbing into the sky, but it was hot enough that Nic found himself still sweating in the shade.

"It's not a bad spot," Nic said. "Let's find the girls and see if they had found somewhere better."

Nic hopped down the steps in front of the market, passing shops with everything from decorative Greek souvenirs to advanced implant upgrades. Nic caught Sophia perusing through Atlantis-themed souvenirs like patches and water bottles. They caught up to her as she finished talking to a man wearing a crimson toga and then pocketed something she had purchased.

When Nic reached Sophia, he asked, "Did you two find anywhere to jump from? It's almost time to go."

"Yeah, Zoe had an idea," Sophia replied. She opened her mouth to say more but paused when a young girl strolled past with her mom. In the girl's hand, she held a metallic ball, which she tossed into the air. When it reached the apex of her throw, it hovered in place behind her. A hatch opened projecting a

Pegasus the size of a house cat. It flew circles around the girl before landing on her shoulder.

"Five more minutes, Nic," Sophia said. "Hey!" she yelled. "Where did you get the Pegasus?"

The girl pointed to the store behind her and then took her mother's hand and wandered down the path heading for the beach.

Sophia ran into the store, Tate trailing behind her.

Nic found Zoe across the path, sitting on a marble bench. He smiled at her as he sat down and asked, "Are you going to get a souvenir?"

Zoe shrugged. "A couple of things seemed like fun, but most technology requires implants."

"Yeah," Nic replied, "they really do everything with them."

Tate left the shop and jogged back to them, followed by Sophia. She left the store and sat on the ground, placing a metal ball next to her. She hunched over it, typing on her dataPad.

They joined Sophia as she stood, holding the ball out in front of her. She lowered her hand, and the ball hovered in place. It clicked open and projected an image of a dragon the size of a cat. "Getting lost in time is now worth it."

"It's cool," Tate said, "but you realize that it's a baby's toy."

"No, Tate. It's like having your very own pet encyclopedia that can teach you over a thousand scientific projects."

"So, it's like going to school whenever you want. Fun."

"It will be. Now I can build solar panels and hover engines out of everyday household items."

"Any ideas on where we should jump from?" Nic asked.

"We could jump from the pier," Zoe replied. "Under it I mean. It's out of the way enough that nobody should be there when we arrive. Although, if people are swimming ..."

"Why don't we use one of those rooms that the play actors were using," Nic said. "They were mostly empty."

"That works for me," Tate replied. "Although, I was thinking—"

A groan left Nic's lips before he could stop himself. He thought Tate was going to try to start some kind of trouble. Nic did regret his unintentional criticism when Tate's forehead creased, genuinely hurt by Nic's slipup.

"Nothing bad," Tate continued defensively. "I was just going to say, I get that we are in a hurry to jump right now, but do we want to take a break on searching for a wormhole? I mean, if we jumped forward a year, we could do some more future exploration, without worrying about police."

"As much as I hate to say it," Sophia replied, "we kind of stick out. And the more our ageless images are spread throughout time, the more likely someone will figure out we're time travelers."

"I agree," Nic said. "We should find the next wormhole."

For a moment, Nic thought that Tate would protest, but he shrugged as he replied, "It was just an idea."

They returned to the garden rooms. Sophia's dragon circled them the whole trip back, periodically pausing in flight to snarl at Tate, a function that Sophia added, much to everyone's enjoyment except Tate's. The room that the actors used earlier was now empty, so they went inside. It was open to the sky, allowing Nic to stare up at the skyscraper as they entered. The Temple of the Gods towered high above them, but its view was blocked out by the tall walls once they were bunched together to hide in the corner of the room.

"Okay," Sophia said, "here's hoping that we have another chance before the Terata War."

"We should," Tate replied. "Timewise, we should have a couple more jumps."

"I agree," Zoe replied, "but that's still just a guess."

"Why are you saying we should have more tries?" Sophia asked. "We are now closer to the Terata War than to home."

Nic thought about the length of time that they had been traveling and then answered, "We started in 2022, and now it's 2156. That's roughly 130 years with four different wormholes, and the first fifty we weren't looking for them. Now we have, how long until the war?"

"Eighty-seven years," Sophia replied.

"Yeah," Nic continued, "eighty-seven years until the Terata War. The way things are going, we have to have another try."

"Time will tell how many tries we have," Zoe added, "but if we did make it to the Terata War, our only chance for a wormhole will be on a Terata-occupied Earth, or as Grandma said, 'On the other side of the Teratas, in space.'"

"So, let's make the next jump count," Sophia said as she prepared the Time Jumper, leaning against the side of the building. "Everyone ready?"

"You're not ready, Sophia. Put your baby toy away," Tate said.

Sophia huffed and opened her dataPad. The ball lowered into her hand, and the dragon was consumed by holographic flames before disappearing. "Goodbye, Fang."

"You named it too?" Tate asked.

Sophia shrugged as everyone knelt around her. "Here we go again."

The lights vanished.

*Thump!*

*Eighty-seven years later*
*June 30, 2243*

Explosions erupted in every direction. The building they jumped from lay crumpled in a pile of rubble, leaving them crouching in a bare patch of its remains.

The smell of burning metal assaulted Nic's nose. Dark specks of rain slowly drifted to the ground like snow. It wasn't until Nic held out his hand that he realized that it wasn't rain that fell from the sky but gusts of ash. He stared into the sky, where Terata spaceships zipped past in dogfights with the future-day human fighter planes.

"Sophia!" Nic said, standing. "Please tell me we have more time!"

"The year is 2243."

"2243!" Zoe yelled. "That's when the Teratas attacked!"

## CHAPTER 17
# ESCAPING EARTH

Nic stared across the island's destruction. Much like the building they were in, the marketplace around them had transformed into ruins that belonged in ancient Greece. The Temple of the Gods was now in view, smoking with an enormous hole clear through to the other side. Despite its damage, the building stood. Panicked crowds ran to it as the only shelter left providing any protection.

A shadowy creature bigger than a bear sprang to the top of a half-fallen building on the other side of the market. Nic fell to the ground, shushing the others, but managed to keep the creature in sight. Everyone collapsed and lay motionless around him.

The creature, which could only be a Terata, landed on all four limbs and crept forward like a lion stalking its prey. It was the same reptilian creature that crashed at home, but larger and with blocky, seaweed-green scales that covered its entire body like a suit. Its eyes bulged unnaturally, and where its mouth and ears should have been were black scales that ran across its face, hiding its true features like a mask.

Nic's heart pounded in his chest, echoing the booming of weapons firing in the distance. The Terata rose onto its hind legs and searched the crumbled buildings around it and then leapt out of sight.

Sophia stared at Nic wide-eyed. "You said we had at least another try before the war."

"All our other jumps were twenty to thirty years. How was I supposed to know that we would jump almost a hundred years this time?"

"Keep it down, guys," Zoe said. "We're here now; that's what matters."

"We've got to get out of here," Tate said in a whisper. "Let's jump now. We could arrive in another time, after all this is over."

"I don't think we can," Nic replied, trying to push the Terata's image from his mind.

Zoe stared back at the Temple of the Gods. "Don't forget, humans lose this war. Whatever time we end up in, it would be inhabited by Teratas."

"Then what do we do?" Tate asked.

"Nadezda is in this time right now, trying to take down the shields, right Zoe?" Sophia asked. "Did Nadezda ever tell you anything that would help us find her?"

"She is here," Zoe replied, "but we can't find her. She told me that when she arrived in this time, she reached the command ship a couple days before it got to the moon. She is somewhere in space, and we would need to be in a spaceship to even look."

Tate stared across the ruins, following movement at the edge of the city, and Nic found what he was looking at. A human had peeled back some cloth that hid half a dozen people. The human got inside what appeared to be a small hiding spot that the Terata could never find. As soon as Nic felt those people were safe, a Terata leapt into view. It was clear to Nic that the Terata had no visual indication of where people hid, but it went straight to their hiding spot like they were out in the open.

Marching across the marketplace grounds, a woman wearing a crimson toga leapt twenty feet into the air, landing on top one of the last standing walls. She held out her arm, toga billowing behind her. Her hand folded back at the wrist, revealing the barrel of a gun, which fired green beams across the former market. The beams struck the Terata approaching the humans' hiding spot, as well as a second Terata that Nic was unaware of until it fell.

Twenty feet away, the crunching of boots on rubble silenced them. A man in robes returned fire on the Terata. A gust of wind blew the toga open, revealing a gaping hole in the man's side. Instead of a wound, a dented metallic plate covered circuitry, revealing the man was not a man at all but an android. The android sprinted away to engage the Terata in battle.

It was shocking that they had been interacting with androids since they got to Atlantis without knowing it. Nic had thought that Hermes, who checked them in, was a statue because he didn't move until they got close. He could have been an android, and maybe even some of the shopkeepers. Nic expected to see robots as they went farther into the future but hadn't imagined interacting with them without knowing.

Nic stood when another explosion erupted in the distance. He turned to the others and said, "We need to get out of here."

"That way!" Zoe screamed. She pointed to a dozen people

being ushered toward the Temple of the Gods by a pair of androids. "Let's follow them!"

Nic ran after Tate and Sophia, pausing briefly to make sure Zoe was still with them. She passed by as he slowed, his eyes focused in the distance on something that made his heart feel like it was attempting to burst from his chest.

On the other side of the market, one of the Teratas crouched, staring directly at Nic. Its head tilted toward him as if peering into his soul. The Terata ignored a barrage of fire coming from a distant android and leapt into the air toward Nic.

Nic stood, rooted in place. He watched in horror when the creature landed and leapt forward again.

Zoe shook him back into reality. "Let's go, Nic!"

Nic nodded and raced after the others like he was being chased by a predator, which he was. Sophia and Tate were waiting for Nic and Zoe at the same repair shop where they had left their car. Right before Nic reached them, he risked a glance back. The creature had gained on them enough for Nic to know they were out of time. He lost sight of it as they crossed around to the front of the repair shop, but they would soon be caught.

One last open stretch separated them from where they stood and safety, but with a Terata now chasing them, there wasn't enough time to get there. Nic stopped in front of Tate and Sophia. "One of those things is coming for us. We need to hide, now!"

Tate searched the repair shop for a place to hide. One wall had collapsed, taking with it half of the ceiling and any possible hiding spots.

"Over here," Sophia said, peeking out from around the outside of the building. Nic chased after her to a car that had been blown upside-down into the wall. It leaned against the wall and provided just enough room for them to hide underneath. Nic crawled after Zoe, hoping their hiding place was good enough. Tate entered last and hunkered down in the remainder of the car's shadow.

"Can you see anything?" Sophia asked.

Tate turned back. "Shh!"

Nic waited, enduring Tate's foot digging into his side. He silently wondered what good hiding was, knowing that the Terata earlier found people hiding in a spot far better than this. All they had was a car they crawled under, and they would be in sight if the creature looked toward them.

Nic listened but couldn't hear anything over the pounding of his heart. A few seconds later, Nic caught his breath as a low growl rapidly approached them. The Terata shot past where they hid, but not far. Sounds of machinery being torn apart in the garage made Nic think he was playing a nightmarish version of hide-and-seek.

The Terata had somehow lost track of them for now, but before they could run again, it returned. Even though Tate blocked most of his view, Nic could still see enough to know that the creature crouched outside only ten yards away.

Nic did get a good look at it, though. Unlike the one they saw at home, this one had no horns. It didn't have any clothes on, but what it did wear seemed to be more of a scaly suit than its naked body. The Terata held a rifle in its hand, which it patted impatiently, and across its back was a spear as long as its arm. Its entire body was scaly like a crocodile but bigger. Besides the weapons, it had a belt with various pouches and a device wrapped around its wrist.

Nic caught a glance of a scaly face, and despite the creature not having a real nose, it repeatedly twitched its head as if it was sniffing. Nic was not that worried about being smelled out. The city was in ruins, and the only thing he could smell was ash, but a simple glance in their direction would let the Terata know they were hidden behind the car.

It spoke into the device in a flurry of grunts and snarls. A single growl came as a reply, which the Terata didn't acknowledge.

More time passed without it moving. Nic considered trying to back out the other side of the car where Sophia was, but they might make too much noise. It would be best to get completely out of sight. Out of desperation, Nic was about to whisper to Sophia to try to back up, when the Terata leapt out of sight.

Tate turned around and said, "I think it's gone." He slowly crept out from under the car to peek around. A loud smack of something heavy hitting the ground caused Tate to fall back, kicking Nic as he did.

The crunch of glass nearby preceded the car flipping through the air like a toy. The car landed with a crash thirty feet away.

The Terata crouched in front of them, and Nic could imagine an evil smile underneath its scaly mask. Despite kneeling, it still towered over them. Its eyes narrowed, head tilting in the same questioning manner one might find on a dog.

Nic scooted back but bumped into Zoe. There was nowhere to run. They were trapped.

The creature flung its rifle onto its back and pulled out the five-foot-long spear. It growled at them and then made grunting sounds similar to an angry gorilla. A translation, in English, barked out of a device around its wrist. *"You four are coming with me."*

The creature pointed its spear at Tate, emitting a guttural croak. "*You first.*"

Tate stood and glared at the monstrous creature and said in a shaky voice, "I'm not supposed to go anywhere with strangers."

"Not now, Tate," Nic said.

The creature stood, reaching its full height, nearly three times as tall as Tate. Its spear now pulsed with an electric blue charge, which it held next to Tate's face.

"Fine, I'm coming." Tate brushed off his pants and stepped forward away from the building.

Fragments of the wall trickled down from above, causing Nic to glance up. Above them, an android wrapped in crimson robes knelt on the edge of the roof, peering down at the Terata. Nic turned back to the Terata, and it hadn't noticed. They were saved, but why was the android not doing anything?

The creature spoke again, which translated to, "*The rest, come!*"

Nic got up, wanting to look for the android but trying to not give its presence away. He stopped next to Tate, and they still hadn't been saved. The Terata's spear crackled, and the heat from it made Nic's hair stand on end. The Terata's gun was behind his back; the android had a chance. Was it defective? What was it waiting for?

The Terata stepped to the side and pointed to the edge of the city. "*Move!*"

From behind, something crashed to the ground. Nic's first thought was the android, but when he turned to see, the android was crawling down the wall headfirst.

The Terata dropped the spear and flipped the rifle around,

blasting a hole in the wall and narrowly missing the android, who had just launched itself over them into the air.

Mid-flip, the android returned fire with a barrage that showered the ground with explosive green beams. Everyone jumped back and covered as they were sprayed with dirt and pebbles that were spit up from the attack. The android landed on its feet next to the toppled car and blasted the Terata inside the garage.

The android approached. It stopped in front of them, its hand snapping back in place on its arm. It faced Nic and stated in a deadpan voice, "My name is Achilles. I will be overseeing your evacuation. We must hurry."

Nic stood next to Tate, waiting for them to be led away, but Achilles didn't move. "I do not see your identification." Achilles held out his hand, and a blue light scanned across the four of them, pausing on their dataPads. "This way. We must get back to our compound before the next attack, which we would not survive out here." He turned toward the smoldering skyscraper and jogged ahead.

Nic ran after Achilles, trying to catch up, but he slowed to stay with the others. As he did, Achilles also slowed, without glancing back.

Once they reached the Temple of the Gods entrance, a panel in Achilles's arm opened, revealing an empty space. He raised his arm into the air, and hundreds of what looked like insects flew inside his arm.

"Gross, what was that?" Tate asked.

"MAV flies."

"What?" Nic asked.

"Micro Air Vehicles. My surveillance nanobots."

"That's cool," Sophia said.

"Yes," Achilles replied.

When they started traveling in time, Nic couldn't imagine what the future would be like. Getting hunted by aliens and chasing after an android never crossed his mind. He pictured Achilles waiting on the roof when the Terata was threatening them. "Hey, Achilles, I noticed that you had plenty of time to shoot down the Terata when you were watching from the roof. Why didn't you do something sooner?"

Achilles turned his head around but continued his pace forward. "I was attempting to discern why the Terata did not kill you on sight."

"Wait! So, we're your guinea pigs?" Zoe asked.

Tate stopped just outside the entrance before Zoe finished her question, and Nic understood why. Should they even trust Achilles to lead them to safety if saving them was not his true goal? If he figured out that they were time travelers, what would happen to them?

Achilles stopped and turned back to them. Despite being a robot, Nic expected him to hide the truth. "I think guinea pigs would summarize the situation. We are unsure of the exact reason the Terata attack and are in the process of acquiring information as it becomes available. The Terata that chased you was acting strange, and finding out why could lead to key information in the war. Keep in mind that any information that we can obtain to help fight the Terata is our top priority."

"Any information," Tate said, "even at the expense of our lives."

"Of course. The Terata have been scouting Earth since they arrived, and in all that time, they have never attempted to capture anyone who did not give them a distinct strategic advantage. They mostly captured military personnel or public figures. So, we have to ask, why are they interested in you? Once there is time, we can debate the topic.  For now, we need to hurry. Despite their interest in you, the Teratas are no longer scouting Earth. This was the first true attack wave, and sensors have reported that we have less than an hour until the second, much larger attack."

Achilles spun around and began jogging ahead again without bothering to see if they followed him. Nic hesitated but then hustled after Achilles into the temple, not because they trusted him, but because they had no other choice.

They raced through the entrance they had used yesterday into what remained of the Temple of the Gods. Toppled statues lined the path, and broken marble columns no longer reached the ceiling. The mural above them was still a masterpiece, but with a crack straight through an unmoving Poseidon. Nic continued, silently questioning the safety of the building that they had run into for shelter.

They entered an elevator, where Zoe stared at her shaking hands. Nic searched for words to comfort her, to say to all of them that things would work out. He attempted to speak but couldn't even bring himself to say *we'll be okay*. He stumbled as the glass elevator shot underground, veering to the side and rushing forward like a hyper-speed train.

They approached an underwater park lit up as clear as day.

"How are we supposed to evacuate from under water?" Sophia asked.

"When we are ready, the park will surface, open up, and allow escape."

The elevator stopped with a ding, opening in the middle of a park the size of a football stadium. A glass barrier separated the park from the force of the ocean. Benches faced a pond filled with now panicking birds that took off and landed, but with nowhere to escape.

They arrived amid pre-departure preparations, with half a dozen androids corralling people into the five transport space-crafts that would soon provide a one-way trip off of Earth. The spaceships were wide and half the length of a commercial airplane, with two stubby wings that held engines the size of a car. The engines roared to life and pivoted independently, generating huge gusts of wind that added tension to the already chaotic evacuation.

Achilles stopped at the center spaceship, where a crowd had gathered anticipating their departure, and said curtly, "You will board here." He then hustled to the ship's docking doors and herded the panicked people on board like cattle.

CHAPTER 18

# ZOE'S SACRIFICE

The ground trembled beneath Zoe's feet from an unseen explosion. She shouted, "What was that?" Sophia pointed behind her, and when Zoe spun around, she stared across the park in horror. The barrier that protected them from the ocean burst with a *crack* that echoed throughout the compound. Water began pouring across the park like a geyser had erupted from the wall, which grew in size with every passing second.

Achilles spoke simultaneously with every other android nearby. "The Teratas have breached the Temple of the Gods! Attack is imminent!"

Zoe's heart raced, and her first thought was to run inside their ship. Before she took a step, the remaining crowd squished her as they rushed forward in panic. Achilles held up his hand, but instead of calming the remaining dozens of passengers attempting to board, he said, "Brace for ascension."

The compound shook again, enough that Zoe felt like a rug was pulled out from underneath her. Everyone around her was knocked to the ground too, including an older man who fell from the ramp.

At first, Zoe thought it was another attack, but the water rushing by the glass walls showed that the underwater park began rising from the depths of the ocean. The park breached the surface, stopping with a jolt. Above them, the ceiling parted, raining down small streams of the ocean like a waterfall and opening up the compound to the smoky sky.

Another explosion roared in the distance. The entire park tilted sideways, dipping the far side under water and flooding the ground underneath a rising spaceship.

The Teratas began pouring into the compound like bees swarming to their hive. The spaceship next to them disappeared. Moments later, a Terata rocket shot at the cloaked spaceship as if it was tracked by a homing missile. An explosion erupted in midair, causing the evacuating spaceship to rematerialize. Its cloaking device sputtered out, and one of its car-sized engines fell to the ground. The entire craft twisted on its side and then began rising again at half speed, powered only by its one remaining engine.

The man who had fallen groaned at Zoe's side, which pulled Zoe's thoughts back from the disaster that erupted around her. She took hold of the older man and pulled him to his feet. "Thank you, miss," he said, his head whirling back and forth as he watched the battle unfold.

Zoe croaked out a response, "Let's hurry." She couldn't bring herself to search the compound again, worried that she might not be able to look away. She followed Tate and Sophia, and assisted the old man up the entry ramp, followed only by Nic.

Once everyone was onboard, Zoe headed for a seat as

Achilles closed their entrance. He then dashed to a side door and flung it open, sticking his arm out to fire his weapon.

The ship was a transport vessel, the closest thing to an airplane that Zoe had ever been on. Ten rows of seats faced the front, with an aisle down the middle and five seats to each side. Zoe found her seat in the back next to her friends, and fumbled with her seatbelt that wrapped around her shoulders and waist.

The spaceship rose, and Zoe turned to see in the gap behind Achilles where a spherical Terata craft crashed to the ground like a meteor, hitting where their escape vessel was mere seconds ago.

Just when Zoe thought they had made it, a crash hit the ship from behind, and the whole craft was yanked back down. Zoe spun around to see a glowing electric-blue grappling hook poking through the closed entry ramp. Achilles turned away from the door, shooting the hook, which seemed to absorb the blast. Instead of flying out into space, they were being pulled to the ground.

Using his arm like a blowtorch, Achilles began cutting a circle in the wall of their spaceship around the alien device holding them in place. He stopped cutting halfway and then charged the door as a scaly claw of a Terata appeared in the doorway. The Terata tackled Achilles, pinning his arm on the floor. Achilles yanked his arm free and kicked hard, only to get tangled up with the monstrous creature and get yanked out of the ship.

Without Achilles to save them, how could they get the hook off their ship? Zoe considered waiting, but they might never see Achilles again. She turned to the others, who stared back wide-eyed. Zoe unlatched her belt and then ran to the glowing hook, but didn't think she could touch it.

Instead, she headed to the door, deciding to peer down to the compound below in search of Achilles. All around the compound below them, dozens of androids fought back, slowing the incoming alien horde to a crawl, but not enough to allow them to escape, and not enough for them to last for long.

A spherical Terata craft had crashed below them. Glowing cables stretched from it all the way to the hook holding their spaceship. The other fleeing human spaceships were also tethered in place, each with its own cable. The only way to break free would be to release the hook next to her or if the spherical Terata craft was destroyed. As if to test her idea, a couple of androids fired on the crystal sphere with no apparent effect.

The park slowly sank back into the water, dragging each of the spaceships with it. A fourth of the park was now flooded, and the thought of them being pulled under water frightened Zoe to the pit of her stomach.

Sophia tossed something at the hook, which sparked bright enough that everyone shielded their eyes until the object fell, charred like it was thrown in a campfire. "If we can't touch it, how do we get it off?"

"That's it," Tate said. "Game over. We're done."

Zoe noticed Nic scoot next to her and peer over the ledge down at Achilles and the Terata fighting. The Terata jabbed at Achilles with its electrically charged spear. Achilles kicked it away but lost his footing enough to be knocked onto his back. Directly below them, Achilles was pinned with his weapon arm missing. He was struggling in a losing battle, and the spear came to a stop ten feet away from their fight.

Zoe heard Sophia whisper to herself, "The spear."

Zoe stared at the alien weapon, wondering if it could disable the crystal sphere anchoring the spaceships to the sinking compound. Nothing else seemed to work, not even the android's weapons, but the Terata's own weapon might.

They were now gathered around the doorway, staring below wide-eyed. The only one who wasn't visibly trembling was Nic, but he was barely able to croak out the question, "What can we do?"

Zoe could tell that they had lost all hope.

They hadn't traveled together long, but Zoe now knew she wouldn't lose the friendship that had developed. Even if she didn't make it home with the rest of them, they would always be friends, maybe not as close as she would have liked, but still friends.

Zoe pulled off her necklace and squeezed it tight. She closed her eyes and exhaled slowly. When she opened her eyes, she set her necklace down in Nic's palm. He took the necklace with brows knitted in confusion.

Their ship had been dragged so close to the ground that once the enormous Terata finished with Achilles, it could probably reach them with a light hop. Achilles was losing, and if he lost, they would all lose. Zoe watched Achilles's fight, waiting for an opening, and then jumped.

Nic's scream followed Zoe as she fell. She crashed onto the Terata's back, tumbled to the compound floor, and rolled over, temporarily stunned. She stared back up at Nic leaning out of the spaceship above, held inside by Sophia and Tate. Zoe rolled over, but before she could drag herself to her feet, the Terata stood above her, growling. She tried to scoot away, but it kicked her onto her back. She lay there in a daze, and before she could move, Zoe felt the weight of an oversized foot stomp down on her chest, pinning her to the ground.

Footsteps rushed toward her, but she could not tell from

where. She grabbed at the huge foot, unable to wiggle away. She strained to take a breath as the Terata's hand reached down. She tried, but it was over. The tips of the Terata's fingers brushed against her neck, and then the hand was gone as the Terata was flung through the air. Zoe rolled onto her side, gasping, and found Achilles fighting the creature once again.

Zoe took a deep breath and then searched for the spear, lying forgotten away from the renewed fight. Still dazed, she staggered to the alien weapon. She grabbed it, surprised at its size. It seemed so short in the Terata's hand but was almost as tall as she was.

She leaned into the spear like a cane and hobbled to the alien device anchoring the spaceships. One spaceship had successfully detached, but the four remaining were still held in place, being dragged to the Terata sphere by electric-blue cables, including the one holding Nic and the others. The entire compound shook, causing Zoe's legs to sway beneath her, dropping her to her knees.

Heavy footsteps approached, prompting Zoe to slowly stare up into the bulging eyes of an enormous Terata. It towered over her, and Zoe barely found the strength to stand. Her lips quivered, and she wanted to scream, but the air seemed to be stuck in her throat. The size of the creature made Zoe's legs shake and got her to unintentionally take a step back.

Zoe bumped into a spike from the sphere that anchored the spaceships. Screams from above, friends she left behind, mentally pulled her back into the dire situation that they were all in. She gripped the Terata spear tightly in her hands, finding a switch and powering it on. Trying to keep her distance, she jabbed the spear toward the approaching creature. The spear's tip sparked with an electric blue that lit up the Terata's scale-covered face.

If Achilles couldn't win a one-on-one fight, Zoe had no chance. Water now covered half of the compound and began approaching Zoe like the tide had come in. She was out of time.

She wouldn't get away and now accepted her fate completely. Zoe stood tall. She glared at the creature with all the disdain she could muster and then plunged the tip of the spear as far as possible into a small opening in the anchoring crystal sphere.

An ear-piercing whistle grew like a steaming kettle, until Zoe dropped the spear to cover her ears. The crystal ruptured, striking Zoe with an energy blast that sent her flying through the air.

---

The spaceship lurched up, slamming Nic to the floor. The whole ship dipped as Achilles climbed aboard through the closing doorway. He no longer looked human; the robotic side of him was the only part that was left. He was missing an arm but was still intimidating enough that Nic backed away, struggling to convince himself that Achilles was on their side.

Nic forced himself to his feet and headed to the door. Achilles sliced away at the grappling hook no longer protected by a Terata's force field, which left a foot-wide hole.

"Wait!" Nic yelled.

Dozens of robotic tarantulas scrambled to the hole, oozing together to form a new wall and ending the sounds of the ensuing battle outside.

Nic fell to the floor in protest as they took off. He grabbed Achilles and pleaded, "We can't leave without Zoe!"

"We have to save her!" Sophia shouted.

"We only made it because of her!" Tate yelled.

Achilles shook his head. "We must leave."

They rocked to the side, causing Sophia to stumble into one of a dozen pods at the edge of the room. "Careful with that," Achilles said. "Those are escape pods. It would do no good to have you launching yourself back to Earth."

Achilles waved his remaining mechanical hand over the newly repaired wall, which created a screen displaying the compound below. They could see Zoe standing in water up to her knees. In front of her were two Teratas, one holding a spear at her neck. Nic's view of the compound zoomed out due to the spaceship's increasing distance from Atlantis, but the last thing Nic saw was a Terata spaceship landing nearby and Zoe raising her hands in surrender.

Their spaceship continued rising as six other identical compounds breached the water's surface, continuing the evacuation of Atlantis. Each compound that surfaced was being swarmed by the Terata warriors.

"We couldn't go back for her," Achilles said. "It was impossible."

"We can't just leave her to be killed by them," Nic said.

"Yet, it will be impossible to retrieve her at this time. You should remember her for the sacrifice that she made. She saved the life of everyone on this ship, as well as the other spaceships in our compound. Remember her for that."

After everything that they went through, in the end, they had failed. Even if they made it home, Zoe was lost. Nic stumbled to the closest seat and collapsed. His trembling hands covered his eyes. Achilles continued to speak, but Nic didn't care what he said.

Nic looked into his hand. He clutched Zoe's necklace and then opened it. The necklace projected an image showing Zoe, Nic, Tate, and Sophia gazing over Atlantis when they arrived. An image that Nic didn't even know was taken.

Nic's body weighed down on him; muscles in his arm strained to wipe the tears welling up in his eyes. He couldn't bring himself to move from his seat.

He woke from his misery to a hand resting on his shoulder. He now noticed the room before him. Every eye was on him, each in a strained expression of sorrow. Nic tried to speak, but his voice cracked, pushed down by a lump in his throat, refusing his words.

"Come on, man," Tate said. "Achilles said we can use the back room." Tate helped him up and walked him past the other passengers. They all lowered their heads with their hands covering their hearts. It was a sign of sorrow for the loss of Nic's friend and thanks for their lives, which she undoubtedly had saved.

# CHAPTER 19

# TO THE MOON

Sophia sat cross-legged on a pullout bed in the spaceship's sleeper cabin. They had spent a majority of the ride in silence, but once the others began talking again, Sophia knew that they would start to argue; Nic would want to somehow go after Zoe, and Tate would say it was too risky.

Sophia would be stuck in the middle, unable to take a side. She wished that she had more courage to take a stand one way or another, but knew, like always, she would probably let things play out without her getting involved. As their conversation approached, Sophia pulled out her new toy, drawing comfort from it, allowing it to distract her from the growing concern over the looming confrontation. Despite only being a projection, her new toy dragon, Fang, now lay in her lap, purring like a cat.

On the bed across from her, Nic was curled up and staring at the locket that Zoe had given him. He hadn't moved since they arrived, except for opening and closing her locket. Through the window, the moon approached. Although the command ship was going to take over the moon before conquering Earth, that's where they were headed. They had no choice. They would arrive at the lunar base soon and needed to discuss their current circumstances, but Sophia couldn't bring herself to rouse Nic from his brooding.

Tate passed time, seated in front of a window made from the spaceship's transparent wall. Despite his disagreements with Zoe, he was unable to hide the fact that he kept wiping his eyes with the sleeve of his flight jacket.

The dread Sophia felt increased by the second, and if they didn't figure out what to do next, they could be taken by the Terata themselves, or worse. Not only was Zoe gone, but now they needed to figure out how to survive. Sophia couldn't take the silence anymore. She rubbed her eyes and asked, "What do we do from here?"

Tate stared blankly at the space between him and Sophia, but answered, "Let's take advantage of the time that Zoe gave us and find a way home. Do either of you have any ideas?"

Sophia stared at Nic fiddling with Zoe's necklace and then back to Tate and shrugged. Nic normally had the ideas, but he hadn't spoken since they got there. Tucking Zoe's necklace under his shirt, Nic shook his head.

"We need to figure this out, Nic," Tate said quietly.

"What do you want me to say?" Nic asked, still facing the wall. "I don't know what to do now. I just don't want to give up on Zoe without trying. I mean, she saved us."

"She did," Tate said, "but what can we do now?"

Instead of leaving and letting the others figure out what to do, Sophia turned to her new toy. She wiggled her fingers, prompting Fang to lean into her. She still expected the dry texture of a scaly hide, but her fingers passed through Fang like the projected image that it was. "I wish. I wish that I could be more like her. Zoe saved us. She stood face to face with a Terata and wasn't even scared. I would never be able to do something like that."

Shrugging, Tate sat down next to Nic's feet, across from Sophia. "You always avoid conflicts, Sophia, but that's not necessarily a bad thing. I act without thinking, and look where it gets me. As much as I hate to admit it, Nic was right before. With the jetpacks. If I waited until Nic was ready too, we might already be home and with Zoe."

Slowly, Nic rolled over to stare at Tate with raised eyebrows. He didn't say anything; he didn't have to. This was the first time Nic had moved since they were stuck in there, and Sophia knew how much Nic appreciated Tate admitting he played a part in their past failure. It told him that them being stuck in the future wasn't only Nic's fault, and he needed to hear that.

"I thought the Terata spear could work," Sophia confessed, "but if I jumped, it would only lead to me getting hurt. I'm just saying, I wish I had the confidence to leap when I saw an opportunity."

"I couldn't have done what Zoe did," Tate said. "Speaking as someone who leaps before thinking, next time it happens, just ask yourself—if you don't act now, will you be too late? You might surprise yourself."

Sophia smiled, considering Tate's words.

A chime from the door interrupted their conversation. The door transformed into a transparent window. Achilles stood behind the door, whole again, complete with a new arm and fresh layer of artificial skin.

At the sight of Achilles, Nic reddened. Zoe would have been nearly impossible to rescue back on Atlantis, but Sophia knew that Nic couldn't stop thinking that a rescue was still possible.

To him, the *machine* that stood on the other side of the door was the reason Zoe was gone. Nic clenched his hands into fists and screamed at the sealed door, "What do you want, Achilles?"

The door slid open to the emotionless face of Achilles. He spoke in his familiar flat tone. "Good evening, children."

"Again," Nic said, "what do you want?"

Achilles stepped inside. "I trust that you find these accommodations to be satisfactory under the circumstances."

While Sophia longed for an update about what was going to happen to them, Achilles made her nervous. After watching him battle one of the Terata warriors, and his disregard for getting Zoe back, Sophia got the feeling that all humans were expendable to him. He was an android, but a little too human, and it was eerie.

Sophia would normally leave Achilles's conversation for Nic, but he wasn't thinking clearly. If Sophia relied on Tate, they were bound to talk themselves into trouble.

Before Sophia could think of what to say, Tate smirked and then said, "Well, the accommodations aren't what we are used to, but they'll do for now."

"What exactly are you used to?" Achilles asked. "I thought you were living the simple life."

"We are," Sophia said, trying to take control of the conversation. "Do you know what happened to Zoe?"

"I am sorry to say, but it would be best for you to honor her sacrifice. She is now a casualty of war."

"No, she's not!" Nic shouted. "When we were on Atlantis, the Terata tried to take us prisoner. The last we saw of Zoe, the Teratas were holding spears on her. That means they wanted to take her prisoner."

"Interesting idea," Achilles said with a smile that was

creepier than it was comforting, "but why would the Terata find a child a person of interest? She is not a general or a politician. She is not important to the war, and it is unlikely that she would warrant such attention. You need to consider her already gone."

"Then why weren't we killed on Atlantis?" Nic asked.

"Unknown," Achilles replied.

Sophia, however, knew the reason—it was because they were different. They were time travelers. However, the Terata wouldn't know they were time travelers by looking at them, so it had to be the only other thing that made them different. "We don't have implants."

Nic and Tate both silently glared at her, probably not wanting to get into their past again, but Sophia continued, "We are living the simple life, but we also don't have implants. Let me ask you, if someone else were to live the simple life but was in need of emergency medical care, what would you do?"

Achilles raised its hand to its chin the same way a human might consider the question and then answered, "The implants still would let us know of the danger."

"So, they are never really turned off," Sophia said excitedly. "What if the Terata were able to track people because of the implants?"

Achilles didn't move, and in his absence of movement, he appeared to be more statue than human.

Tate jumped up and said, "That has to be it!"

Nic smiled for the first time since they lost Zoe. "Zoe is a person of interest, because they want to know why they can't locate her."

Sophia considered that Achilles having a hand on his chin might be a default thinking position used to appear more human. Now that she knew he was an android, the action didn't work.

After a moment, Achilles spoke again. "That is an interesting theory and will be examined thoroughly. However, those deemed a person of interest are evacuated back to the command ship, rather than risking them being rescued. In your highly improbable scenario, Zoe as a person of interest still will not survive. You need to accept that Zoe is beyond saving. Now—"

"*Interesting theory*," Nic interrupted. "Why wouldn't everyone know this already?"

"Everyone has an implant," Achilles replied. "Tracking us was not something that came up. Now, this was an enlightening conversation, but we will be arriving at Marius Base soon. You three will be assigned to a colony ship for evacuation."

"Evacuation to where?" Sophia asked.

"There are three colony ships ready for launch. You will be assigned to one of them. One ship will travel to Gliese-667, twenty-three light years away. One ship will travel to Kepler-186f, four hundred ninety-six light years away. The last ship will create a colony at an undetermined location. There is hope for you, if you are assigned to Gliese, you might even get to see a new world."

Sophia remembered Nadezda saying that her colony ship was the last to survive. "Are the colony ships even safe from the Teratas?"

"Safer than staying on the moon," Achilles replied. "If you think of anything or have any questions, please message me. Eat what you can. We will dock at the lunar base soon, and before you know it, you will be traveling out of our system." He bowed, and then turned to leave.

"Wait! Where is the food?" Sophia asked.

Achilles paused at the door, pointing to a two-foot square panel on the wall next to him. "You are authorized to use the replicator unit."

Sophia got up, pressed on the panel that slid into the wall, revealing a plain two-foot cube alcove. It had a tray at the bottom and was similar to a microwave oven. Sophia linked her dataPad with the replicator and ordered three hamburgers. The replicator lit up with an electric-blue light, and a dozen pipettes poked through the sides of the unit to spin in circles, squirting materials that solidified into the bottom half of hamburger buns.

Tate joined Sophia at the replicator and leaned in to watch the burger print. "Ugh, I think I lost my appetite."

Sophia turned away, no longer wanting to see how it was made, greeted by a wide-grinned Nic. "You heard that, right?" Nic said. "Zoe is alive on the command ship, and if she is not there yet, she'll be there before we can get there."

"I don't think that is what he said," Tate replied, voice subdued. "He said that Zoe is beyond saving."

"Nic," Sophia said, "she is on the command ship."

Nic's eyes narrowed, and he said under his breath, "You talk about her like she's dead. She's not." He stood and glared at Tate. "Did you know that while on Atlantis, Zoe confided in me that she didn't feel like she was one of us? That's on you, Tate."

Tate just sat there. His eyes welled up, but instead of lashing out like Sophia expected, he calmly said, "You're right." He wiped his eyes and then added, "I never wanted her to come along, but she was one of us from the beginning."

"Was she?" Nic asked. "I told her that she was one of us, and just like she didn't leave me behind with the jetpacks, *we* would never leave her behind. And what are you talking about doing now? Leaving her behind."

"It's not about leaving her behind, Nic," Tate said, raising both his arms. He shook his head and lowered his voice. "Look, I would rather get her back too, but we don't even know if she's still alive or how we could get to her. She sacrificed herself so that we would survive. So that we can get back to Nadezda and everyone could survive. We can't go back to Earth." He stared out to the approaching moon. "And we all know that the colony ships aren't going to make it. If we don't find a way back to the wormhole, we're not the only ones who are doomed; everyone is."

Nic closed his eyes and sat back down. He ran his fingers through his hair and said, "If we make it home without Zoe, our lives will continue. I'll move away, and the two of you will return to life as we knew it before all this started. But Zoe will never be rescued. We will spend the rest of our lives knowing that we might have been able to save her. She is one of us, and without us, Zoe will be left to a fate worse than death."

Sophia felt sick. They couldn't travel through a wormhole when their biggest conflict was merely finding one, but now they not only had to find one, but had to do it during an alien invasion? What's worse, they'd lost a part of their group—a person who sacrificed herself for them when they never felt they breached the inner sanctum of their friendship.

Sophia didn't want to give up on Zoe, but she looked at their situation from all angles and had no idea what they could do. "Maybe we should consider coming clean to the locals. They might be able to use the time machine. We no longer can. I mean, maybe whoever we give it to will be able to stop the

Terata by going back in time like Nadezda did when she tried to take out the shields."

"No!" Nic said, shaking his head. "Anything they did would end Zoe's chance at surviving. They would take the time machine, and we would *still* be trapped in the future on a colony ship we know will not make it. It's better if we can find a way to do it on our own."

Nic and Tate both looked to Sophia.

Sophia felt like she was cornered. She didn't want to be the one to make a decision like this. "I think," Sophia said, "that getting Zoe is the right thing to do. But taking on the Terata on their own command ship seems like a fight we can't win. Why don't we figure out our options? We still have to find a way to the wormhole in space, so let's just take it one step at a time."

Nic and Tate nodded in agreement.

"Well," Tate said, "if Sophia is considering a fight, then the least we could do is find out if rescuing Zoe is possible."

Nic put his hand on Tate's shoulder. "I'm sorry, man. I didn't mean to come down on you as hard as I did. We need to try; that is all I'm asking. If we work together, I'm sure we'll figure something out."

Tate's smile returned. "We'll do what we can, Nic." He walked to the replicator, which Sophia forgot had printed a meal. When the replicator panel opened, it released an amazing aroma that reminded Sophia of the local burger place back home. Tate handed out the 3D-printed burgers and then took a spot by the window to watch them begin their nighttime orbit of the moon.

Sophia examined her burger, peeling off the top bun to take a deep sniff. It smelled like a barbecued burger, and even the lettuce leaf snapped in half like a real piece of lettuce. If she didn't watch it print, she would have thought it was the real thing.

Expecting it to taste rubbery, Sophia sank her teeth into the juiciest and most flavorful burger she could have imagined. Despite being a little grossed out by the process, she devoured it in a couple bites and then printed up a basket of fries before joining Nic and Tate by the window.

By the time they reached sunlight again, they clustered around the window. More structures covered the moon, but now in the daylight, it was easier to see what they were. Countless cannons pointed into the sky, each labeled *Asteroid Particle Blaster* on Sophia's dataPad. However, their true purpose as a defense against Terata became obvious once they saw dozens of construction bots building new ones across the lunar landscape.

Tate peeked outside. "The moon looks different than I remember."

"No kidding," Nic said. "It's bigger."

"No, look. We're on the light side of the moon, but I don't recognize that crater being on the moon in our time. I wonder if an asteroid hit it."

"We're still on *the dark side* of the moon," Sophia said, frowning at Tate, and then turned back to the moon below.

"Huh," Tate said. "I thought it would be darker."

"It's called the dark side because we can't see it from Earth. It still gets sunlight."

Tate opened his mouth to speak and then stared at the floor.

Nic pointed to a structure on the horizon that extended far above the rim of a huge crater. "I think we made it to the moon base."

The structure resembled a humongous submarine. As they

approached, numerous vehicles sped around, performing tasks that Sophia could not guess at. She held her dataPad up to identify the structure. "Guys, that's not the moon base. That's the *Niña*, one of the colony ships."

"Unreal," Tate said. "It's the size of a city."

"It would have to be," Nic replied.

Two more identical colony ships came into view, looming over the horizon. They passed over the *Niña* and then veered toward a hole near the center of a huge crater.

They approached the giant hole surrounded by igloo-shaped mounds of various sizes. The mounds were made of glass, and people could be seen rushing around the underground city below. As they descended, they passed through an enormous hole that acted as the gateway to the Marius Lunar Research Facility.

# CHAPTER 20
# MARIUS LUNAR BASE

Under the surface of the moon, Nic stared across an immense cavern that left him breathless. The lights that lit up the cavern came from the ceiling itself, which was covered in a moss-like substance. It had to be artificially created but still provided the feeling that they were in a submarine navigating through an underwater cave, instead of on a spaceship traveling across a lifeless moon.

The cavern had been transformed into a spaceport, and based on science lessons in school, Nic thought that the tunnels could've been carved out by lava. It was over a hundred feet deep and wide enough to fit a sports stadium, stretching far beyond Nic's vision to where the tunnels sloped underground.

The sheer volume of spaceships littering the cavern floor made Nic wonder how many people were still on Earth. There were thousands of ships below them, and those were the ones he could see. Parking the ships, though, was more of an afterthought. Each one rested at an odd angle, some packed so tightly together that they wouldn't be able to take off again.

Tate nudged Nic and then nodded to the ships below. "I

guess we found our way off the moon. Now we just need to find a way past the aliens' shields, get Zoe, and find the wormhole. This will be easy, right?" Tate shook his head, and then held up his dataPad, scanning the parked ships they passed. He began pulling up charts and reading about different makes and models and what each ship could do.

Nic turned his attention back to the cavern, where they now lined up behind others that had fled from Atlantis. They landed in an overcrowded patch of tunnel, nearly on top of an abandoned spaceship, and waited for a line of five trolley-like lunar shuttles to fly them into the base itself.

Evacuation to the shuttle began, and Nic trailed behind Tate and Sophia. His step faltered as he entered the ten-foot-wide metallic tube. Gravity is much lower on the moon, but Nic forgot about the change while he was under the artificial gravity of the spaceship. He tripped forward, raising his hands in front of him in preparation for a fall that he easily caught.

With one-sixth his normal weight, Nic's stomach hung a little too high in his chest, and he felt like he was hopping across the bottom of a pool. When he entered the shuttle, he was reminded of a commuter train. While some people sat, others chose to stand holding on to bars.

Instead of sitting in the shuttle next to Nic and Sophia, Tate raced over to Achilles, who was detaching the tube between the shuttle and the Atlantis spaceship being left behind.

The shuttle rose, and they pitched forward until they flew through the center of the moon's cavern. In the shipyard below, a family stepped into a lunar shuttle. They abandoned their spaceship without even bothering to shut it down, and they weren't the only ones. Lights from a few other abandoned spaceships left Nic with an empty feeling of lost hope.

To get into Marius Base, they had to enter through a passageway at the side of the tunnel. They flew toward a circular metal door, which slid open just before they arrived and slammed shut behind them. They came to a stop inside a room barely big enough for their shuttle.

Sophia rose from her seat and stared outside. "Oh, they're filling the room with air. I was wondering how we would be able to breathe while in the base."

"That makes sense," Nic said. He made sure nobody could overhear and then whispered, "Sophia, do you have any idea how to get past the Teratas' shields?"

Sophia responded in a whisper, "I'm not sure. We might be able to do it with the Time Jumper, by jumping past the shields. Although, even if I figure that out, we still need a place to jump to."

"Then I'll see if we can find a blueprint for the command ship somewhere. Maybe people were able to figure that out already."

Sophia nodded and then stared blankly at the seat in front of them. Her smile returned again after the shuttle took off. They sped through a second door that closed behind them, arriving in a small terminal similar to one found in an airport. As people disembarked, some hopped almost ten feet into the air, testing out the gravity difference.

Nic, Sophia, and Tate lagged behind everyone else, leaving last. Nic considered staying behind and trying to take a shuttle back to the shipyard right away, but saw Achilles staring at them at the shuttle's exit.

Tate led them into the corridor. "It's time for a moon walk." He bounced into the air ahead of Nic, a little higher with each step, followed closely by Sophia. By the time Nic joined them, Tate had almost reached the ceiling twenty feet above them.

Nic didn't jump, though. He was still unsettled by the low gravity, but he reluctantly headed down the long hallway that led to the main section of the lunar base.

Within the terminal, behind a long window that lined the corridor, many hundreds of people stood in a line. They were being ushered into more lunar shuttles. Nic guessed that these shuttles would ferry people to one of the colony ships.

Each step Nic took gave him more confidence. It wasn't the same as walking on Earth; on the moon, he found it was easiest to hop from foot to foot like a game of hopscotch, and it felt awkward. His stomach rested in his chest, and the lack of true gravity left him feeling buoyant.

Ahead of him, Tate bounded forward to a circular door with a large sign above it reading *CAUTION: ARTIFICIAL GRAVITY – 1G.*

Nic jumped after Tate. He leapt higher than he expected, but still in control. Nic took hold of handrails and stepped through the doorway, pulled to the ground by the moon base's artificial gravity. The queasiness that came with the low gravity faded, leaving Nic with no lasting ill effects.

The statuesque Achilles stood in front of them. "You three will be heading to the *Santa Maria*. Your scheduled boarding time is at 0400 hours lunar time. It is now 0130 hours, leaving you two and a half hours before you board."

"Thanks, Achilles," Sophia replied.

"Thanks to you and your friend, Zoe, many more people survived. Zoe will be remembered for her courage and sacrifice."

Nic glared at Achilles and then stepped away a couple of

feet. He knew they would have to get back to the shuttles, but as the android didn't leave yet, it would have to be later. It was probably for the best, though, as they still needed to figure out if they could get on board the command ship.

Nic strode into Marius Base knowing they would never board the *Santa Maria*. He wanted some privacy, so he led the way through a sea of people who filled every nook and cranny of the facility. Marius Base was not designed for this many people, giving it the appearance of a small airport terminal overcrowded from flight cancellations. With lines of people inching toward the lunar shuttles, the moon base would empty out eventually, but Nic wanted to find a place to talk privately with the others now.

The best they could do was on a slightly raised platform under a glass dome, which provided a vantage point to the lunar surface. It wasn't a room and was in sight of all the people waiting for a shuttle to a colony ship, but it did provide enough privacy for them to talk. Nic sat at the bench next to Tate and stared up at one of the colony ships at the edge of the crater. "Okay, we're safe to talk now."

Instead of joining them, Sophia sat on the floor against the wall. She pulled out the Time Jumper and dove into the controls, only pausing long enough to pull out her projected dragon, Fang. It rested on Sophia's shoulder once again, but no longer snarled at Tate.

Nic searched for blueprints to the command ship, but there was nothing besides images of it from a distance. Unsure of where else to look, Nic stared outside where one of the colony ships rose above the lunar atmosphere, heading for outer space. Nic was watching it leave when Tate asked, "Do you think

Nadezda is out there right now, trying to take down the command ship's shields?"

"Don't know. My guess is that she's probably in our time by now," Nic said, shrugging. "If, uh, we get into a spaceship, will you be able to pilot it?" Tate's face turned sour, so before he could respond, Nic added, "I'm not saying this to be critical of you. I just want to know if you think it's possible."

Tate waved his dataPad around. "This does everything an implant does, just not as well. I flew the spaceship simulator in the arcade, I flew the car, *and* I'll be able to fly a spaceship too."

"But you crashed in the arcade," Sophia said, glancing up from the Time Jumper. "And you crashed the car too."

"In the arcade, I got better. Just don't expect me to win any races. And in the car, I had minutes to read through the instruction manual. If we get a spaceship, I will manage."

Sophia returned to the Time Jumper and didn't question Tate's abilities anymore. Nic was sure she still had doubts, like him, but it wasn't like they could stay on the moon or board a colony ship.

Nic nodded, unsure if Tate was still just being hopeful, but decided to take him for his word. "What about a spaceship? Are there any that will work for us?"

"Yeah," Tate replied, smirking. "We need a spaceship with a sub-light drive, which are used for traveling around the solar system."

"Are any of the spaceships with sub-light drives in the shipyard?"

"Yep. Those will be the ones with four engines. Two of the engines navigate short distances like on Earth, and the other two will be the sub-light drives. If we get one of those ships, and *only* if we get one of those ships can we actually make it to the wormhole, or the command ship. Otherwise, anywhere we go, we just won't be fast enough."

Tate opened his mouth to say more but remained quiet. The whole lunar base was quiet too, with only the sounds of shuffling feet heard from people scooting toward their fleeing shuttles. Nic imagined that the people here thought that they were moments away from a Terata attack, and any second it would be too late for them.

As if to confirm Nic's thought, the silence that hung in the air was broken by a thud of irregular drums, beating to the rhythm of impending doom. Every person in sight stopped and stared in front of them with grayed eyes.

Rumbles in the distance continued as if they were in the finale of a fireworks show. Nic and Tate both opened their dataPads and pulled up a video of the Terata attacking. The video first showed images of Terata fighters leaving the command ship, and then switched over to a local video of them attacking a fleeing colony ship. The booms that shook the base were mostly human defenses, but it meant that the Terata were close enough to fire on.

"Guys," Nic said, "the Terata are trying to stop the colony ships from leaving."

"Ready or not," Sophia said, "we need to go. The command ship is almost at the moon, and that signifies that our time is up."

"It's okay," Tate said, looking up from his dataPad. "It doesn't look like the command ship will get here for at least a day, and Marius Base holds until they arrive, right?"

"But that means it's almost here," Sophia said. "We need to get on the command ship before it arrives, and a day is not a lot of time."

Nic stood up and stared out at the colony ship leaving. "Well, Sophia, if we leave now, we need to know if we can get Zoe or not. Can you get us past the shields?"

"I believe so," Sophia replied. "We need to find out where in space the command ship is going to be and get there first. It's on its way to the moon, so it's a matter of meeting them halfway. From there, if it takes an hour for the command ship to reach us, then that is how long we jump. That way we will return in time inside their ship, shields and all."

"Will that really work?" Nic asked.

"I don't see why not," Sophia replied. "Although, we still don't know where to jump to. If we jump into the command ship, we might land inside only to crash. We need an actual location in the command ship to time jump to, or we just can't do it."

Nic pictured the video he just watched, and the number of Terata fighters that already attacked Marius Base. "Wait, we saw Terata fighters leaving the command ship on video. Can we just go in where they came out?"

"Yeah," Tate said. He returned the video of the Terata attacking, back to where the Terata space fighters left their command ship.

If they time jumped there, it would get them past the shields. It could work, as long as they didn't run into any Terata space fighters when they returned in time. It would be risky, but it could work.

Tate stared at Nic with his arms crossed. "Then we have a way to rescue Zoe. Are we really going to board the command ship?"

Nic nodded, and Sophia said, "Yes."

"Then we have a plan," Nic said, clapping his hands

together. "We *commandeer* a spaceship, fly it to the Terata command ship, and then time jump inside their flying fortress without being noticed. We only have to figure out how to find Zoe once we're inside."

Sophia shrugged and then quietly added, "What could possibly go wrong?"

None of them wanted to poke holes in their plan, now that they had one, so they remained quiet. Nic took their lack of response as a cue to move on. The steady *thud-thud-thud* from the moon's defenses pushed them into action and provided a constant reminder of the danger they were in.

Nic hustled back toward the shuttle they came in on. Crowds had thinned to less than half the people who were there when they arrived. It seemed impossible moments ago that the colony ships could board in time, but now they were nearly done.

A motionless woman with a blank stare stood nearby. Now that they knew how common the androids were, they were easy to identify, despite this one being in a military uniform. The android appeared to be on standby and wouldn't be able to stop them from getting back to the shuttles.

Nic crossed through the line of people waiting to board a shuttle that would take them to a colony ship. The lunar defenses continued firing as they approached the circular door for the lunar shuttles. The sign above the door on this side read *CAUTION: LUNAR GRAVITY – 1/6 G.* In the time since they'd arrived, Achilles had left, as well as people arriving from fleeing spaceships. This allowed them a clear path to the shuttles.

Nic followed Sophia through the circular doorway. This time Nic braced for the loss of gravity and found his footing easily before bounding next to Sophia, Tate behind them. They entered the first empty shuttle and headed to the front. Sophia leaned over the controls with a creased brow, unsure of what to do, but reaching for the controls, nonetheless.

"I've got this, Sophia," Tate said. He straightened his jacket, patted his jacket's patch, and took the controls. He pulled a lever next to him, sealing the shuttle. He tugged on the control rods in front of him gently, and the shuttle lurched forward no faster than a walk.

Behind them, the android near the shuttle entrance had moved close enough to watch them depart. They flew down the passageway, with a brief stop to return the air pressure around the shuttle to what it was on the lunar surface. The final doors opened, and they passed into the cavern making up the abandoned spaceport.

Nic stuck his face next to the window, searching below. He spotted a rectangular spaceship with four engines that reminded him of a school bus with its lights still on. "That one has four engines."

"Ugh, I don't know," Tate said. "Wait. That one." He pointed to a spaceship that was a small version of the one they fled Atlantis in. Instead of having two wings, though, it had four, each with an engine half the size of the core of the ship. A small room on the side remained open with its lights on, letting them get inside without breaking in.

Their shuttle approached, and despite the slow pace that Tate flew, the shuttle didn't stop. Tate groaned, and then yelled, "Nic, see if you can—

Before Nic could do anything, the shuttle slid along the roof of the spaceship below them. The ship vibrated with a shrill screech. Nic cringed as the ships ground together in a thunderous screech that ended with Nic airborne. He caught himself easily, thanks to the low gravity, and was still breathing, so at least the shuttle wasn't open to the moon's atmosphere.

Tate laughed from the controls as he extended the metal tube to their soon-to-be-claimed ship. The tube sealed around the opening with a hiss, and air rushed from the shuttle to the spaceship's open room. "Never mind, Nic. I landed just fine." He laughed again and then pulled himself through the tube as Nic caught a notice flashing on his dataPad. "We have a message, guys."

"Yeah," Sophia said. "We got that when we left Marius Base."

Tate twisted around in the middle of the transfer tube. "Forget it. It's got to be someone trying to stop us. Hurry up, I've got a spaceship to fly!"

Nic snapped his dataPad closed over his wrist. "I'm coming, Tate." He hopped after Sophia through the transfer tube, his heart pounding in time with his dataPad's message alert telling him that they were being contacted. The spaceship's door sealed shut behind them. Nic turned to watch the transfer tube withdrawing, removing their last chance for a *safe* retreat, even if it was on a doomed colony ship.

The room they were in now was an airlock for getting on and off the spaceship. Sophia stood at the controls, attempting to get inside. "Oh, I can adjust the gravity from here."

"Just open the door," Tate said.

"Got it," Sophia replied as the door slid open, revealing the spaceship's bridge.

"The ship is ours," Nic said.

Tate grinned. "Well, guys, we're officially space pirates."

# CHAPTER 21

# SPACE

Without waiting for the others, Tate strode over to the pilot's chair in the center of the room and tossed his backpack behind him. Multiple computer workstations were built into the walls, two of which were now occupied by Nic and Sophia. Nic was using his as a seat, not to help fly the ship. Sophia madly searched the computer for information of one kind or another.

Tate noticed at the back of the ship was a row of escape pods similar to the ones in the spaceship they used to flee Atlantis. Beyond the escape pods was a second door and more computer stations.

Tate leapt onto the pilot's chair. When he did, two joysticks floated out of the side of the chair and stopped in front of him. Tate opened his dataPad, leaving it strapped to his arm, and swiped away the messages ordering them to return to Marius Base. He linked his dataPad to the ship's controls and asked, "You guys ready?"

"Yes," Nic replied, but he seemed hesitant.

"Sophia?" Tate asked. "What are you looking up?"

Sophia sat at the workstation next to the door and poked around on the computer. "I'm just trying to find the command ship." She scrolled through the spaceship's schematics and then a map of the inner solar system. She nodded, turning to Tate to give him a thumbs-up. "Go ahead."

Instead of taking the controls, Tate stared at Nic, who still seemed unsure. Tate had considered trying to fly them out of the cavern before, but with his poor navigation with the shuttle, he was having second thoughts. He might be able to get them out by himself without a problem, but he needed a hand when he failed with the car, and he might need one now.

As if reading his doubts, Nic asked, "Are you going to be able to fly this thing?"

"Well," Tate said, "after *landing* the shuttle, I'm once again having second thoughts. We still don't have a choice, though; we have to leave. But maybe you could see if it's possible to maintain the power in the engines on that workstation. I think that was my biggest problem when I flew the car."

Nic spun around and began searching through the controls.

"Sophia," Tate continued, "you already found information on navigation. Why don't you see if you can handle what is going on around us? Look out for Terata space fighters, asteroids, or just the *space* around us."

"Got it," Sophia said.

Nic easily found controls for the engines. "I'm ready."

Tate smirked, rested his hand over his dad's aviator patch, and said softly, "This one's for you, Dad," and then reached out, grabbing the joysticks. Straps zipped around his body, securing him tighter than a standard seatbelt. The pilot's chair rose to the center of the room, and he was engulfed in darkness.

Light crept into Tate's vision, revealing the crisp view of his surroundings. He gazed into the cavern as if their spaceship had no walls. Half a dozen shuttles zipped by on a course to exit the cavern, on their way to fill up a colony ship.

Tate's grip tightened, and he gently pulled back on the joysticks to follow the shuttles leaving ahead of them. Behind them, a single shuttle piloted by one android followed, but it was too late to stop them.

Just like the car he flew, thrusters fired on full, pushing them past the spaceships on the ground around them. Unlike last time, though, Tate stayed his course. Nic had made the adjustments needed for them to leave the ground smoothly.

They rose, only staying afloat using the controls that were meant to rotate and stabilize the craft, something Tate didn't think would work unless he was in the moon's limited gravity.

Tate tilted his controls, and the spaceship mirrored his movements, creeping through the spaceport toward the exit. "All right, guys. Here we go!" He yanked back, flipped a switch on his dataPad, and sent them out of the shipyard and into the moon's limited atmosphere like a rocket.

One colony ship remained below them, while a plethora of the small shuttles ferried the remaining Marius Base refugees on board. Tate could barely make out the second of the three colony ships escaping in the other direction. The first was nowhere in sight and had clearly already started its mission through the galaxy. Tate knew from Nadezda that none of them would survive without the Terata being defeated, but he still found hope that they would escape eventually.

Past the crater's edge, the asteroid blasters pointed deep into space. Tate aligned their ship in the same direction as one of the lunar defense weapons and then punched maximum acceleration, launching them toward what he thought would be the Terata command ship. After releasing his controls, a view of Earth caught Tate's eye. He spun his chair around and sat motionless as the moon-sized Earth shrank from sight.

"What are you looking at, Tate?" Sophia asked.

"Watching humanity disappear," Tate said. "Where are we headed, Sophia?"

"I left a marker of where you need to go on your screen. Head for that."

Tate found a bright-red dot and veered toward it. He briefly searched for the controls to the sub-light drive and then called out, "We're lined up, Nic. Engage the sub-light drives." They shot forward again, the moon disappearing in a blink of an eye, yet Tate didn't feel the effects of their sudden movement, the ship's inertia dampers doing their job.

***

They managed to make it to the spot between the moon and the command ship, as directed by their ship's computer. They couldn't time jump yet, though. Tate needed to turn around and head back toward the moon and then match the command ship's speed. That way they would be going the same speed as the command ship and in the same direction. Otherwise, they could appear inside the command ship and fly into a wall, which was not ideal.

Taking hold of the spaceship's joysticks again, a smile grew on Tate's lips. He had always dreamed of flying a plane, and now he was flying a spaceship. Space relaxed him, somehow allowing him to forget how the success of their plan was in his hands. Stars didn't shoot by like in the movies, but the vastness of space made him think that the Teratas could never find them out there; nothing could.

Tate stared into the stars and turned the spaceship around. Once he did, he couldn't tell when to stop, as all he could see were distant stars. The emptiness of space surrounded him. Tate's grin faded. Without the moon to guide him, he couldn't focus. Before he knew it, the stars circled around them faster and faster. The ship spun, and when Tate took his hands off the controls, it kept spinning.

Attempting to sound as calm as possible, Tate asked, "Sophia, can you mark where the moon is?"

"Oh yeah, sorry."

With trembling hands, Tate once again took hold of the joysticks. He took a deep breath and nudged the controls just enough to gradually straighten their spaceship. The spinning slowed, allowing Tate to find the spot Sophia indicated for the moon. The red light spun from his right side around to his left side repeatedly. Tate twisted the ship back until the moon drifted but remained in front of him.

"Tate?" Nic asked.

Tate didn't respond. He concentrated on their spaceship until they no longer spun, facing the red dot indicating the moon in front of him.

"Tate," Nic said, "are you okay?"

"Yeah," Tate replied. "We were in a bit of an outer-space tailspin. We're good now." Tate set the spaceship to autopilot, released his controls, and lowered his chair back to the bridge, hands still shaking from his lack of control. With a sigh, he sank into his seat. "Nic, engage sub-light speed."

Tate's nerves got the best of him, causing him to spend the last hour sitting in the pilot's chair, staring off into space. Before that, though, he had time to study the ship's controls and managed to figure out how to maneuver the ship more easily with his dataPad. He would still rely on the others, but now he thought he could pilot on his own, if only a little slower than with help.

The controls were a bit clunky, but if he wanted their ship to spin, turn, speed up, or reverse, he could do it. He now thought of flying like he was playing a video game, but with delayed movements. If he knew what he knew now, back when they had the car, they would've been home already. Not that he could test out the controls without sending them off course. The real test would happen in mere moments.

They had lined up their ship, matched speeds, and now the only thing left to do was to time jump inside the command ship. Sophia had said that she was able to pinpoint where they needed to be using their ship's computers. "According to these calculations," Sophia said, "the command ship will catch us in fifty-three minutes and twenty-two seconds. As long as we are matching their speed, that time won't change."

"How do we know the jump will work?" Tate asked.

"The time field is surrounding our ship. The settings are in the Time Jumper. So, as long as the command ship continues at the same rate and doesn't decelerate, in fifty-three minutes and twenty-two seconds, we will be inside. If all goes as planned, we'll make it. If things don't go as planned, we should appear in space and can try again.

"Or, if things really don't go as planned," Tate said, "we will never know, cause we'll be dead."

"Exactly," Nic said cheerfully. "All right, Tate, you're the pilot. You say when."

"When," Tate said.

"Here we go," Sophia said.

Tate held the joysticks tight, took a deep breath, and waited.

*Thump!*

---

*Fifty-three minutes and twenty-two seconds later*

Hundreds of Terata fighters appeared in front of them. Tate yanked on the controls to avoid crashing into the one directly in front of them, only to head straight for a wall. They skipped off of the wall, putting their ship's inertia dampers to a test as Tate felt the pressure of their hit almost wrench him from his seat. He lost control and spun wildly through humungous hangar doors before smashing into the roof and then sliding through a warehouse full of crates.

Sparks flew as the ship slid, stopping with a light bump against an inside wall of the command ship. They stopped moving.

They made it.

Tate sighed in relief. The wall they leaned on extended farther than he could see. At first, he thought they might have reappeared outside the command ship, but remembering all the crates, he realized that they landed inside a room that was open to a vast space. Maybe they landed right on target and the larger room was where the smaller Terata spaceships disembarked from. He twisted around, getting a closer look at the dim room that they landed in.

Metal crates spread across the roof above his head, but not on the floor. The room's door met the ceiling instead of the floor. Tate pictured himself walking on the ceiling, and then it hit him. "We're upside down, guys."

"Then don't turn off the gravity," Sophia said.

"Like I know how," Tate replied. Tate scratched his head and called out, "Hold on, I should straighten us out."

"Why bother?" Nic asked. "We don't need to straighten out to time jump out of here. Besides, if the aliens heard us arrive, we need to get going. If they didn't hear us, then we don't want to risk making more noise."

The straps around Tate retracted as his seat lowered. He joined the others smiling. "Another successful landing."

"Another?" Nic asked. "You've crashed every time."

"Yeah, but we're still alive. Let's find Zoe and get out of here so I can do it again."

"Well, someone should teach you how to land," Sophia said.

# CHAPTER 22

# THE COMMAND SHIP

Nic stood next to Tate in their spaceship's airlock. Fiddling with the controls, Sophia shut the door to the bridge and then opened the outer door to the command ship. The smell of urine and rotten eggs assaulted Nic's nostrils, causing a cough chorused by the others.

Overhead lights made of the same crystals that their ships were made of lit the room with a soft red hue, giving their surroundings an unnatural tint. The light could have been brighter, but he could see just as far as if he were home. He considered that wherever these aliens came from, their sun could have been red.

Nic stared out of their spaceship into the alien one. He searched around for the Teratas and didn't see any, but what he did see confused him. The ceiling of the room was below him, and when he stared up at the floor, his head spun. Tate had said that they were upside down, but Nic didn't realize how disorienting it would be. It was like he hung upside down over a cliff and that any second he would fall up into the sky. He wasn't sure what bothered him more, looking up at the floor of the command ship and not the ceiling, or the putrid smell. Shutting his eyes, he turned away from both.

"Why does the air reek?" Sophia asked, coughing.

"You saw what they look like," Tate replied. "Did you think their home would smell like flowers?"

"Is it safe to breathe?" Sophia asked.

"Let's just try not to stay too long," Nic replied.

Sophia moved to the airlock's control panel. "When I was looking through the controls earlier, I saw where I could flip the gravity in just this room. That way we could match the Teratas' gravity before we climb down."

With a beep from the computer, Nic began to rise slowly into the air. He grabbed on to a bar that ran from the floor to the ceiling and rose into what used to be the ceiling. He spun around, setting down on his feet.

The cool air gave Nic the chills and reminded him to put on his jacket before leaving. Nic and Tate left their backpacks inside. Sophia stuffed hers with some water, food bars, and the Time Jumper. She rested Fang's ball on her hand, getting ready to turn it on.

Tate shook his head, blurting out, "Don't you dare have that thing fly around us. The last thing we need is for the Terata to find us because they spot Fang."

Sophia shrugged. "I thought it might be able to look around corners, but I guess you're right." She spun it in her palm and then tucked the metal ball into her jacket pocket.

Nic returned his gaze to the command ship, still with no Teratas nearby. He peered over the edge to the ground, noticing controls for a ladder at the edge of the airlock. After opening a panel and switching on the ladder, one dropped to the floor from a compartment on the outer hull. It hit the ground with a clang and securely attached itself to the command ship with no extra slack.

Swinging his feet over the edge, Nic kicked around for the ship's ladder. His foot stopped on the first rung. Instead of swinging around like a rope ladder as he expected to, the ladder held firm. Once out of their ship, Nic felt weight press down on him. At first, he thought Tate might be pushing him down, until he looked back up to see Tate beginning his own descent. The Teratas had higher gravity, not much, but enough that they would tire out quicker than they would on Earth.

Stepping off the ladder, Nic took his first step onto an alien world never willingly touched by mankind. "One small step for a man, huh?"

Tate hopped down next to him and added, "And into the lair of what will cause the extinction of mankind."

Breathing in the atmosphere, Nic coughed again. Behind their spaceship, humongous hangar doors opened up to the edge of a vast chamber with no end in sight, allowing them to peer down the endless wall of the command ship. There was enough room for them to fly their spaceship out of the storage area, which could come in handy if they needed to flee in a hurry.

In front of them, rows of steel containers were stacked to the ceiling, reaching far into the depths of the room, like a huge, abandoned warehouse. The closest stacks of containers had been knocked over upon their arrival and were scattered around their spaceship, some crumpled from their landing. Nic could only imagine that the Teratas used the room for the storage of spare parts and hoped none of these parts would be needed anytime soon.

Sophia rushed past them to examine the toppled crates. She

reached deep inside a broken ten-foot-cubed container and said in a muffled voice, "They have crystals in here."

"Are they weapons?" Tate asked, running to Sophia's side.

"I don't think so," she replied. "They seem like they are a bunch of large panels on stands."

Tate ran to a second oddly labeled crate and pried open a section that had shattered when they landed. He managed to drag a box out and opened it up. When he dumped the contents across the floor, seeds spread everywhere. "Why do they need seeds for war?"

"These could be supplies for after they have conquered Earth," Sophia replied. "I don't think we will find anything useful here."

"But what if we could find a weapon?"

Nic left the crates behind and called back to Tate. "If we don't have any weapons, then they might not shoot us on sight. Let's just get going before they come in here and find us or our spaceship."

They headed toward a humongous brick-colored door at the side of the room. Next to the door, an oversized and unoccupied chair sat under a desk. On top of the desk was a powered-down computer. Everything was taller than what seemed natural and gave Nic the impression that they were in a house built for giants. Though double in size, the computer and furniture could have been found on Earth. Nic couldn't help but think that their two species weren't that different after all, despite the atmosphere.

The door extended wide enough that the three of them couldn't reach both sides if they stretched across it hand in hand. In the middle of the door was a sky-blue button roughly the size of Nic's hand, in reach only if Nic jumped. He searched for a doorknob but guessed the button was it.

While the others headed his way, Nic turned back to their ship. It lay upside down, out in the open, and would be spotted the second a Terata entered this storage room. It had dozens of the crates that had landed on it when Tate crashed into them, but there was no real way to hide the fact that humans had come aboard. Given the seeds, the storage room appeared to be for future use, and that possibility was the only real protection their ship had from being found. Nic only hoped that they had enough time to get to Zoe before it was discovered.

Once the others had joined him, Nic jumped up and slapped his hand against the circle on the door. It whooshed open, sliding into the wall and revealing a shipyard that dwarfed the one on the lunar base.

In front of Nic, several dozen crystal Terata space fighters lay forgotten, at least for now. These spaceships were in different states of disarray: parts missing, cracked in half, or riddled with weapons fire that had to come from human defenses. Each space fighter was the size of a house, lined up in rows that reminded Nic of the streets you may find in a housing tract. He searched for Teratas nearby but couldn't see any in the area. He strolled down the outside of the Terata space fighter *neighborhood* toward the shipyard filled with working ships.

Beyond the repair yard, countless crystalline spaceships spread as far as the eye could see. So many that it looked like the they were actually docked in outer space rather than inside the command ship.

Nic stepped to a balcony overlooking the shipyard and gazed across row after row of the Terata space fighters. Thousands of them were docked on space piers that extended deep into the cavernous room. A hundred feet above him was an identical shipyard extending out of sight, and a hundred feet above that, another.

Tate joined Nic and stared up at the shipyard. "I know we are already here, but are you sure we can do this?"

"Yes," Nic replied without hesitation and then added, doubting himself, "We have to."

"I'm just saying. When you look at this ..." Tate waved his arm in front of them. "It makes me think that maybe *this* is bigger than us."

"We aren't fighting *this* ..." Nic waved his hand, mimicking Tate. "And we can rescue Zoe without even being seen."

"You mean like, if we are careful, stick together, and avoid wandering off."

"Yes." Nic sighed and then searched for Sophia. A damaged Terata space fighter had a big enough chunk missing that the inside of the cockpit could be seen, if Sophia hadn't climbed halfway inside it.

Shaking his head, Nic headed toward Sophia. Movement across the shipyard caught his eye. He ducked behind the damaged space fighter that Sophia was examining and whispered emphatically to her, "Get down!"

Sophia crawled out of the cockpit as Tate said, "We're not alone."

"When I was up there, I found the door to the rest of the command ship," she whispered, pointing.

Nic shushed the others as the two Terata approached. The stomp of boots passed by, stopping at the Terata space fighter closest to the storage room, which was barely visible when Nic peeked around the corner. Nic couldn't get a good look at the

Terata, but when the spaceship they were working on rose into the air, Nic took that as a sign to leave.

If Nic wanted to get back to their ship right now, they couldn't do it without being seen. So, as they were currently out of sight, they ran in the direction Sophia indicated was the entrance to the command ship. They made it to the open patch in front of the door when a large group of Teratas passed by a window. It was like break time was over, and an entire shift was returning to their work fixing broken-down spaceships. In seconds, they would enter the shipyard to find Nic staring right at them.

"Under there," Tate yelled, pointing to the damaged space fighter closest to the door. They ran for cover, ducking behind a long crystal fragment resting on the floor.

Despite them being hidden under a spaceship the size of a small house, Nic felt cornered. Like their hiding spot was shrinking as more Terata came in.

Barely visible from their hiding spot, Nic watched the Terata pass by, as if on parade. The Teratas' heads hunched over, and rows of short, stubby horns spread across their scalp. The alien version of hair, just like the one they saw on Earth before they time traveled. And like the one back home, these Teratas were smaller—still twice as tall as Nic, but smaller than the ones that attacked Atlantis. They were slightly different shades of green, but weren't covered in scales. They had clothes.

They wore maroon shirts lined with a golden trim, with billowy sleeves that stopped around their forearms. They had vests with black-and-green swirls, and loose brown pants that were tied around their waists and calves with lace. Their long arms dangled to their knees with lengthy, slender fingers covered by gloves that matched their skin, and they carried what resembled power tools. They even wore boots.

They spoke to each other with grunts and snarls, and unlike the Teratas at Atlantis, these had a small bump of a nose and nostrils that flared open and closed with every rumble of speech.

Nic hunkered down as the footsteps drew closer, stopping next to the terminal controls. His heart pounded like a drum in his chest, loud enough that he thought the Teratas might actually hear it.

A few more grunts, and the space fighter that they hid under began to rise into the air, their hiding place slowly fading away. Nic crept forward, risking a peek before they were completely exposed, and found the two Teratas were making their way around the space fighter.

"Now," Nic whispered and then raced for the shipyard exit as quietly as possible. The light slap from his leather-soled shoes seemed to call out *"over here,"* with each step. He made it to the door, though, and hit the sky-blue button in the door's center, harder than he meant to. The door slid open, revealing a wide hallway. Sophia and Tate passed through the doorway and hid around the corner, Sophia out of breath and Tate with a slight cough.

# CHAPTER 23

# LIFE OF THE TERATA

Nic hung on a windowsill, staring into the shipyard a moment longer before lowering into a crouch. He glanced around, trying to take in his new environment. The walls had hexagonal plates of different shades of gray, sticking out at various but similar lengths. Thirty feet above them, the ceiling had a series of crystalline tubes that wrapped around like tentacles, glowing a light red. It was just a hallway, albeit an oversized one, but it still felt wrong.

While it was bright enough to see, it reminded Nic of lighting a person might find in a darkroom used to develop photographs. The smell was better, though, but Nic guessed that was more because he was starting to get used to it. Now, it just smelled like someone had tried to cook a meal with rotten food.

Pushing past the eerie feeling, Nic nodded to the others and then sneaked down the hallway at a snail's pace until the hallway branched into multiple directions. He glanced both ways and whispered, "It's clear," and then headed down the corridor leading them away from the shipyard.

The maze of hallways was in no discernible pattern, and would get them lost before too long. One positive thing though, was that Nic wasn't worried about losing his way back to their ship. Every intersection they had come across had signs akin to street signs pointing off in various directions. While they couldn't make out the language, they were able to figure out which Terata symbols pointed to the shipyard.

A periodic odd clank or a woosh of doors meant the Terata were around them, but it was impossible to figure out how far, and in some cases, which direction. The hallway's gradual curve didn't help either, allowing them to see no more than twenty yards ahead of them. While the curve kept them out of sight, a Terata could literally be just around the corner and they wouldn't know. Nic shook off that thought before he lost his nerve.

They inched their way to an intersection, and not for the first time had to turn back and find another way. Steadily they did make it farther into the command ship, but they still didn't know where to go next.

While most doors didn't have windows next to them, the ones that did gave a glimpse into alien life. They stooped under the windows they passed but saw numerous Teratas sitting at computers and working at jobs Nic couldn't even guess at. It occurred to Nic that human and Terata technology was similar enough that when the Teratas took over, they might even adopt a form of the human implants.

Slowly, they made progress, hurrying down the hallway toward the center of the ship. They sneaked around until they came to a large spherical room roughly the same size as a baseball field. Nic hung on the windowsill again, his muscles aching from the extra weight due to the increased gravity, despite its small difference.

Through the window, Nic saw a spherical room, and while it was roughly a hundred yards across, it was mostly empty. A walkway ran around the outside, connecting four chambers, and a small room in the center was mounted on a pedestal, indicating its importance. Bridges connected the four chambers to the central room, and tubes underneath the bridges pulsed rhythmically, feeding some kind of power into it.

The chamber on the right was powered down and swarmed by dozens of Terata workers. The workers went in and out of their door, pulling equipment onto the walkway, which was littered with charred circuitry, coils, and mechanical devices—remnants of a fire or explosion.

Nic hopped down from the window, as Sophia peeked inside, saying, "I wonder if this is the ship's bridge."

"I doubt it," Tate replied. "Maybe it's the controls for a death ray."

Nic shook his aching arms. "Well, it's not the prison, so let's keep going." They started down the next hallway, but as more paths opened up to them, Nic couldn't help feeling that even if they went the right way, they would never know. At the pace they were going, Nic thought they could make it back to the shipyard in a couple of minutes if they ran.

The next window they passed remained dark. Tate pulled himself onto the windowsill and peeked inside. "I think this one's empty."

The whoosh of a door opening nearby silenced them. Footsteps approached, and the grunts and growls of the alien language sent shivers down Nic's spine.

Sophia slapped the button opening the vacant room next to

them. The lights flashed on as they dashed inside. The room was sparsely decorated, with a single computer desk, chair, and a purple plant striving for life. It reminded Nic of his dad's office back home, if his dad's office was clean.

They dove under the desk and then stared at the window, with a clear view of the hall. If a Terata looked inside, they would be seen. They scrambled out from under the desk and then flattened themselves against the wall under the window. Nic counted each passing second with the pounding of his heart. The shadows of more than one figure passed by, but Nic still didn't move. Seconds ticked away before he relaxed enough to peer through the window to an empty hallway.

Another minute passed before they ventured back into the command ship. At the next branch in the hallway, they found a hexagonal room decorated with purple ferns that draped down walls on both sides of a lone hexagonal door. Besides the path they came from, which continued deeper into the ship, there were two more hallways that sloped to the floors above and below them.

With no window to show what lay beyond, Nic paused at the hexagonal door. "This room seems to be special in some way. What do you think is in there?"

Sophia leaned forward and rested her ear at the door's seams. "That's strange," she said. "It's getting louder."

Tate grabbed Sophia, and they all rushed up a side corridor to an upper floor. Distant voices stopped them, and when Nic turned back, four Terata walked out of sight from what lay beyond the hexagonal door.

Sophia ran back and peeked inside the new room as the doors closed. She waited for the Terata to get out of sight before she said, "It's okay. The room is empty." She opened it up and stepped inside.

Nic followed her, turning around to find a plate next to the door covered in hundreds of buttons. "Guys, I think this is an elevator." A series of symbols written beside each button indicated where it would take them.

"Well," Sophia replied, "I doubt it only goes up and down in a ship this size. We could probably take it across the ship."

"Then it's the ships transport system," Tate said. "Should we just pick a symbol?"

"No," Nic replied. "Unless you we know where it will take us."

Sophia returned to the hexagonal room, just outside the transport. "Where to now?"

They stood silently, awaiting any answer, looking to Nic. He had hoped that they would have a plan by now, but he had no idea where to go. Standing in silence, Nic could make out a faint murmur coming from both the upper and lower hallways. He shuffled closer to the one leading up.

"What are you doing?" Tate asked. "Nic, I can hear them up there. We need to stay away, remember?"

"They aren't getting closer. Besides, we don't know where to go, and maybe this will lead to an answer."

Nic headed up the path, the sounds growing louder with each step. He stumbled forward, doubting if he should continue, but unsure what else to do. The murmur was clearer here, gradually transforming into the grunts of the alien language.

Their path had turned into a hallway that curved out of sight. The first room they came across was occupied by a pair of Terata lounging with drinks in their hands. Nic hurried past their room and continued to the next one, which was unoccupied and led to a balcony.

"It sounds like a crowd," Sophia said.

"If it is, then we should turn back," Tate said. "We should only go where we know all of us will make it."

"Let's find out what's going on first," Nic whispered, creeping forward. "Maybe we can find where they are keeping Zoe."

Tate sighed, and Nic turned around to see him silently pleading with Sophia.

"What else can we do?" Sophia said, shrugging. "We'll just take a peek."

They inched forward until they reached the ledge of a balcony, where a fake red sky lit up a city far below. Nic had thought the Terata were similar to humans, but it wasn't until now that he thought their society matched his own. It made him sick to his stomach, though, that common Teratas were going about their peaceful lives, as others of their kind fought to destroy humanity and conquer Earth.

On their left was a huge park with magenta-colored grass and dark pathways weaving along violet streams. In the distance, Nic could make out a field where a growing number of Terata gathered on the sides as if getting ready for a sports match.

On the right was an orchard filled with a variety of funny-shaped trees. Some Terata roamed through the trees, stopping to eat bits of their various oddly-shaped fruit.

In front of them was the metropolitan life of a major city. The buildings all around were made of the same crystalline materials as their space fighters, mixed with standard frames you might find in a building in downtown Los Angeles. Each of the buildings stretched from the ground all the way to the ceiling far above, like a skyscraper contained inside a humongous cave.

Countless Teratas roamed around their downtown area, going about their daily lives as if they weren't in the middle of a war. No matter their reason for attacking Earth, their civilization was still thriving. It gave a real clue as to what life was actually like on the Teratas' home world, and it was just like what was found on Earth.

Tate backed away, stifling a cough. He tried to clear his throat, but the atmosphere seemed to be taking a toll on his respiratory system.

Nic turned to him, wondering if he would be okay, but he seemed to be recovering for now. The longer they were there, the more problematic it would become.

Tate caught his breath and then croaked, "Guys, let's go. Now!"

If Zoe was held in the city below, they would never find her. Heart sinking, Nic backed up to join Tate, while Sophia continued to gawk at the city. On the walls all around them, more balconies overlooked the city, some even occupied by the Teratas. Nic returned to Sophia and dragged her back into the halls.

The sounds of the city faded as they ran, and they were unwilling to stop until they made it back to the ship's transport.

"Where are we going, Nic?" Tate asked, now recovered from his troubling breathing. "We could be here for days and not find anything."

"I'm open to ideas," Nic replied.

"I don't know," Tate said, "but the longer we're here, the

more likely we'll get caught. We can't go searching blindly through cities."

"That's it!" Sophia said. "Cities have maps. We have to find a map."

"I guess," Tate said, shaking his head. "Do you think we could actually find one we could read?"

"They have cities, doors, windows, hallways, and computers. They even have some ugly plants." Sophia rustled the purple fern that hung on the wall, hanging down to the floor. "I'm sure if we can find a map, we'll be able to use it."

"A computer," Nic said. "We can try that room we hid in."

"It's right down there," Tate said, pointing down the hall. "I guess anything is better than waiting here." He took off, stopping to check that the room was still empty before slapping the door open.

Sophia pulled herself onto the armless chair made for a giant, standing in order to reach the computer. She pressed a button next to the screen, which turned it on, displaying a hundred keys that lit up with a slight glow in front of them.

They stared at the symbols written in another language. Tate shook his head. "We'll never be able to figure out their language. I mean, ask my teachers. I struggle enough with English as it is."

"We don't have to read it," Sophia said. "We just have to find a map."

Nic stared at the screen displaying the language created by the aliens. The thought of guessing what to choose filled Nic with dread. Sophia selected icons on the monitor seemingly at random, managing to navigate a little, but mostly just picking something and then backing up to the home screen again.

After ten minutes, Nic jumped down from the chair and

joined Tate at the door. The door was shut, but Nic hoped he might be able to hear something that could give them a warning. The only thing that gave Nic hope of not being caught was that if a Terata did walk by, they would see the chair's tall backrest and the monitor. They might even believe the computer was left on.

Anticipating a long wait, Nic closed his eyes as Sophia announced, "Jackpot!"

"Really?" Nic asked, climbing back up the chair.

A three-dimensional image of the command ship rotated on the screen. Sophia zoomed in on thousands of lines and boxes meshed together in what could have been a blueprint for a circuit board and was just as confusing. Nic guessed that a series of rectangles were a variety of rooms, each with strange symbols. Some symbols were recognizable, like a drop of water or a bolt of lightning, but not many. Most rooms were labeled with what had to be letters from the Terata language.

"Can you figure out where we are?"

"Yeah," Sophia replied. "This place must be the shipyard, and the small room next to it is where we crashed."

"Landed," Tate corrected.

"Fine, Tate. *Crash landed*," Sophia said, pointing to a room along the hall. "We're down this hall in one of these rooms. This one I think."

Tate reached out and pointed to another room. "That one is that humongous circular room." He pointed to a word containing a symbol. "That's the same symbol that turned on the computer. Maybe it means *power*."

Nic stared at the symbol and remembered the charred parts they were replacing. Nadezda came to mind and how she thought that she had taken down their shields. "Do you think this Terata word could have to do with power for their shields?"

"Possibly," Sophia said.

"If this is the word for shields," Nic said, "and if their prison is shielded, maybe they have another one next to their prison."

"It's worth a try," Sophia said, fumbling with the controls unsuccessfully. She was only able to zoom in and out or rotate the map.

"Can we scan the map with our dataPads?" Nic asked. Without a response, he held up his dataPad and selected the scan program, which copied the map as Sophia rotated it. It took some time, but Nic was able to project a nearly identical three-dimensional blueprint in front of them with his dataPad. Nic sent both of them the map file and then searched on his dataPad for anything that could be used for a prison.

The map created by the dataPad was equally detailed, with the added bonus that they now navigated through options they were familiar with. He selected the word that they thought could mean *shield* on the dataPad and highlighted every other instance of the word throughout the Terata command ship.

Time ticked away, but their search led to success.

"I think I found it," Sophia said, pointing to a long corridor marked with the alien word. Moreover, the corridor was organized in the same way that cells might be in a prison.

"I can't believe this worked," Tate said. "How do we get there?"

"I believe the quickest way is to take the ship's transport up a couple of floors, and then head to the ship's center," Sophia said. "We could avoid taking it, but that would add a fair amount of time."

"If the transport is the fastest way, then we should take it. Let's go before our luck fails us."

Tate grabbed onto the windowsill and pulled himself up enough to see into the hallway. "It's clear right outside the door."

Nic slapped the door's button and looked in both directions. Seeing no sign of the Teratas, he crept back to the transport. Inside, he stared at the panel filled with hundreds of buttons, most too high to reach. "Which one is it?"

"This one," Sophia said, displaying the map in front of them, highlighting the alien word that they hoped meant *prison.*

Nic found the symbol in the middle of the panel. "Tate, let me climb on your back."

"I don't think so. I'll climb on you."

"Whatever." Nic knelt, leaning against the wall. Tate climbed up his leg and then onto his shoulder. He pushed the button and then hopped to the floor.

Sophia pulled the Time Jumper from her backpack. "I'll be ready to jump us a couple minutes forward, in case when the door opens a Terata is there. And then, hopefully they would be gone, by the time we return."

The door shut, and Nic prepared to be lifted to another floor. He stumbled as the transport lurched sideways, like a train leaving a station. It took a couple minutes before they slowed, but without knowing how fast they went, Nic had no idea how far they traveled. They came to a complete stop and then shot up like an elevator. The transport stopped once again, and the doors flung open to an empty hexagonal room exactly like the one they had come from.

Nic crawled into the room and carefully peered down each

of the four hallways branching away from them, half expecting to find a Terata. Despite the cool temperature, Nic wiped sweat from his brow. He got up and crept next to Sophia, waiting for her to point them in the right direction.

"Quit skulking, Nic," Tate said. "You're freaking me out."

"I'm just being careful," Nic replied.

The map displayed a 3-D image above Sophia's dataPad. A line showed the path they had traveled so far and pointed them where to go, as if they followed Google Maps. "That way. It's not far."

Nic took the lead and stopped when their path branched in two directions. Sophia directed them down the next hall, where Nic made out a guttural conversation in the distance heading away from them. They followed the voices until they were cut off by a door closing. Next to the door, a window allowed them to view what was inside.

Nic peeked in, finding two Teratas dressed in the same decorative robes as the ones in the shipyard, except without gloves. They held a muscular human, half their size, wearing a military uniform. They stood facing a counter that reminded Nic of a reception area in a doctor's office. The waiting area had chairs around a table and a mahogany vine that draped across the wall where a picture would have been on Earth.

A third Terata stepped into view. This one was not in robes but in one of their exosuits. It shoved the human down a short hall toward the cells, only pausing long enough to power down a force field in front of the cell block. It would be much more difficult to rescue Zoe right under the watchful eye of one of their Terata warriors, but that couldn't be helped.

The two Teratas that brought the human typed on a device similar to a tablet. They waited for the guard to return after he imprisoned the human. One of them glanced in Nic's direction, causing Nic to fall back to the floor to avoid being seen.

"Do you ... Do you hear something?" Tate asked in a hushed tone.

Down the hall, faint footsteps drew closer, like a drummer marching their way. With the curved hallway, Nic couldn't tell how long they had. He crept to the closest room and peered inside, revealing a dozen Teratas, and then ducked down before seeing what they were doing.

Nic shook his head and then joined the others in a huddle as the door to the prison slid open.

A long, green, scaly arm swung through the doorway, followed by a comically large black boot. Its head came into view, whirling toward them, and then disappeared with the light.

*Thump!*

---

*Ten minutes later*

Nic stared at the now-closed door and listened for footsteps but only heard Sophia shuffling next to him.

"Nice timing, Sophia," Tate said.

Nic took a deep breath and waited for his pulse to slow. "Well, I think we found the right place." He peeked back into the prison, where the only remaining guard, the one in the exosuit, sat facing away from them, typing at a computer. "Any ideas on how to get past the jailer?"

# CHAPTER 24

# ZOE'S RETURN

The door to the prison slid open, and grunts of the alien language announced the Terata jailer behind the counter, possibly questioning who entered the room. Sophia sneaked inside and got behind a chair, waiting to see if they were noticed. She knew if they made any noise, then the Terata in its exosuit would hear them. However, the clacking of keyboard keys indicated that the Terata continued to work at its computer.

Nic crawled in front of Sophia and stopped under the counter, only pausing long enough to wave Sophia forward. Sophia crept forward hesitantly on all fours. She got next to Nic and then flattened herself against the wall under the counter, waiting for Tate to join them.

Nic scrambled forward, crossing into the hallway leading to the prison cells. Once he made it halfway down the hall, he stood and waved again for Sophia and Tate to follow.

Staying low, Sophia reached out her hand to crawl when the door whooshed closed behind them. A large, scaly head peeked over the counter, freezing Sophia in place as it looked over her and Tate back to the door. The jailer grumbled, but a creak from its chair indicated it had returned to its seat, leaving them unseen for the moment. Sophia debated waiting to give it more time to relax, but Tate gently prodded her forward.

Starting forward again, Sophia halted once more as an alarm blared overhead. Her first thought was that they were found, but the Terata behind the counter didn't move, and a light tapping of what might have been its finger indicated it still didn't know they were there. The only other things that Sophia could think of were either an attack on humans, or the discovery of their spaceship in the storage room. If it was the latter, they would have to figure out how to get there while it was guarded.

Heart pounding, Sophia swallowed her nerves and turned back to Nic. Ahead of her, he stood in front of the force field barring their path to the cell block. An emerald-green glow from the shield lit him enough to outline his frame. Reaching out to the panel on his side, Nic shut off the energy field.

The field powered down with a loud crackle, similar to the sounds of a roaring campfire. The Terata hopped over the counter, landing an inch from Sophia's outstretched hand. It charged forward, freezing Nic in place, staring back, eyes wide and mouth open.

Sophia reached out to trip the monstrous creature, only to grasp at air as it launched forward at an inhuman speed. She wasn't fast enough, but instead of panicking, what Tate said on the way to the moon flashed into her mind: *"If you don't act now, will you be too late?"* Without a second thought, Sophia sprinted after the Terata, watching it tackle Nic inside of the cellblock.

Sophia raced forward as the Terata grabbed Nic by the neck and lifted him a foot off the ground. Hunching over, it pulled

Nic closer until they were inches apart, face to face. In its off hand, its spear crackled to life as a series of deep grunts escaped its mouth, which translated from the device on its wrist to, "Now, where did you come from, little human?"

The closer Sophia got, the bigger the thing looked. She knew she had to get Nic out of its hands but didn't know if she could budge the Terata, even if she tackled it at full speed. With the Terata stooped down, staring into Nic's eyes, Sophia could reach its head, though.

As she ran, the hard shell of Fang's ball struck her hip with each stride. Sophia pulled it from her pocket and leapt into the air, and then slammed the ball down on the Terata's head. Pieces of Fang's ball rained down on them, and the momentarily stunned Terata dropped both Nic and its spear.

Nic collapsed to the ground. Still gasping for air, he scrambled toward a cell and attempted to release the field holding a prisoner. The Terata caught his leg and tossed him across the floor into Sophia.

Behind the Terata, the five-foot-long spear rolled to a stop. Sophia scrambled out from underneath Nic and darted sideways, dodging the snarling creature grasping for her. She dove for the spear, only to be snatched out of the air by a hand as long as her arm. The air rushed out of her in a wheeze as the grip tightened around her waist.

Sophia hit the ground hard and then was yanked across the floor by one of her legs. She spun around, kicking at the Terata's meaty fingers, unable to loosen its grip. Slowly she was lifted off the ground, held upside down next to an equally struggling Nic. Sophia watched the features of the Terata's mask stretch, and despite the scales covering its mouth, she knew that it was grinning.

Sophia imagined being thrown into a cell and locked away on an alien spaceship hundreds of years from home. The whole thing was over in seconds, the two of them no match for a single Terata. Sophia stared into its eyes, all hope lost, until the creature crumpled to the floor on top of her.

---

Nic gasped as he sucked in the putrid air. Above him, Tate held the sparking spear against the now-motionless Terata. At his side, Sophia was pinned underneath the creature. She looked stunned but still attempted to free herself, though unsuccessfully.

The crackling charge at the end of the Terata's stick that Tate held flickered out, and Tate rushed to help Sophia, but he couldn't quite budge the Terata enough to get her out. "Are you two okay?"

Nic scrambled to his feet, grinning. "I'm fine. I'm just trying to figure out what happened. I mean, Sophia charged in without thinking, and you calmly used your head."

"Well, with Sophia of all people rushing to your rescue, I thought maybe I should try to figure out if there was another way to help. Turns out, fighting the giant alien monster wasn't the best idea." Tate set the spear on the ground next to him. "Help me get this thing off her."

Nic grabbed onto the side of the Terata's exosuit. It was oily, and the scales were smoothly interlocked like a giant snakeskin. They barely managed to move it, but it was enough for Sophia to wiggle out from underneath.

"Are you all right, Sophia?" Nic asked.

Sophia groaned, but not from an injury. She shuffled across the floor to her broken toy. "Fang was so young."

Nic smiled and then turned around to face a grinning old bald man standing behind the first cell's force field. Nic's head throbbed, but he felt better with each passing second, and soon the only pain remaining was the scratchiness in the back of his throat caused by the environment. He turned to Sophia and Tate and said, "Let's release everyone before more Teratas show up."

Nic went to the cell containing the old man, releasing him, while Sophia and Tate ran down the cellblock to release the rest of the prisoners.

Stepping out of his cell, the old man greeted Nic with a light slap on the back. "I don't know how you kids escaped, but we'll be in your debt for the rest of our short lives." Pulling Nic along with him, he knelt next to the Terata, verifying that it wouldn't get up. "Do they know you're here?"

"No, sir," Nic replied. "Well, an alarm went off when we came in here. They might have found our spaceship."

"Call me Lucien."

The military man they originally saw when they got to the prison ran to Lucien's side. He grinned widely, staring at Nic before speaking to Lucien. "It looks like we have a second chance to do some good here."

"We do, Hoyt." Lucien stood, gazing down the hall to the reception area. "Hoyt, lock this thing up, and then secure the entrance. Let's hope that we have enough time to do some real damage."

"Yes, sir." Hoyt picked up the spear that Tate left behind, looping it through his belt. He dragged the much bigger creature into Lucien's former cell and then ripped the bracer it used as a translation device from its arm. He turned on the force field, locking the Terata inside, and then hurried back to the reception area.

Lucien directed the released prisoners as they arrived to follow Hoyt and said to Nic, "Tell me, how is it that you got here without being detected?"

Nic took a deep breath, air continuing to irritate the back of his throat. "We figured out that the Teratas use human implants to track them, and we don't have implants."

"Ah, then you really weren't prisoners?"

"No. Actually, we came here to rescue a girl our age. She has black hair, with a purple streak in it."

Lucien's sighed. "I saw her when she was brought in. I don't know if she is still here, though."

"Where else could she be, if not here?"

"Well ..." Lucien said, waving at a pair of prisoners with weather-beaten faces. They grinned, waving at Nic with newfound determination. Despite their apparent optimism, Nic wasn't sure they should be walking around. They had not been fed well, and their continual hacking coughs revealed just how sick they were. What they needed was a hospital. Lucien went on, "Humans don't last long in this environment and are only kept alive as long as they prove worthwhile. If she is here, you'll find her in one of these cells. Now, how did you know how to find—"

"Sorry," Nic said, racing down the cellblock. "I'll be back."

Ahead of Nic, Sophia and Tate had almost reached the end of the cellblock, and now they weren't the only ones releasing the prisoners.

Tate waved them over and shouted, "You guys, come on. It's Zoe! She's here!"

Sophia ran to her, arriving when the field powered down. Nic caught up to them as Zoe stood from her cot.

The purple highlights had spread across her disheveled black hair, which was still pulled into a ponytail. Puffy, wide eyes betrayed the fact that she had spent more time crying than she would admit. With a quivering smile as captivating as ever, she stepped toward them.

Nic rushed past Sophia and Tate and embraced Zoe in a hug, not quite believing that they had actually gotten her back. She held him, not letting go until after both Sophia and Tate had joined in. When they finally did part, Zoe's eyes gleamed with unshed tears. "Were you captured too? What are you doing here?"

"No, we weren't captured," Nic said. "We came to rescue you."

Sophia put her hand on Zoe's shoulder. "After what you did for us. We couldn't go home without you."

"So, you," Zoe said, her voice cracking, "you risked your-selves, for me?"

Tate took some time before responding, "We owed you for saving our butts back on Earth." He shuffled his feet, never good at expressing himself. "Besides, you're too important to us to let you rot away on an alien spaceship, lost in time. When we met, you were searching for a place to belong. That place is with us."

Zoe opened her mouth to respond, but instead smiled. They didn't speak as another freed prisoner passed by. Their silence finally broke when Zoe began to cough. Once her coughing subsided, she asked, "But how did you even get here?"

"We, um," Sophia replied, glancing around the cellblock, "we time jumped inside the command ship, shields and all."

"It was on the way to the wormhole anyway," Tate said, smirking and downplaying his part.

A prisoner jogged by, calling to them, "You four are the last of us. We need to hurry."

"Thank you," Sophia shouted back without turning around.

"We really should hurry if we're going to make it back to our spaceship." Nic hustled back toward the reception area, unable to hold back his wide grin. He rested his hand on Zoe's back as they went. "How are you feeling? You don't look too good."

Zoe replied, beaming, "You're too kind."

"You know what I mean," Nic said.

"I have a headache and a cough, and my feet are a little numb. Though, I feel much better now."

They reached the first cell as two of the former prisoners dragged an unconscious Terata dressed in a gold trimmed turquoise robe that covered a maroon shirt and brown pants. The Terata warrior that they fought was no longer unconscious. It paced back and forth across its cell, eyes narrowed, and a low guttural growl escaping the mask that hid its face. Tate danced past it, laughing, causing it to slam its fists against the force field that imprisoned it.

With a prison filled with humans, Nic thought they might have a small army to help them make it back to their spaceship, but he was wrong. When they arrived back at reception, Hoyt sat on the oversized coffee table addressing a dozen people, which made up the human resistance. Despite Hoyt's size, he still appeared childlike in a room made for creatures much larger. "We have two missions ahead of us."

As soon as Nic stepped into the reception area, Lucien stopped them. He rested his hand on Nic's shoulder, but before he spoke, Sophia asked, "How is everyone going to get back home?"

"We're not leaving," Lucien replied. "This is our last stand. We're going to take down their shields and send a message back to Earth telling them to attack. Now, if you weren't a prisoner, then how did you find us?"

Nic motioned toward Sophia. "We found a map."

"Without implants, what did you copy the map to?" Lucien glanced down to Nic's wrist. "To a dataPad? Let me see."

Nic removed his dataPad. "You can have it. We have two more."

Lucien studied the map and asked, "How did you get on the command ship?"

"We have a spaceship," Nic replied. "Though, it's possible that the alarm was set off when they found it."

"We're ready," Hoyt said from behind, holding an oversized rifle of Terata design. A second prisoner had one as well, taken either from one of those two new Terata prisoners or found in the office.

"Take a look, Hoyt," Lucien said.

Hoyt leaned in.

Holding the dataPad out, Lucien zoomed into an unexplored area of the map. "We should be able to send our message from here." He zoomed out again, then zoomed in to the circular room Nic had found after leaving the shipyard. "And the shields must be powered from this room here."

"Take mine too," Sophia said, handing her dataPad to Hoyt. "We can get back with just Tate's."

"You can get back?" Lucien asked. "We can't just leave you alone. You're going to have to come with us."

"I don't think so," Sophia replied, more forcefully than Nic was used to. "You said yourself that you are not leaving. We are."

"Yeah," Nic added, "we can go with you for a little while, since we are heading to the shields, but we're going home."

Hoyt took Sophia's dataPad and strapped it around his arm. He narrowed his eyes at her but spoke to Lucien. "We need to go now, before the Teratas learn we escaped."

Lucien sighed, glancing to Nic and the others, clearly seeing the determination in their faces. He took a Terata spear from Hoyt and handed it to Tate. "Thank you for the dataPads. Just know, if you really want to go separate ways, you are on your own. We're going to shut down the shields and send a message back to Earth."

"We understand," Nic said, nodding. He put his arm out, motioning to the door, and then added, "After you."

# CHAPTER 25

# THE COMMAND SHIP'S UNDERBELLY

Hoyt opened the door and led them down the empty hall. They moved at a brisk pace, much faster than Nic had before, still ducking below windows on their way. The two small groups of former prisoners trailed behind Hoyt, followed by Nic and the others.

Tate used the spear as a walking stick, with a periodic tap on the floor that caused Nic to whirl around in search of the Teratas. Once Nic glared at him, Tate stopped tapping the ground and instead rested it across his shoulder. "Would it be so bad if we stuck with them? We are going the same direction as one of their groups."

"I think we should go on our own," Sophia said quietly. "We do have the Time Jumper, and I don't want to find us in a situation where we could use it to escape but can't because of the others."

"That's a good point," Tate replied, "but ..."

Their discussion was cut short once they reached the ship transport. Hoyt and Lucien huddled together outside the transport's door. They had pressed the door to call the transport, but nothing happened.

While the transport's door stayed shut, Nic's uneasiness grew. When a light flashed above the door, Nic offered a warning to the former prisoners. "That light never turned on when we rode the transport earlier. Maybe we should err on the side of caution and find another way."

They both nodded but remained in place. Hoyt opened up his dataPad and knelt down as a blue energy beam flashed past him, scorching the door where he stood a moment before. The Terata knew where they were but approached from another hallway, out of sight.

Even though Hoyt's team was going in the same direction as them, Nic thought that now would be a good time to go out on their own. "We need to split from the others."

"This way," Sophia said, backing down the hallway they came from. She peered inside a window next to a darkened room, with the time machine in hand.

The room's light shone down on them as Sophia opened the door, but besides knowing the room was empty, they didn't have time to examine it. Nic entered last and shut the door behind them. He gripped the windowsill and lifted up high enough to spot a dozen clothed Teratas zipping past the window from the direction of the prison.

Zoe covered her mouth and was stifling a cough, but the short run seemed to be too much for her. She let out a barking cough that continued long enough that a pair of Teratas turned back.

"We've got company!" Nic said.

Still coughing, Zoe grabbed Nic, yanking him down next to

Sophia and Tate. Nic shut his eyes. Without waiting for the door to open, Sophia sent them into the future.

*Thump!*

---

*Ten minutes later*

Nic opened his eyes and turned to the door, half expecting to see a Terata staring down at him. The lights turned on, revealing an oversized but empty storage area that Nic hadn't noticed when they first entered. He reached up and grabbed the windowsill, pulling himself up again.

Zoe was still coughing, with Tate patting her back, but it seemed that the coughing spell was dissipating.

Sophia held the Time Jumper tight across her chest. "We can't keep doing this. It's only a matter of time before they're here when we return from a jump."

Once Zoe was breathing easy again, Nic reached for the door release. "I'm going to check it out. Wait here."

Zoe frowned, clearly wanting to stick together.

Nic left anyway, wanting to make sure they were safe before they all continued. He glanced down the empty hall and then crept toward the transport on his hands and knees. He saw one Terata in turquoise robes, but it marched away from them. Nic turned back to get the others' attention and met Zoe's eyes as she crawled directly behind him.

She shrugged, smiling. "Is it clear?"

"Clear enough." Nic took one more peek down the halls. "But the others are gone, so it's up to us. Are we going to take the transport?"

"No!" Zoe replied.

"What's wrong with it?" Tate asked. "We took it on the way here."

"For one," Zoe said, "now that they realize there was a prison break, the transport won't be safe. How did you guys figure we would make it back to your spaceship?"

Nic ran his fingers through his hair. He didn't want to say that he planned to take the transport.

"We took it here," Tate said, shrugging. "I thought we would take it back too."

"Well, Zoe's right." Nic decided that for all they knew, the Teratas could wait for them to board the transport and then shut it down with them inside. Then they would be trapped in the transport, and even the Time Jumper couldn't get them out. "It's too bad that we can't just take the same path as the transport."

"Why can't we?" Sophia asked. She always seemed to doubt herself when it came to deciding what to do next, so it surprised Nic that she was taking charge. "You said the same path as the transport. If we could find a way into the shaft that the transport travels through, we could run across the ship while staying out of sight."

Sophia ran over to a panel on the wall next to the transport door and opened up a service hatch big enough to crawl through. She waved to the others and said, "Through here," then climbed into a dark void left by the ship's transport system.

Entering last, Nic closed the hatch behind him, enveloping them in darkness. He barely had to duck down as he crossed into a small alcove, which would be a tight fit for a Terata, but easily managed by a human. He put his hand on the floor, feeling the vibrations from the transport system. Even after he lifted his hand and continued forward, his hands felt numb.

In the tunnel ahead of him, the still silhouettes of Zoe, Tate, and Sophia stood among more figures. His first thought was that the Terata knew they would take the transport's tunnels, and then how they could escape. As Nic's eyes adjusted to the dim lights, he could make out Lucien waving before taking off down a side tunnel to send a message to Earth. Lucien and his team were also using the shafts to travel across the ship. Hoyt was not in sight and had either already left or taken another route to the shield room.

Glowing a faint white, a pair of steel tracks were sunken into the floor like in a subway, except identical tracks also ran along the two sides and the ceiling as well. The tunnel was thirty feet around and branched into three horizontal routes and a vertical path above and below them. It reminded Nic of oversized ant tunnels.

Nic cautiously peered over the edge of the vertical path where the transport could descend and stared into the depths of the ship. Ladders made for the Teratas were embedded into the walls, but the ladder rungs were too far apart to comfortably climb. Ascending would be a problem, but descending was more feasible, since they could drop down instead of climbing up. Nic backed up before his growing vertigo got the best of him.

Since the transport took them most of the way there, all they had to do was run down the tunnel to make it back to their ship and then drop down a couple of stories. Tate projected his dataPad's map into the tunnel, and then he pointed down the obvious path. With their route chosen, Tate closed his dataPad, shutting them into the darkness once again, until their eyes adjusted to the dim light provided by the tracks.

"We could see better if I used this thing," Tate said, flicking on the spear like a five-foot-long torch. Instead of the crackle of electric blue that they saw when the Terata used it to take prisoners, the tip burned hot like the tip of a high-powered welding tool. Tate ran the tip along the ground, which melted everything it touched into a heap of metal. "Hey, it has two settings, shock and melt."

Zoe shook her head. "While that may be useful, it could also have a limited charge. Besides, we can see well enough with the light from the tracks."

Without argument, Tate nodded and then powered down the spear. He held his hand toward their path. "After you."

Nic led the way, walking at first, to make sure Zoe would be able to keep up. The tunnel continued in one direction, with the only break in it being the service hatches and alcoves like what they came in through, which ran roughly fifty yards apart throughout the tunnel. They stopped briefly to drink water and to let Zoe eat a food bar that Sophia brought in her bag. Halfway past the third alcove, red lights behind them brightened.

"What's happening back there?" Tate asked.

"Maybe it's a Terata patrol," Nic replied. "Stay still."

Seconds ticked away, and they remained frozen in place. The tracks continued to brighten, but the only thing they could hear was a growing hum. Finally, they spotted something heading their direction, but it was not a patrol.

"Incoming!" Sophia yelled as a ship transport shot toward them.

"Run!" Tate shouted.

Zoe stumbled over Nic, falling to the ground coughing.

Sophia grabbed her and pulled her to her feet. They ran for the next alcove ahead of them.

The ground quaked below their feet, and the deep hum advanced at their heels. The hair on Nic's neck stood on end as if pointing toward their approaching doom. With ten yards to go, Nic risked a glance back to find the transport was now at the point where they started running.

Sophia jumped for the cover that alcove provided, followed by Zoe. Nic dove inside and was immediately tackled by Tate.

A blur shot past, taking with it the lights in the tunnel. The quaking ground reduced to a light hum.

They gasped for air, hacking in the alcove's temporary safety. "Sophia," Tate said between coughs, "why didn't you just jump us?"

"It slipped my mind. Besides, *you* said to run."

Nic took a deep breath, coughing up the stale air. The red glow returned again until a transport zipped by in the other direction.

Zoe laughed, bringing a smile to Nic's lips. "I really missed you guys. And not just because I was in prison." She stood in the tunnel in front of them. "Well, are we going?"

Nic's laugh was cut short. Muffled shouts came from behind the wall—alien or human, they couldn't tell. Everyone remained silent. Nic motioned for the others to get away from the service hatch. They ran down the tunnel, hoping to get far enough away that *if* the Teratas did search inside the tunnel, they would be long gone.

They reached the next transport stop but skirted around the outside of the shaft that led to lower floors. Once on the other side, Nic paused to allow everyone to catch their breath before they started again.

"I hate to say it," Tate said with a cough, "but maybe we should keep running until we get there. We have a long way to go."

"Are you sure you can make it if we run?" Nic asked. He had a sour taste in his mouth and was continually clearing his throat, but was able to manage moving around in the Terata environment without coughing. While Tate had been there just as long as Nic, he coughed just as much as Zoe. Sophia didn't seem to be affected by the atmosphere like the rest of them but would still collapse at every brief stop they made, likely from the extra strain caused by gravity. While gravity was not much more than that on Earth, it made Nic feel like he'd run a mile every time he did more than walk.

Zoe coughed into the crook of her arm. "I'll do what I can, but I have been breathing this air longer than you guys."

Tate cleared his throat. "I don't think we have a choice. The sooner we get out of here, the better."

"Then maybe we should run between the alcoves," Nic said. "We can take breaks as needed when we don't have to worry about getting hit by a transport."

Sophia nodded and then jogged ahead, with Tate next, followed by Zoe, leaving Nic in the back. Despite Zoe's periodic cough, she kept up with their pace. Nic worried that she was pushing herself too hard, but it didn't show yet.

The farther they traveled, the more Nic's concerns about Zoe faded and his concerns for Tate grew. Zoe might have been there longer, but Tate had developed a wheezy sound whenever he took a breath, which would not have been present from this much running at home.

They continued for well over an hour until their tunnel ended. "I think we're here," Sophia said when they came to the dead end. The tunnel continued to the floors above and below them, but they could no longer head in the same direction. "Can you check the map, Tate?"

If they continued like this, they would make it to their spaceship and be safe in no time. They only had to reach the shipyard without being seen.

Tate opened his dataPad and projected the map above it. He located their spaceship. "We have to go down two floors, but we're almost there."

Zoe pointed to the dataPad. "You have messages from Nic and Sophia."

"Lucien and Hoyt, you mean," Nic said. "I wonder if they were able to shut down the shield."

"I must not have noticed when I got them because of the tunnel's slight vibration," Tate said, holding out his dataPad again and opening the messages.

*47 minutes ago – Lucien:*

*Sent a message to Earth. We're heading to you.*

*31 minutes ago – Hoyt:*

*We made it but are caught behind one of the Teratas' staging areas for our search. There is no way we could proceed without being noticed, but if you can get to a shield entrance, we'll cause a big enough distraction to allow you time to complete the mission.*

*8 minutes ago – Lucien:*

*We couldn't get there. They are now checking the transport tunnels. We made it to the shipyard, but they're close to us. Stay there, and we'll meet up with you when we can.*

"Hoyt is pinned down somewhere, and Lucien is in the shipyard," Tate said. "They can't shut off the shields." He hesitated before adding, "Can we?"

"When we make it home, Grandma might have another chance," Zoe replied. "But maybe not? Maybe we should take a look."

Nic sighed and then switched back to the map on Tate's dataPad. If they climbed down the two floors, they would be right outside the shield room at the exact spot they found it before. If Hoyt created the distraction, *they* could get inside the shield room. "We need to shut down the shields."

"How?" Sophia asked.

"We'll have to figure it out," Nic replied. "Nobody will ever get a chance like we have right now. We have to try, for the sake of humanity."

# CHAPTER 26

# SHIELD ROOM

The ladder in the transport tunnel was definitely not made for humans. Nic grabbed on to the top rung and had to hang down into the shaft before his feet reached the next rung. Then he grabbed the rung he stood on and swung down again. The increased gravity made the descent exhausting, but two floors and twenty minutes later, and they had all made it to the service hatch next to the shield room.

"Well, we're here," Tate said. He opened his dataPad, displaying the ship's map. He pointed to the shield room and then back to their location in the transport tunnels. "Any insight as to how to blow that thing up?"

Sophia shushed them with a finger across her lips, and then whispered. "Let's go one step at a time. The first thing we have to do is get inside the shield room. Let's see if that's even possible."

Nic listened at the hatch, but the only sounds he could hear were Zoe's periodic stifled cough and Tate's raspy breathing. Tate handed the spear to Sophia after showing her how to turn on the stunner part of the weapon. He then backed up with Zoe in order to avoid alerting the Teratas of their presence from an unexpected cough.

Slowly, Nic clicked open the transport hatch enough to peek into the hall. The door to the shield room was directly in front of him. At its side, a Terata guard stood facing the window. A large gun was slung from a strap across its shoulders. Thankfully, its alien robes and its horned scalp were clearly visible, which told Nic that it was not protected by an exosuit.

Nic considered messaging Hoyt for a distraction, but then he figured that he had no idea if this Terata would leave its post anyway. He pushed the hatch door open and set it aside without making a sound. He climbed out and turned back to take the spear from Sophia. It was lighter than he expected, weighing no more than five pounds. Nic felt like an ancient hunter carrying a spear, preparing for a hunt. On tiptoe, Nic inched his way toward his prey until he stood directly behind the towering creature.

With a flick of the switch, the spear crackled to life. The Terata spun around, spotting the open transport hatch, briefly missing Nic below him. Tilting its head down, its black, marble eyes bulged, and its jaw dropped in surprise. Confusion wiped from its expression, replaced with a snarl as it reached for its gun, too late. Nic thrust the spear at its chest, and the Terata crumpled to the floor. Its rifle, now laying on top of it, pulsing with the same electric blue as the spear.

Tate rushed out of the hatch after Sophia. He leaned over the creature and unhooked the rifle laying on the creature's chest. He tried to lift it, but it fell from his hands, smacking into the wall, making a loud *clank* that echoed down the hallways. "Whoops. It's too heavy." He reached down to its waist and unstrapped a spear. "Now we have two of these."

Zoe glanced around, searching for any approaching Teratas that might have heard them. "Maybe we should try to hide this thing before any more come this way." She stared at Tate. "Especially if we don't want to announce our presence."

Kneeling at the creature's head, Nic grabbed its robes bunched up around its neck. Zoe pulled it from the other side of its head, while Tate and Sophia took hold of its arms. Pulling with all their strength, they dragged the unconscious Terata no more than a foot. It slipped from Nic's hands and fell limply to the floor.

Tate took a step back. "At this rate, the thing will wake up before we get it to the transport hatch."

"Well," Zoe said, "I suppose that means we're even more pressed for time."

Nic grabbed onto the windowsill and peeked inside the shield room. The four chambers around the sides of the room fed some kind of energy into a central room.

Sophia hung next to Nic and nodded toward the central room. "It looks like it is up to us to take the shields down."

Tate had the dataPad open, and he zoomed around the map. Nic hoped for new messages from Lucien and Hoyt, but there were none. "Hoyt had a plan to take out the shields. If we contact him, we might be able to find out what his plan was."

"You know," Zoe said, "it's been like half an hour since the last message from him. If we send a message and they have been captured, then the Teratas would learn that we're still out here."

"Okay then, no message." Nic studied the others' expressions, but only blank stares returned his gaze. "I'm open to ideas. I mean, we're here. We have to try."

"The only thing we have that can actually damage their

systems is this spear," Tate said, jabbing it into the dataPad's projection, causing the image to flicker. "And that's if we are lucky."

"That spear might be all that we need to destroy their shields," Zoe said. "Can you imagine hitting computers back home with that thing? And don't forget, it worked on that Terata device that held the fleeing spaceships on Atlantis."

"Let's just hurry," Nic said as the shield room door whooshed open.

Everyone froze, then they turned to face the open door, only to find Sophia standing in the middle of the doorway staring back at them. Nic sighed, glaring at Sophia.

"What? I peeked through the window. We were clear to go. You said hurry."

Tate spun the five-foot spear around in his hand and flicked it to the welding setting. He skewered the Terata weapon, rendering it useless. Before joining Sophia, he flipped it to the shock setting and then shocked the immobilized Terata again. "One for good measure. The one in the prison wasn't down for long."

Nic shrugged and then followed Zoe across a metallic mesh pathway that clinked with each step that they took. He was reminded of a balcony in an amphitheater, except here he over-looked the inside of a baseball field–sized sphere. Ten yards in, Nic stopped at the rail, preventing accidental falls below.

Sophia was right about being able to get inside. While there were Teratas visibly repairing the chamber on their right, they were clearly too preoccupied to cause an alarm.

The three other chambers that powered the shields were equally spaced out around the far edges of the room. At the shield room's center was the core room, which was accessible from one of the four fifty-yard bridges that came from each of the side chambers.

They hustled down the walkway, partially concealed by the railing. Above them, windows showed other sections of the command ship. Through those windows, dozens of Teratas walked the halls and would be able to see them if any happened to look down, which thankfully none of them did.

Sophia ran ahead and slapped her hand on the door release. After everyone entered the chamber, she turned around and kept watch for Terata through a window by the door.

Dim red lights flickered on, revealing a classroom-sized chamber. A clear ten-foot-wide tube stretched from the floor to the ceiling, fifty feet up. Large coils wrapped around it, and inside radiated an emerald glow that swirled through the tube at an incredible speed. There was a door on the opposite side of the chamber and a bridge that led to the spherical room in the shield room core.

Nic could see through the grated floor. A clear conduit attached to the tube traveled under the bridge heading toward the core room.

The door closed behind Zoe, and she said, "Even if they haven't noticed us yet, one of them might see the lights are on in here or discover the unconscious Terata in the hallway."

Tate flicked on his spear. "Nic, let's get to destroying this place while we can."

Nic hesitated, staring down at his spear. "Wait, Tate. There are four of these chambers. Nadezda said she took out the command ship's shields briefly. We can assume that the repairs being done on that other chamber are due to what she did with her spaceship's weapon. That means that if we destroy this room, the Teratas could still have shields from the two other chambers, and we would have let them know we are here. We either have to destroy all four chambers or take out the core room."

Sophia shook her head. "The second we disable anything, they'll be all over us."

Zoe peeked down the bridge. "Then the only way to take out their shields for good is to destroy that core room." Zoe led the way but stopped once she was able to see the windows at higher levels. She backed up and didn't say anything until they had returned to the empty chamber room. "The Terata in the windows above us are looking down here. If we cross the bridge, they will see us."

"We can't even escape anymore," Sophia said. "Nic, what do we do?"

Picturing the Teratas in the windows above them, Nic once again stepped onto the bridge to take a closer look at the core room. It remained unoccupied, but it was impossible to tell for how long. They were wasting time. "We still have to take out the shields. And that means get to the core room."

"Right, Nic," Tate said. He held out a hand in the shape of a gun, and then pretending to fire it, he added, "We'll just run in there with guns blazing."

Nic swung his spear like a baseball bat. "That's right."

"I was just kidding, Nic. We can find a way that won't get us caught."

"We're running out of time," Nic said. "And I don't hear any better ideas. We might not make it home, no matter what we do. You were right back in the Terata's shipyard, Tate. This is bigger than us. We have a real chance right now to make a difference for the survival of the human race. And the more time that goes by, the more likely we'll get caught. It has to be done, and now."

"Maybe it's time to contact Hoyt," Tate coughed out.

"That's right," Nic replied. "The Terata already know we're here. If Hoyt is still able to cause a distraction, now is the time. Maybe he can buy us time to take down the shields and get away. Do we have any other thoughts?"

When nobody replied, Nic continued, "Tate, you contact Hoyt and see if he can get the Teratas away from here. I will get into position on the bridge and wait for a chance for us where we won't be noticed. We won't go until we can make it." Again, nobody objected, probably for a lack of better ideas.

Tate looked up at Nic and asked, "Are you sure about this?"

"Yes," Nic said. He was surprised to find that he wasn't nervous. It had to be done, and he was ready.

Nic nodded to Tate and didn't wait for him to contact Hoyt. He took his first step down the bridge to keep an eye on the Teratas when he felt Zoe's hand on his shoulder pulling him around. "In case we don't make it." She leaned forward and kissed his cheek, and then ran away to check for Terata patrols through the chamber windows.

Nic continued to smile even though Zoe was around the corner, now out of sight. He stood dumbfounded, until Tate softly called to him, "You okay, man? I'm ready to send a message."

Nic nodded and then inched forward until he couldn't get any farther without being noticed by a Terata on an upper floor. There was another forty yards before he got to the core room, and the thought of falling off the bridge made his head spin, so he stayed centered. Careful to stay out of sight, Nic searched around for the Terata. Above him, half a dozen Teratas gathered at various windows, all looking down as if notified of their presence. With so many Teratas searching the shield room, Nic could hardly believe the four of them had made it as far as they did.

Then, the reason the Teratas knew they were there became obvious. Nic spotted a Terata leaning against the same door that Nic and the others had used to enter the shield room. Its clothes were seared in the center of its chest from one of their spears, marking it as the same Terata that Nic had knocked out.

"Nic!" Sophia whispered. "Come back!"

Nic turned to see the others in the middle of the room, waving him over in a panic. There wasn't enough time for Hoyt's distraction, so something was wrong already.

Nic raced back to them, hoping to make it in time, but he was too late. He stopped at the end of the bridge at the chamber room's entrance, spotting a Terata that had entered through a side door. It was equal distance to Nic and to his friends. The Terata caught sight of Nic but then ran for the others. It would be able to reach them far faster than Nic could.

Without Nic there, though, they would be able to survive by time jumping to safety, so Nic let them go. Instead of racing the Terata to his friends, Nic turned and sprinted down the bridge to the core room. A gentle *thump* came from behind, preceding a roar, which told Nic that his friends escaped without him.

When the roar stopped, it became eerily silent. The only sound he heard came from the clanking of his shoes as he ran. With only ten yards to go, distant shouts that were more of a growl than words called out to him. But he didn't look to see where from.

Inside the core room, an oscillating hum rumbled from every direction, and Nic's hair stuck out like a mad scientist's.

Nic ran over to a ten-foot-wide globe resting on a pillar in the center. A red fog swirled around inside the globe, sparking with the same emerald green that emanated around the alien shields, like in the prison.

His spear flicked on, sending sparks to the floor. Arcs spit out as he swung the spear into the globe with all his might. It bounced off, leaving the globe without a scratch. He flipped it to the welding setting, but again it left no mark.

Nic returned to the core room's entrance, spotting the Terata racing toward him. He searched for a way to destroy the shield, and the coils under the bridge caught his eye. The coils encircled the room, combining with the ones from the other chambers, and fed up into the globe through the pillar.

Nic crawled around the base of the pedestal, searching for a way to access the coils. Spotting an access port at the side, he popped it open, revealing glowing circuits. A tube in the middle had the same electric glow as the chambers.

Barely audible over the room's hum, a growl alerted Nic to the Terata behind him. He spun around. The creature's lips trembled, and rows of its sharp teeth glistened.

Nic grinned and said to it, "This looks important," and then stabbed the globes circuitry with the spear, sending sparks arcing all around inside the device. The hum from the globe came to an abrupt stop. It began again, quietly at first, and then quickly rose in pitch.

Nic faced the Terata, leaving the spear behind, still inside the pedestal, still sparking. The Terata approached but winced in pain as the globe emitted an ear-splitting shriek that grew louder by the second. Nic smacked his hands over his ears and fell to one knee.

The Terata fell to the floor, covering its ears too, not even able to crawl, the sound affecting it more than Nic.

Nic pushed himself to his feet, and with his hands still covering his ears, he scurried past the Terata's feeble attempt to grab him. He dashed back across the bridge, making it halfway, when it shook, causing Nic to stumble to the floor. He spun around to see the core room tremble, and then an explosion erupted from within, causing a shockwave that blasted Nic through the air.

CHAPTER 27
# ESCAPE

Nic didn't remember hitting the ground. When he came to, one of his legs dangled off the edge of the bridge. Ears buzzing, he looked around as his blurred vision began to focus. Lying on his back, Nic saw Teratas through the overhead windows, shock clearly evident in their open mouths and wide-eyed expressions.

Momentarily unable to stand, Nic rolled back to the center of the bridge and pushed himself to his knees. The core room in front of him sparkled, either from a fire or from the Terata power source gone haywire, Nic couldn't tell. Smoke rose out of it too, obscuring his view, but not enough to hide the Terata stirring on the ground.

Nic had destroyed the shields, given humanity another chance, and survived for now. He laughed and wondered if the others made it back to the ship. If they returned while he was out, they might have started for their spaceship. He might be able to catch up to them, depending on how long he had been out.

Nic pushed himself to his feet, stumbled to the floor, and

then stood again. He staggered the rest of the way down the bridge, until he reached the chamber where the others had disappeared. He silently hoped they were there when he arrived, but they weren't. He was still on his own.

Nic headed for the exit but turned back in time to see the Terata from the core room was racing toward him. Its clothes were in tatters, and it ran with a limp, but it still moved faster than Nic could. It was just a matter of time. Nic made it to the chamber room door before falling to the ground. The Terata stooped above him, reaching out as Nic raised his arm in defense. Instead of being grabbed, the Terata collapsed at his feet. Sophia and Tate crouched behind it, while a wide-eyed Zoe stood above it, still prodding the creature with her spear.

Nic laughed and said to the fallen Terata, "Buddy, it is not your day." Nic's ears still rang, and Sophia pulled Nic to his feet. She said something, but Nic could only make out *go*.

Tate was on his dataPad, messaging Lucien and Hoyt, and Zoe pushed all of them through the doors. They could still make it.

Sophia sprinted ahead of them along the walkway, heading back to the same door where they first entered the shield room. Tate pointed across from them. The core room had collapsed into a crumpled heap below, but more Terata chased after them from the walkways that connected each of the chamber rooms.

They made it back to the door that led to the rest of the ship. Slapping the door open, Sophia froze, rooted in place. A Terata in an exosuit stepped forward, looming over her while raising its gun. Nic lunged forward and tackled Sophia to the ground as a shot blasted over his shoulder.

Nic rolled over as the Terata collapsed to the floor, taken out by Zoe and her Terata shock stick. This Terata warrior was guarding the exit, but more were coming. Blasts pelted the wall around them, and Nic scrambled after Sophia into the hallway.

The door shut behind them all, blocking the Terata in the shield room long enough for Zoe to run the spear, in the welding setting, along the door's edges. The door's seams were melted shut as a Terata crashed into the door, causing Nic to jump. His hearing had returned, and he was able to make out what the others were saying again.

"Let's go!" Sophia yelled.

"Lucien's waiting for us," Tate said. "He said they would help us get to the ship. We just have to make it to the shipyard."

Nic waited for Zoe to finish sealing it as Sophia ran ahead with Tate.

Together, Nic and Zoe chased after them. Tate slowed to check their path on a Terata sign, but Sophia dashed past him, without waiting for Tate's confirmation on which way to go. She shouted back, "We're almost there!"

Nic and Zoe chased after them. Sophia opened the shipyard door and waved for Nic and Zoe to hurry up, and then ran ahead again with Tate. Nic made it to the door and ran into the empty shipyard. Sophia and Tate were already halfway to the storage room holding their ship, when they stopped and raised their hands over their heads.

Countless Terata stepped out into the open from behind their damaged spaceships. The Terata knew they were coming and had waited for them. Tate and Sophia knelt down in surrender. Nic and Zoe began raising their hands.

The Terata that approached them snarled but then spun around. Every Terata in sight spun around and raised their weapons as the door leading to their spaceship burst open in a ball of fire. The silhouette of a human dashed forward, and a renewed battle for survival began.

Before seeing who had the advantage, Nic took Zoe's hand and pulled her to the back side of the closest Terata space fighter under repairs. The last sight of the shipyard battlefield Nic saw was of the snarling Terata turning back around to see that Nic and Zoe were no longer there. Nic didn't stop, though. He had dropped Zoe's hand and raced around the edge of the shipyard, until their doorway came into view.

Nic assumed that the human resistance would have dug in, guarding the door so they too could escape with Nic and his friends in their spaceship, but they were gone. Sophia and Tate were there, though, and passed through the door as soon as they caught sight of Nic and Zoe. Nic would have wanted them to wait but understood that the quicker they got onboard their spaceship, the faster they could leave.

Shouts from both sides seemed to be more distant, and Nic considered that the battle had moved away. They sneaked forward as fast as they could, racing across the last open stretch and making it safely to the storage door. It wasn't until they got to the door that Nic saw how far away their rescuers were. The resistance fighters had made it to one of the piers full of working Terata space fighters. The shipyard was still filled with countless Terata, either mesmerized by the fight as it unfolded or running to chase down the humans as they fled.

Before opening the door, Nic spotted Lucien hiding with some others behind an alien structure being blasted by Terata rifles.

The storage door opened with a whoosh. Zoe grabbed Nic's arm and pulled him into the storage bay. When the door closed again, Nic let out a sigh of relief. Their spaceship lay in front of them, in the same position as when they left. This time however, fallen Terata were spread around the corners, taken out by the freed prisoners.

Nic could hardly believe that they were successful in finding Zoe and making it back to their ship. While Lucien and the others were rescued by Nic, now they had sacrificed themselves to let Nic and his friends escape. As their ship lay in front of them, Nic wondered if he could have done more for them.

They jogged forward.

As she ran, Zoe was gawking at their ship, seeing it for the first time. She chuckled and said, "Let me guess, Tate's the pilot."

Nic unsuccessfully stifled a laugh. He forgot that when they left the ship, it was upside down. From where he was now, Nic could see that the closest crates that made up the towers of Terata storage had tumbled onto the top of their ship. "Yeah, Tate flew here," Nic replied, running forward. "He did his best to cover the ship. Pretty good idea, right? It's *camouflaged*."

Zoe coughed out a laugh but kept up with Nic.

They made it halfway to their ship when Nic heard the familiar whoosh of the door behind them, accompanied by a blast at Nic's feet that froze him in place. His first thought was to sprint to their spaceship, but they might not get another warning shot. Slowly turning, Nic saw two Terata warriors standing in the doorway with weapons pointed at them. The smell of burned metal wafted up from the warning shot, and Nic trembled at the thought that they could be next if they took another step. Unsure what else he could do, Nic raised his hands in defeat. Zoe set her spear on the ground and raised her hands too. The spear rolled away and stopped, leaving them in silence.

The Teratas glanced around the room, eyes lingering on their fallen companions, and then began their approach. Nic stepped in front of Zoe, unsure what to do. He turned back to the ship, hoping that Tate saw from the pilot's chair that they didn't make it. Lucien and his team wouldn't rescue them this time.

Nic crouched as their ship rose behind him. The screeching of metal on metal pierced the silence, causing Nic to clasp his hands over his ears. The ship flipped over, narrowly missing them, and sending the crates that were on top of it flying across the room. It spun around, landing between Nic and Zoe and the two Teratas.

"Run!" Nic yelled.

Together, Nic and Zoe ran to the ship as a ladder swung down in front of them. Nic followed closely after Zoe. An odd electrical pop rang out nearby. It got closer as he climbed the ladder and crawled inside.

Once inside, Nic turned to find one Terata had circled around their ship and was firing plasma blasts, which created the odd popping when the ship was hit. Staying low, Nic crawled along the floor to the door controls and sealed their spaceship with a hiss. They had made it inside; now they just had to get away.

---

Tate sat in the pilot's chair in his sphere of darkness. Sophia operated the nearest computer, helping to adjust the spaceship's controls, not that Tate could see her. When Tate heard the door to the airlock open, he knew it meant that Nic and Zoe were finally safe on board. Tate shouted, "Everyone here?"

"Yes," Nic replied. "We made it."

Tate gently pulled on the flight sticks and then spun them toward the shipyard. They lifted off the ground as the two Teratas continued their assault behind them. The Teratas' weapons didn't seem to have any effect on their ship, and Tate wondered if it couldn't penetrate their hull. Tate pushed them forward, leaving the storage room behind, entering the shipyard's docks.

Blasts continued to streak past them as their ship got out of range. Tate turned them, diving under a Terata space fighter, but the movement was sluggish, bumping it enough to knock the space fighter off the docks it was attached to.

"Sophia?" Tate shouted. "What happened? I can't maneuver correctly anymore. Is the ship damaged?"

"Sorry," Sophia said. "As soon as we left the storage room, I've been trying to jump us out of here. I still need a minute."

"Nic, take over the controls," Tate said. "Sophia, wait until I say it's time. I want to see if I can help Lucien and his team."

"Are you sure?" Nic asked.

"Yeah," Tate replied. He didn't know if he could help, but he knew he didn't want to leave Lucien and the others to get killed without checking on them. "They got us out. It's the right thing to do. Now let me concentrate."

Tate slowly wove their spaceship through the docks filled with unused Terata space fighters, locating the small squad of humans near the repair yard, hiding behind a mechanical arm. Dozens of Teratas were charging while firing blasts that would soon reach the human resistance.

"We're ready to jump!" Sophia shouted. "Just let me know when, Tate."

Tate pushed them forward, heading for the oncoming

Teratas, who stopped their assault on the former prisoners to begin firing at Tate's ship. Moments before Lucien's team was overrun, Tate stopped their ship directly in front of the charging Teratas. He was about to call down to Nic to open up the airlock to pick up the prisoners when an alarm blared around them. Tate second-guessed the integrity of their ship and whether it could withstand the shots it was taking.

Tate had to leave already and glanced toward the humans below. Grinning, Lucien and some of the former prisoners stared up at them. Tate imagined their pleading words, begging to be picked up, to escape. Instead, smiles lit their faces that reminded Tate of his reunion with Zoe. Balled fists crossed their chests, and they bowed before sprinting for the closest docked Terata space fighter.

As the last human entered the space fighter, one controlled by the Terata swooped into view. It shot a rocket that exploded on their hull, rattling their entire ship, and sent them skipping across the docks. Before coming to a stop, Tate was yanked to the side, feeling the full effect of gravity for the first time since they got in their ship. He couldn't be more thankful that he was strapped in.

The pier spun in circles outside, and Tate wouldn't be able to control their spin while bumping into the pier. He pushed down on the control sticks, managing to lift them into the air just in time. Below them, a second explosion severed the pier in half, causing hundreds of the empty Terata space fighters to fall to a lower level.

Their ship was out of control, and Tate couldn't keep them in the air. They crashed into the floor beneath them once more, sending sparks that ran along the ground as their ship slid to a stop, facing three Terata space fighters positioning themselves for an attack.

Another alarm blared from below as Sophia shouted, "We can't take another hit like that!"

"Your turn, Sophia!" Tate yelled. "Get us out of here!"

Dozens of rockets shot at them from each Terata space fighter. Before hitting, though, Tate's vision was plunged into darkness.

*Thump!*

---

*Thirty minutes later*

Nic gasped for air, and a sudden drop in temperature gave him the shivers. Although, if there were a hole in the ship, it would have been worse. All around him, previously hidden robotic tarantulas crawled across every surface. They had appeared just before the time jump, and Nic guessed that without them, they would not have made it. If there was a breach, it was already sealed.

Weightlessness had sunk in, though, and alarms blared around them. Without the belts strapping him in, Nic would have floated into the air.

Sophia reached out to the controls, and the deafening alarms ceased. "We're thirty minutes later," she said with a heavy sigh of relief. "We lost some minor systems. Gravity is out, but the ship is okay—damaged, but okay."

Zoe sat next to him and fiddled with controls until the wall in front of them dissolved into a transparent viewscreen. Nic froze, staring at the Terata command ship looming between them and a baseball-sized Earth, orbited by a marble-sized moon. Zoe zoomed in until the command ship took up most of the screen.

The pilot seat lowered, revealing a smirking, pale-skinned Tate.

In the thirty minutes that passed during their time jump, the command ship had almost made it to the moon. Its silhouette covered the moon like a partial eclipse.

"I can't believe we made it out of there," Zoe said. She coughed and then began to laugh.

"Even better," Sophia said, chuckling, "we can still make it through the same wormhole that Nadezda used. That will get us back home to our time."

"We're going home, guys," Nic said, smiling. He stared back at the command ship. His only hope now was that the Teratas weren't able to get their shields operational again. In answer to this hope, explosions erupted from the command ship like solar flares escaping the sun.

"Wow!" Tate said.

Explosions erupted all over the command ship, brought about by hundreds of ant-sized dots moving around it, which could only be spaceships in battle. The command ship was turning away from its path to the moon as pieces of it drifted apart.

Everything they set out to accomplish was finally within their reach. The wormhole was close, and they would make it home shortly. Nic stared in wonder as the command ship devolved from an impenetrable force to one being destroyed by the defenders of humanity. The people of this time might not know what the four of them had done, but it didn't matter.

A new alarm blared, piercing through Nic's newfound

serenity, after which Sophia said, "We're not done yet. We've got a Terata space fighter heading our way."

Tate's chair rose, and then he disappeared behind his dark sphere. "Sophia, where do I go?"

"We're actually quite close," she said. "The coordinates are already on your screen."

"Got it," Tate replied. "We're pretty beat up, but we'll be there in less than a minute."

"The wormhole is dead ahead," Sophia said. "Make sure you go through its center."

Nic stared, transfixed by the explosions on the command ship, until Tate spun them around. Seconds later, their ship shook violently. "What was that?"

"They're firing at us," Tate replied.

"They're gaining on us," Zoe said.

"Stay on target," Sophia said. "The wormhole is expanded. You can see it now!"

Far in front of them, but approaching quickly, a gray sphere of ooze ebbed and flowed as if tossed around by a wind not present in space.

A second shot struck them, sending them spinning, but still in the direction of the wormhole. More alarms blasted in protest of the ship's diminishing condition. Nic's heart stilled as a chunk of metal spun across the ship's bow. They straightened out, revealing the metal was one of their wings drifting through space.

"Did we ..." Nic muttered, "lose a wing?" It floated past the wormhole that approached, mere seconds away.

"Forget about it. We're still heading for the wormhole," Tate said, "and besides, we have three other wings. How many do we need?"

Nic held his breath as they flew through the wormhole nearly sideways.

Traveling backward in time was different than Nic was used to. The *thump* and being plunged into darkness that accompanied a trip into the future never came.

The wormhole caused everything in Nic's view to expand. His muscles tightened, and his skin began to tingle. He tried to take in a deep breath but couldn't capture any air. Light burned into his eyes as if he had looked into the sun. It didn't hurt, but when he looked down, his hands were glowing. Before he could freak out, they had returned to normal, and the Earth appeared on the viewscreen in front of them.

———

*221 years earlier*
*July 10, 2022*

Nic's body shuddered as he regained control, gasping for air. The viewscreen that had shown the beginning destruction of the command ship now displayed the city of Sunland below. Instead of being in outer space, as they were in the future, they were now close enough to Earth to find their houses.

After flying through the wormhole weightless and then suddenly entering Earth's gravity, Nic was pulled so hard toward Earth that he thought he was going to pass out. He heard a groan from Sophia next to him and the clatter of something tumbling across the floor, followed by a loud *crack*. It wasn't until Tate had managed to steady their ship that Nic felt gravity return to normal.

"We made it!" Tate shouted.

"The Terata space fighter is right behind us," Zoe said.

The ship spun around and hovered in place. Their spaceship's engines rattled, causing Nic's extremities to grow numb. They were tossed around either by turbulence or from instability caused by the missing wing. The ship flew at an angle, and with gravity returned, Nic found himself pulled to the side as if he was on the brink of sliding down a hill.

"Sophia," Nic said, "can you close the wormhole?"

"I dropped the Time Jumper."

Nic spotted it at the front of their ship and unlatched his seatbelt. Hopping off his seat, he slid across the slanted floor. The Time Jumper was splintered down the middle, with cracks that spread across the screen like a spiderweb. The image behind it was frozen in black-and-blue illegible shapes. "It's broken."

Nic climbed up to Sophia and handed it over.

Sophia rubbed her finger over the cracks and then tucked it in her backpack.

"We can't let them attack Earth," Nic said.

"What do we do?" Tate asked. "They will get here any second."

"Let's ram them," Zoe replied. "Tate, move us directly in front of the wormhole so that the second they come out they will crash into us."

"Then get to the escape pods!" Sophia added.

Their ship shook violently, but Tate managed to stop them in front of the shimmering wormhole, exactly where they came through. Tate's chair lowered. "Autopilot is on, let's get out of here!" He leapt from the seat, landing on the uneven floor, and then scrambled behind Sophia to the escape pods.

In the corner of Nic's eye, he spotted the viewscreen with a trembling wormhole. The Terata space fighter was coming through. He clambered up to the escape pods after Zoe, unsure if he would make it in time.

Tate and Sophia entered separate pods and dropped out of sight.

Nic reached for a pod when the spaceships collided. Flying through the air, Nic hit the roof and then crashed back to the floor. A long crystal shard stabbed through their ship right below Nic's feet. Jumping off of it, he grasped for the escape pod's edge, but his grip faltered, and he was lifted into the air again. Instead of falling back into the ship, Zoe took hold of him, yanking him into her escape pod.

The escape pod's door sealed, silencing the crashing space-ships before ejecting them below. Nic's stomach lurched into his chest, and Zoe squeezed him tight. They watched their escape through the glass ceiling of the pod. Their spaceship ripped in two as the Terata space fighter exploded in a blast that chased them in their descent and sent debris raining down on them and the city below.

# CHAPTER 28

# HOME

The escape pod plummeted into the wash at the edge of the city. It came down like a comet, slowing its descent only once it passed below the highest mountain peak. Inside the pod, Nic stiffened, bracing for impact. Instead of a rough landing, it felt more like he reached the bottom floor in an elevator, complete with a ding before the door opened into Ebey Canyon.

They were home.

Nic stepped out of the pod and onto Earth for the first time since he left Zoe behind on Atlantis. He held his hand out to her, and she took it, stepping next to him.

Above them, the remnants of their spaceship's crash formed thick tendrils of black smoke that reached across the sky. Helicopters passed overhead, following the smoke trails that would lead them to wreckage that didn't belong in this time. Nic and Zoe stood, searching for the others in the wash that made up the canyon.

Nic couldn't imagine their situation turning out better.

Sophia and Tate made it to their escape pods and should be safe. They had saved Zoe, and the future of the human race in the process.

Still holding her hand tightly, Nic guided Zoe toward his home. The sun shone down on them from above, having just started its morning crawl across the sky. They roamed through the wash until they reached the city's edge. Zoe's smile faded as she asked, "What do we do now?"

"Head home, I suppose," Nic answered cheerfully.

"Yeah," Zoe replied, releasing his hand. "Whose home is that? Nadezda is my grandma, but in this time, she doesn't even know I exist. And even if she did, she doesn't have a home either."

Nic stood dumbfounded. They had saved the future of humanity and made it home, achieving everything they set out to do and more, but trapped Zoe in this time as well. With the Time Jumper broken, she would never return to her own time.

Nic sighed and then hustled forward, taking Zoe's hand again. Instead of pulling away, she held tighter. Nic blurted out, "You could stay with me." Nic felt the heat in his cheeks rising, hoping she would say yes.

"*Right*," Zoe said, rolling her eyes. "I forgot that in this time, parents happily allow their son's girlfriend to live with them."

Nic stared at her, eyes widening.

Zoe averted her eyes, her face reddening. "You know what I mean. I can't stay with you."

Zoe had acknowledged their relationship was more than friends, but the fact that Zoe had no place to live and couldn't go home left him feeling that he had failed her. Nic remembered the dread he felt about the possibility of never making it home, but he always had hope. She no longer did. "You won't know what Nadezda will do until you talk to her."

Zoe sighed deeply, meeting Nic's eyes again.

Nic wanted to say more but couldn't find the right words. He turned away, and when he looked back to her, she pulled him toward the nearby houses.

Sophia shouted, "Hey!" She was sprinting toward them from the edge of the suburbs. When they reached each other, Sophia hugged them both tightly. She stepped back and then jumped around. "You both made it!"

"Yes," Nic said. "What about Tate?"

As an answer, Tate jogged over. "I can't believe you two made it. I thought one of you was a goner for sure, since only one escape pod left after mine."

"Zoe grabbed me when the Terata fighter crashed into us."

"Do you know what day it is?" Sophia asked.

Tate glanced at his dataPad. "It's Sunday. The morning after we left. We've only been gone for about twelve hours."

"What now?" Zoe asked.

"Let's grab our bikes from the park," Tate said. "Everyone can head home from there. Hopefully, we can get back before anyone fusses over us too much."

"Then what are we waiting for?" Zoe said. "Lead the way."

---

They crossed into McGroarty Park, expecting it to be empty, with their bikes ditched under the jungle gym. Instead, a crowd of people had gathered outside the closed gate, arguing with a police officer on the other side.

The officer pointed at them as they approached, prompting

a mob of family and friends to rush over in a crazed panic. Unable to contain his relief of being home, Nic raced to them as well. He ran into his parents' arms and welcomed their embrace. When his parents finally released him, his mom wiped away the tears welling up in her eyes. "I thought something terrible happened to you."

His older brother, Ethan, rustled Nic's hair. "You had us worried, man."

Nic's dad knelt next to him. "Where have you been?"

Nic stared into the sky at the remaining contrails left by the spaceships. He was unsure what he should say. If he told the truth, nobody would believe him. He shrugged and decided to keep it simple for now. "We lost track of time."

"*Right*," Ethan said with raised eyebrows. "We used to hike back there all the time. You would have known when to head back. What *really* happened? Did you find the plane crash? It's been all over the news, and there was another one like an hour ago. Though, it's more likely that you were just trying to get out of finishing your packing on moving day."

In all the excitement of making it back to their time, Nic had forgot that he made it back the morning he was leaving. He was home, but it was now time to move away. "No, Ethan, I think I'm ready to go," Nic said with a sigh. His dad's eyes narrowed, and he tilted his head to the side in clear doubt. "And Dad, I am really sorry about how I've been acting over our move."

In response, his dad hugged him. "It's okay, Nic, we'll talk about it later. I'm just glad you're home."

To his side, Sophia was sitting on a bench chatting with her parents. Both of them had wide smiles and their arms around her.

Tate freed himself from his mom's embrace. His oldest

sister, Emma, slugged him on the shoulder. Tate chuckled and said, "Yeah, I missed you too." His sisters stared at Tate in puzzlement, but he ignored them.

Behind Tate, Zoe stared at Nadezda, who was among the small crowd of neighbors and friends who were probably going to search for them. Zoe turned back to Nic and smiled. He waved her over and she reluctantly joined him, stopping in front of Nic's family. Nic laid his hand on her shoulder. "This is Zoe. She helped us get home."

"Well," his mom said, narrowing her eyes as she glanced between the two of them. She smiled again and gave Zoe a quick hug. "Thank you," she said, looking around, and then asked, "Is your family here too?"

Zoe bit her lip and watched Nadezda as she made her way around the edge of the crowd. "Um, I'm not sure."

A black SUV pulled up next to the police officer. A tall, bald man stepped out, and Nic instantly recognized him as the military officer who pulled back the tarp on the Terata from the crashed spaceship. The police officer chatted with him briefly and then called all the parents together for a debriefing of sorts.

While their parents were distracted, Sophia grabbed Nic and Zoe and pulled them over to Tate. She pulled out a small aviator patch and held it up to Tate, who took it apprehensively. Nic leaned in and stared at the round, embroidered patch, depicting the same type of spaceship they used to flee Atlantis. On the patch, the spaceship swooped in front of the city of Atlantis at its prime with the insignia *Wonder of Atlantis* written across the top.

"It's for your jacket," Sophia said. "I found it in an Atlantis shop. I thought, if we ever made it home, you would want something to remind you of your flight experience. At that time, it was just crashing a car, but still."

Unable to speak, Tate stared at it, mouth parted. He rested his hand over his father's patch and then examined his new one. A grin slowly grew on his lips. He held it up to his jacket and then reached out, giving Sophia a hug.

Zoe put her hand on Tate's shoulder. "Humanity might never know it, but you're without a doubt the most important pilot in history."

"Your dad would have been so proud, Tate," Nic said.

Tate stared between them. "Thank you, guys. This means a lot."

Nic nodded toward Nadezda. She stood behind them, pretending she wasn't listening. Nic put his arm around Zoe and then said quietly. "Even if Nadezda doesn't know you exist, she's family. She doesn't belong here either. So, she could probably use someone to talk with about the future. Might as well be someone who also hasn't even been born yet."

Zoe smiled and then took a step toward Nadezda. Before she could take a second, Tate called to her, "Lose something, Nadezda?"

Nic groaned. "Always the diplomat, aren't you?" He glanced around, confirming that nobody would overhear them.

"What?" Nadezda replied. She took a quick look around and then joined them, eyebrows raised. "Who are you, and what did you kids do?"

"We made it home," Tate said.

With clenched fists, Nadezda glared at Tate.

Nic unlatched Zoe's locket from around his neck and returned it to her.

Zoe immediately clicked it open and closed and then took a

deep breath. Clicking it open again, she showed Nadezda a three-dimensional image of Zoe with her arms wrapped around a much older Nadezda.

The moment she recognized the image as her own, Nadezda gasped and then froze in place, staring wide-eyed. With a deepening frown, Nadezda stared at each of them. She took the locket from Zoe and cycled through images of her future. "How exactly do you know me?"

They told her about the years to come, her garden atrium fifty years from now, the Vegas wormhole, the jetpacks in Paris. The whole time, Nadezda stared with a fixed gaze, which only broke with a wry smile when they told her how they boarded the command ship. Zoe ended by saying, "The last we saw of the Terata command ship, it was being destroyed by a human fleet."

Nadezda didn't move. She looked at Nic and then laughed. "Then, it's all over." She stared up into the sky with a wide smile. When she turned back, she asked Zoe, "So, if I knew you fifty years from now, what does that make us?"

Zoe shuffled her feet and stared down at the ground. "Hi, Grandma."

Without saying a word, Nadezda examined Zoe's face, as if searching for some resemblance. The drawn-out silence made Nic sick to his stomach. He couldn't imagine what Zoe was feeling.

When Nadezda finally spoke again, she asked, "Where are you going to stay now, Zoe?"

Zoe slouched, crossing her arms in front of her, avoiding eye contact. Unable to respond, she shrugged.

"Well," Nadezda said, "I can't stay in my ship anymore, but we can figure out where to go from here, together."

As soon as she said *together*, Zoe leapt into Nadezda's arms. It was a somewhat awkward embrace, due to Nadezda not really knowing Zoe. It was cut short too, when Tate cleared his throat. He pointed to the bald military officer heading in their direction.

"What are we going to tell them?" Sophia asked, cramming her hands into her pockets.

"Nothing about the time machine," Tate replied.

Zoe pointed to Tate's dataPad. "You should hide that."

They remained quiet until the military officer reached them and said, "I'm sorry to interrupt you, but can I please speak with these kids for a moment?"

Nadezda nodded and then stepped away with Zoe.

The military officer glanced over to their parents, who were deep in a conversation with the police officer from the gate. Tate's mom glared at the military officer, but he ignored her. "Let's make this quick. Could you please explain your absence? Where were you last night?"

"We found the crash in the hills," Tate replied, rubbing his empty wrist.

"Then we hid in the mountains until morning," Sophia added.

"Sure, kids," he said, shifting his stance. "And what exactly did you see at the plane crash?"

"Crystals, and a big, green, scaly creature with horns instead of hair," Tate replied.

Seconds passed without comment. The military officer's expression didn't change, but his voice softened to almost a whisper. "Did you take any pictures?"

"No, we aren't allowed phones yet. Our parents can tell you that."

He nodded, and then noticing their families heading their direction, said sternly, "You three will tell anyone who asks you that you found a plane crash. No details, though." He spun around and then walked to intercept Tate's mom. "Hello, Ms. Booker. I need a brief word with you." He led Tate's mom away, leaving Nic alone with Tate and Sophia.

Nic's dad returned to him and said, "We need to get going, Nic. Can you say bye to your friends?"

"Sure thing, Dad," Nic replied. "Just give me a minute, please."

Nic's dad left, heading over to Nic's mom and brother, who were adding Nic's bike to the rack on the back of their car.

Zoe returned without Nadezda and gave each of them a hug. "We have to keep in touch."

"Of course," Nic replied.

"I'll get you Zoe's contact information, once she knows it," Sophia said.

"Then," Tate said, "I guess this is goodbye."

"Goodbye for now," Nic replied. "We'll get together again."

Even though he had to move, Nic no longer thought of it as a curse. Now, he looked forward to it. He would of course miss his friends, but he knew they weren't gone forever. He could still meet up with them online, and before he knew it, the high-speed rail would bring them all together again.

Nic gave Zoe one last hug and then wrapped his arms around Tate and Sophia a final time. He stared into the sky, finding the spaceship's smoke trails had finally faded, returning their city to a semblance of normal.

Nic waved goodbye and slowly walked away to his waiting family.

The four of them had done the impossible. They made it

back to their time and home to their families. Even if less than a day had passed here, the world would never be the same. It was a different place now, for the future, and for them. In the future, mankind would survive. For them, their future was yet to be written.

# THANK YOU FOR READING!

**Please consider leaving a review!**

As an independent author, one of the biggest struggles is getting your name and book out there. If you enjoyed the story, there's no better way to show your support than leaving a review.

If you are interested in learning more about me or have any questions, please check out my website:

www.adamcrozierbooks.com

# Acknowledgments

I am so happy to have been able to write this story. It started with a simple enough idea, but got more complicated quickly. You have now seen what almost ten years of work got me, and I couldn't have done it without all the people in my life. Especially my wife, Carrie, who helped me through learning to write and supported me even after seeing the first draft.

I am deeply grateful to my writing group who taught me far more than they realize:

evan austin https://www.facebook.com/evanaustinauthor

Shami Stovall sastovallauthor.com

I want to thank my beta readers and all the people that helped or put up with me as this story was being made: Brian Skidmore, Dan Skidmore, Don Crozier, Edward Letts, Erin Glavich, Greg Kastigar, Jeanette Glavich, Jeffrey Hawthorne, Meghan Crozier, Matthew Crozier, Niki Turkovic, Sandy Crozier, Sean Crozier, and Tom Glavich.

And special thanks to, YOU, my reader. You read the story that I always wanted to tell, and for that, I'll be eternally grateful.

# About the Author

Adam Crozier is a writer living in Sunland, CA. His hobbies include camping, cooking, gaming, hiking, and adventuring with his wife and two kids.

He has spent a good part of his life with his head in the clouds, imagining strange distant worlds that loosely resemble our own.

To learn more about Adam, you can take a look at his website: www.adamcrozierbooks.com

www.ingramcontent.com/pod-product-compliance
Lightning Source LLC
Chambersburg PA
CBHW021224310726

48971CB00006B/1675